I0744635

Published by: Cinnabar Moth Publishing LLC
Santa Fe, New Mexico

Cover Design by: Ira Geneve

ISBN-13: 978-1-953971-79-1
Library of Congress Control Number: 2023933428

Prophet's Lamentation

ROBERT CREEKMORE

Dedication:

This book is dedicated to the memory of Josephine Strasnicsak; dancer, choreographer, mother, grandmother, and grande dame.

I talk to God, but the sky is empty.

- Sylvia Plath

"Even after your enemies' defeat, they are still with you."

Those are Nate's words. I hear them whenever I wake up screaming and fighting in the middle of the night. Tiffany has similar episodes.

How do you build an ordinary life when you're not, well, ordinary? Terror and fury molded me for eleven years. That abruptly ended with the death of Vernon Proffit and his acolytes. Sure, there was a period of celebration following. After vengeance, the anger never completely subsides. Don't interpret that as regret; some motherfuckers need killing.

What bothers me is that before I fed Vernon to the Atlantic Ocean, the screams that woke me were my own as I relived trauma.

The abilities my guide, Mara, gifted me are still intact, but I choose to shut myself off from them. However, now something new comes pulsing forth from the ground that I have no control over. I'm stirred from sleep by the horrors others are experiencing. They cry out for help, but I don't know how to save them. Mostly, they're abused young people. Their voices drive me mad. If I could only find them, maybe I could stop their suffering. Last night, it was a young man named Vincent. I couldn't see where he was. I could only hear him wail in pain as he experienced abject hopelessness.

But I attempt to tarry forward.

Today, I should be happy. It's July twentieth, two-thousand-six; my twenty-seventh birthday as Naomi Pace. Legally, as Hannah Sillman, I'm thirty-four and will turn thirty-five on Christmas day. That birthday is celebrated more ominously, as the real Hannah rests with her mother, Milly, under an old oak tree high up in the hills of Yancey County. Her father, Al, gifted me with this new life by giving me her identity for my eighteenth birthday. He was more of a father than my own, Amos, who beat me mercilessly when he found out that I was in love with Tiffany. I still am. Their hate and violence couldn't destroy that.

I won. Why am I still so sad? Why do I disregard my own life, feeling guilty about those I couldn't save, like Charles? He died during our escape. There was nothing I could do. I know that, logically, but I can't convince my heart of it. It eats at me with each heartbeat, saying, 'you could have done more.' It does so now, at four-thirty in the morning. I'm sitting up in bed with no one to speak with. I don't dare wake my beautiful bride, Tiffany, as she sleeps soundly next to me.

After completing my Ph.D. in marine biology, I took a job with North Carolina Fish and Wildlife. It lasted a year. I simply lost interest one day, walked out, and never returned. I ran my own dive business for six months afterward but found myself feeling listless about that as well. I don't need the money. I was seeking a normal life.

Tonight, our friends Nate and Herschel are coming down from Little Washington to our house on Wrightsville Beach. We are supposed to celebrate my birthday at Spectrum in downtown Wilmington.

I'm done trying to sleep. All I can see of Tiffany are her red curls as she sleeps on her left side, rolled up in the covers like a burrito.

Gently, I rise from the right-hand side of the bed, which is closest to the door. I dress in a black t-shirt and pajama pants. I leave my feet bare and tiptoe across our new seafoam green carpet. I open the door and exit quietly. There's a large picture window to the left outside our bedroom that faces the sound side of Wrightsville Beach. At the moment, all I can see are the lights from the boat docks framed by darkness, and my reflection. I still keep my blond hair very short. I don't feel that I look any different than I ever have, even though I'm a year older today. My outside is still fit and strong, but the interior of my mind feels like a sun-worn, faux leather car seat.

There's a loveseat and chair-and-a-half positioned in front of the window. Past the furniture, in the far corner of the room, is a black spiral staircase that leads upstairs. An open floor plan takes me to a kitchen whose counter goes along the wall to my left. There's a square island in the center. To the right of it is a large bathroom that also connects to our bedroom.

I boil water in a black electric kettle, impatient for physics to catch up with my desires. My coffee is made in a Pyrex French press. Caffeine in hand, I ascend the spiral staircase deliberately. When I reach the top, I see the cream-colored sectional facing the wall to my left, which has a large flat-screen television attached to it. In front of it sits a glass-top coffee table. Beyond the couch is a pool table in the center of the room, and a bar behind that. There's a guest room to my right. Along the same wall is a bathroom, and in the far-right corner is Tiffany's office, where she writes, draws, and does calligraphy.

Holding my coffee cup with my left hand, I slide the glass door to the second-story deck open with my right. I sit in one of our two rocking chairs and look out onto the water just as the day stirs from its slumber. Across the bay, fishing charters and dive boat crews are already up, prepping their vessels.

After rescuing Tiffany and bringing her back here, we spent a lot of time out on the water. Learning to maneuver the boat gave Tiff something to focus her energy on during recovery. She's a natural. Out there, it was just the two of us surrounded by quiet. There wasn't a lot of talking during the first month. We sat, looked out onto the blue, and held hands, just being together after so long. When the time came, I told her everything that had happened to me. I could tell Tiffany was skeptical at first, especially about Mara. A silent, ominous bodyguard appearing from nowhere seems like a delusion. But the day we left Vernon on the rotting whale carcass, out at sea, Tiff saw Mara transfer the light I carry in my chest to me. That's why Tiffany didn't question my sanity when I asked her if she can hear the strangers' voices in her sleep. She only hears hers and mine, and the terrors wrought upon them in our past.

Since shuttering my dive venture, I've done as I have today; slept very little, drank a lot of coffee, and stared at the water. Everyone else dashes around me, going places and having a purpose.

While seeking one, I asked Tiffany to let me call on those who hurt her while we were apart. She told me no. I never agreed, but I've followed her wishes so far.

I pour two more cups of coffee over the next hour and a half. Right before six in the morning, I start the kettle again to make a cup for Tiff. She's taking a summer writing course at UNC-W that meets from eight to twelve on Tuesday and Thursday mornings.

I place Tiffany's cup on her bedside table.

"Coffee," I say quietly.

She groans.

"Did you sleep at all, baby?" she asks.

"No. I don't want to hear them."

"Your body will eventually force you to sleep."

"I'm not like other people."

"You're not that different," she says softly."

"You know that's not true, Tiff."

She sighs in begrudging agreement.

"How can I sleep? There are so many. Their cries vibrate through the ground and into my ears."

"Even if you knew who they were, you can't stop it all."

"I know," I say, frustrated, then turn and walk out the door to drink even more coffee and stare.

I'm not walking away because I'm angry at her, rather, the truth breaks my heart. Being inside makes me claustrophobic and I need to breathe.

Tiffany dons her robe and joins me, taking a seat in the rocking chair to my left.

"After I leave, I want you to go to bed. It's your birthday. You should enjoy yourself this evening instead of sitting in the corner delirious from lack of sleep."

"I don't know how to enjoy myself anymore," I reply.

Tiffany kisses my cheek and goes about her morning routine.

As she prepares to leave the house, I admire how beautiful she looks in her black dress with white polka dots and adorable red glasses.

She kisses me on the lips and says, "I love you," before walking about the front door.

"I love you too," I respond.

I do as Tiffany instructs, and take myself to bed. It feels as though my head passes through the pillow and into oblivion.

2

I wake up on an isolated set of train tracks cutting a corridor through a dense pine forest. It's cold enough that I can see my breath. That can't be right. It's summer. My clothes are different. I was wearing an old pair of gray pajama pants and a faded black t-shirt. Now, I'm in jeans, a greenish-black flannel, and equipped with a nice set of hiking boots.

I sit up and look around. There's nothing but moonlight, a starlit sky, train tracks underneath me, and trees on both sides. I begin to feel foolish for remaining on the tracks, so I stand and move off to my left. Though, I don't dare go too far. The woods are close. It's dark in there, and I'm not sure if it's safe.

Then I glimpse a light ahead on the tracks. It's not a train. It's too slow and quiet. As it grows closer, I see that it's a woman carrying a lantern. She's in a long black dress, accessorized with a black shawl. She has shoulder-length, straight black hair, olive skin, round features, and green eyes.

Holding the lantern to her chest, she announces, "I am Frieda," in a soft, wandering voice.

"What the hell do you want?" I inquire, tersely.

"Oh Naomi, whose rage has served her well, not everyone

wants to harm you."

"Enough do."

"Your abilities frighten you."

"My anger frightens me because of what my abilities make me capable of. What if I lose control?"

"What you're capable of is why those voices cry out in your direction."

"There are too many."

"Terrifyingly so. Whatever gifted this to you doesn't want it stuffed away in the attic of your mind. Rather, it seems to want you to hone your skills like a knife edge upon a stone. As you learn, you will be able to focus on the voices of those you can help. Right now, it's like a radio, tuned in between stations."

"The convergence of these stations is unraveling my mind," I reply.

"Reality is already unraveling. Recognizing this when others ignore it isn't insane."

"I have ignored the sphere of light in my chest for two years, never once using my ability to manipulate the Earth. The only time I find myself wanting to is when I'm angry."

"What creates a power, fuels it."

"And what are you, exactly?"

"A Ceraphirian."

"Jesus-fucking-Christ," I say, kicking at the gravel the tracks are laid on, launching several to disappear into the forest. Then, it seems, the wilderness growls in protest.

Frieda pauses and looks toward the trees with a hint of concern. There is stillness again.

"Ceraphirian are equation-minders. There were twelve of us. Each is responsible for an aspect of reality. My function is the regulation of consciousness. That's why I'm the one who was sent to speak with you. One of our sisters passed into your plane, hundreds of years ago, as you would understand it. She never returned. Her responsibility was terrestrial functions. It's her light we believe you possess. That's why your abilities center around the Earth."

"The tracks are a netherworld between realities. It's a representation of the human plane, where time exists. Everything rotates around it, like a wheel on an axis. For some, this could be seen as a road, a river, a wagon trail, or any other mode of human transport. It clicks forward, around, and around, like the hands of a clock.

"And the train?"

"Those who choose to ride it have forfeited their time and consciousness. They travel placated and blank, awaiting an unfortunate destination."

"Suicide?"

"Yes. Besides having the light of a Ceraphirian, it's the only way into this nether plane. What most humans don't understand is that they occupy one of three realities. Existence is akin to the layers of a cake, sandwiched upon one another. Most sentient species are only aware of their own. We Ceraphirian can view all three, and time as a whole instead of linearly. While that might make us seem god-like to humans, we are not. It could be said that your reality is the center layer, ours the upper, and the one where Mara originated, the lower. They work in harmony as one unit. On the rare occasion that something passes from either the Ceraphirian or Mara's existence into yours, it is extraordinary and capable of bending what is considered real."

"All I want is to grow old with the woman I love, catch some fish, and hang out with my friends. I've had enough."

"I have no doubt the girls buried in Vernon's sarcophagus felt similarly. They didn't get what they wanted either."

"Shit," I remark as I scoff and cross my arms.

Pointing toward where I kicked the rocks earlier, Frieda says, "That world is home to the dreadful beasts who haunt the imagination of your species. They can only be tamed with the light of a Ceraphirian, and only when that light is wielded by a human. You're the only one who has ever accomplished this. We don't fully understand how, but what I can tell you is that your discontent stems from the fact your path has not met its end and you refuse to move forward."

"Are y'all in control of this debacle?"

"Absolutely not. No one is."

"How convenient for you," I reply with sarcasm.

"Solid Rock is just a phantom limb now. But the ones who gave birth to their ideas are curious about you. Their tendrils grasp and explore the very air you have occupied. They seek to unleash the nightmare contained within Mara's world onto yours. Their cult believes God wishes for them to punish those they deem wicked and then bring about end times. Their deity, like all human deities, is a fiction created by fragile minds compiling a stream of data zipping past their limited view."

"What do they want with me? Revenge?"

"They want the Ceraphirian light that resides within you. That would allow them to wield creatures of Mara's plane like a weapon of war. And war is exactly what they want."

The sound of a train's horn engulfs us, and its light barrels down the track in our direction.

"There is only one way off your path. The train. If you find yourself here again and want out, all you have to do is jump on one of the freight cars and ride. The passenger compartments are for those who boarded in your Universe by their own hand. Your light won't allow you to commit suicide. Though you're still vulnerable to harm by others' hands. If you choose to do so, your body will dissolve from the physical world. You will enter a stasis. Awareness of everything from your life will leave. You will become perpetual joy without agency or complexity. Tormented people run toward it. But it's our thoughts that give us meaning. And to abandon them is to become nothing."

I step back away from the train, toward the side occupied by the beasts. Frieda moves to the opposite side of the tracks.

"Don't get too close," Frieda says, raising her voice, as the sound of the horn grows. "The creatures are contained, but the boundary is always in flux. After their deaths, men like Vernon are dumped here to chase the train, only to find it's always just out of reach. Beasts from the tree line collect them as they stumble across the rocks. Their screams can be heard from time to time as they ceaselessly run through the forest in horror. There is always a creature on their heels. They are eventually caught, torn apart, eaten, digested, and defecated, only to re-form and repeat the process for eternity. Everyone else bypasses the train to either be reborn or retire to a small world of their own based on their happiest memories. I see you living simply in a cabin surrounded by friends."

The train passes between us. While waiting, I look into the woods. I see a strange oblong shape that I soon realize is something's head peeking around a tree at me. Its claws slowly appear as they grip one side of the trunk. It's then that I get a scope of its size. The creature is likely eight feet in height. Its long legs gradually propel a small, plump torso my way. As the moonlight illuminates this thing, I see that its skin is the color of school paste. Deep, bright, shimmering indigo-colored veins are easily apparent underneath. There are no eyes, just black holes. The creature's upper mouth is teeming with human-like teeth, but there is no lower jaw, only a flappy hole leading to a gullet.

Instead of running, I walk directly at it with focused intent. This confuses the beast, bringing it to a standstill. The orb in my chest glows through my skin. Having heard the train pass, I quickly look in Frieda's direction. She's no longer there. When my head whips back toward the stalker, I see it galloping straight toward me, long, black claws, a foot in length, extending in my direction. Then, the orb ignites a piercing white light that extends from my chest like a spherical, illuminated bomb, filling up the space around me. The beast flees back to the safety of the dark woods, all the while releasing a high-pitched scream.

3

Awakened suddenly, I have the instinct to catch myself as I experience the sensation of falling through the ceiling and into bed. This is prompted by the front door shutting. Is it that far past twelve already? I sit up as Tiff enters the room with a glass of ice water for me. She knows that I will often go all day without drinking anything but coffee. Tiffany regularly states how she wants to keep me around as she forces water and green vegetable matter on me. I quit smoking after killing Vernon, just like I promised.

Tiffany has taken up a very healthy routine. She does yoga daily and rarely eats meat other than broiled or grilled fish. Often, I can catch her dinner right off our dock without much effort.

"It's a quarter-till. Don't you want to get lunch?" Tiffany questions.

"Okay," I say, feeling a bit dejected after my conversation with Frieda. Should I tell Tiffany? How do I start a lunch conversation about the multi-dimensional being who told me that I'm being pursued by a cult, while simultaneously encouraging the use of my abilities to bring about their destruction?

My mind is at a point where I'm not sure if I am dreaming while awake or awake while dreaming. Frieda could be a figment or paranoia. I can't rightfully discuss it with a therapist. I'd likely be placed on an involuntary seventy-two-hour stint at a psychiatric hospital, for fear that my tenuous grip on what is real could pose a danger to myself. It doesn't sound therapeutic at all.

It's decided that we're to have lunch at Allen's. It's a restaurant with outside seating on the sound. Tiff drives me there in her gold-colored Camry. She says my Jeep isn't a safe vehicle. I have shrimp and grits. Tiff eats a Caesar salad with shrimp. I drink three painkillers. At Allen's, they're little more than a glass of coconut rum with a splash of orange juice. The questionable slurry food and cheap booze in my stomach make me feel ill.

On the way home, I hang my head out the window while we cross over the drawbridge and vomit profusely down the passenger-side door of the unfortunate Toyota.

I can tell Tiffany is unhappy with me. I don't blame her.

I sleep dreamlessly most of the afternoon.

Nate and Herschel arrive at seven, and we head to downtown Wilmington in Herschel's car. We eat at a restaurant called Caprice. It's French, which, until last year, I'd never had. I have escargot and striped bass.

Here's the thing about Herschel: something about getting his pinky chopped off by two Nazi-redneck pricks made him snap. He began taking martial arts and working out regularly. His physical transformation has been dramatic. Since he already had a tendency toward arrogance, it's become mildly annoying. But, yeah, he's kind of a badass now. Herschel has done well financially. He drives a God-awful BMW, which I have to admit, is comfortable as hell.

Nate, though, is the same soft-spoken, brilliant man he was the day we met.

Herschel parks the large, black, four-door sedan in a parking lot across the street from Spectrum for a five-dollar fee.

The four of us jaywalk with brisk strides to the front door. The entrance has a small foyer where they check IDs and take the ten-dollar cover charge. Inside, there's a bar to the left, bathrooms to the right, and a large dance floor in the center, taking up most of the building's square footage. Behind it is a DJ booth. A few high-top tables surround the dance floor.

Sweaty bodies move to the beat of house music, oblivious to anything but the rhythm and feeling. I personally don't understand the appeal. My friends know this, which is why we walk around the dance floor and take the stairs behind the DJ booth to the rooftop. There are a dozen high-top metal outdoor tables, with four matching chairs at each. All of them have umbrellas that are closed, as it's a clear, comfortable night. Directly across from the door is a covered bar. If you look over the edge of the roof by the stairs, you'll see a courtyard hemmed in with a large stone wall. That also belongs to Spectrum. Like the rooftop, it gives those who want to have conversations without screaming over music a place to sit and drink. Unlike the mountains, Wilmington is warm enough to allow the use of outdoor spaces year-round.

Beyond the courtyard is a bar called The Helm, frequented by Marines. Across the street, facing both Spectrum and The Helm is a Baptist church that permanently has signs posted out front that say things like, 'God hates queers,' or 'Matthew Shepard is burning in hell.' We try to ignore them, but it still hurts.

I order a painkiller. Herschel has a Jameson served neat, and Nate, a dry gin martini. Tiffany has quit drinking altogether, so she's our designated driver.

Herschel goes on about a new cannabis strain he bred. Even though we've gotten out of the illicit cannabis trade, he keeps a personal grow for himself and as medicine for his mom, Diane.

After a few drinks, Nate is approached by a man named Claude, who asks to dance. Claude is five-foot-six, wiry, with dark hair, and thick eyebrows over an equally thick brow. He's not a stranger. We've spoken to him a few times before. Nate takes his hand and is led enthusiastically by Claude back downstairs.

Herschel is approached several times. The men compliment his physique, and he loves it, though he never takes any of them up on their offers. I know Herschel is straight, but he never has a girlfriend. At this moment in his life, I believe he prefers compliments to commitment.

Tiffany doesn't drink, she does smoke cannabis and is now enthralled with Herschel's impromptu presentation. I'm on my fourth drink.

The booze has caused me to withdraw into my mind. I think about Frieda while I stare off into space pretending to listen. It's not that I'm not interested in what Herschel is saying. I love him dearly, but I'm on edge. My mind vacillates between concern over my own sanity or fear that what Frieda said is true.

That's when I hear it.

"Nate," I scream, as I leap to my feet!

Herschel immediately does the same, like a soldier reacting to the command of a superior officer.

"What is it?" Tiffany asks, still seated.

"Something is wrong. I can feel it," I reply.

"Where," Herschel responds.

"There, in the alley," I say, pointing over the edge of the courtyard toward the building next to us.

We can't see into the alley because of the stone wall.

"Let's go," Herschel shouts.

Tiff rises to her feet.

"No," I say sternly, looking at my bride.

I can tell by the look on her face that Tiffany is pissed, but she knows I'm right.

Tiffany may be mentally strong, but she doesn't have the constitution to deal with the trouble I sense.

Herschel leads the way, running toward the stairs. When we make it to the courtyard, we see that the security door has been propped open. Herschel runs into it at full force, causing it to smack against the wall as it swiftly articulates one-hundred-eighty-degrees. He turns right toward the alley, with me fast on his heels.

It's the space between the courtyard wall of Spectrum and the Helm. There, we see five young Marines confronting Nate and Claude. All are young white men in their early twenties with the typical jarhead buzzcut. Slews of them drive over on the weekend from Camp Lejeune in Jacksonville. Sure, plenty come to have a good time, then head back. But a substantial minority travel here to catcall, harass and force themselves on young women. When that fails, they often go out looking for fights, or as is far too common near Spectrum, to gay-bash someone. A large muscular man of six-foot-four appears to be their unofficial commander. He leads the taunting. The others are men of average height, and very fit, as they had all recently finished basic training.

"Y'all boys out here kissin'," I hear him say.

I can't make out much in the way of facial features because it's dark, but I can clearly see Nate standing directly in front of Claude to protect him. I know it's Nate because he almost always wears a crisp white shirt that shows up well in the dark.

It dawns on me now. After dancing, Nate and Claude stepped out the security door, propping it open, so they could make out in the alleyway.

"Yes, we are," Nate replies as he stares down the large Marine, not flinching, or capitulating to his demands by making excuses.

Nate is proud of who he is, which is something I adore about him.

"You got a fucking problem," Herschel screams down the alley at the imposing marine as we approach.

"Why? Is this here your boyfriend?"

"My best friend," Herschel says as he reaches the man.

Seeing me, he says, "So, you two are coming out of Rectum too?"

'Rectum' is a pejorative, guys like him use to describe the only gay-friendly establishment in Wilmington. Occasionally, when referring to women, they call it 'Speculum.' I suppose they think it's clever.

"Are you planning on doing something about it," the brute inquires?

"I'm planning on going home with my friends, safely. That's all. No one is bothering you. Just go back to your bar and have a few more drinks, and we'll go back to ours," Herschel responds.

"Are you telling me what to do now," he asks.

"It's a friendly suggestion. They haven't done anything to you."

"They're fagging the place up. That's enough to piss me off good."

Nate and Claude begin to move away from the courtyard wall, toward us.

"Wait a second, bitch-boy. Ain't nobody said you could go nowhere," the large Marine says, grabbing Nate by the collar with his left hand. "Whatcha gonna do? There are five of us against two skinny homos, you and a girl."

"Whatever it takes," Herschel responds.

The hulking Marine, while still holding Nate's collar, rears back his right hand in a fist. It's a drunken, profusely telegraphed punch. Before he can land it, Nate quickly jabs the man's liver with his left fist.

Surprised, and in excruciating pain, the Marine stumbles backward toward his friends. I'm instantly proud of Nate. I taught him that. A proper liver shot is devastating and can take down the largest of opponents. That's why they're illegal in boxing.

The other four immediately dogpile Nate and Claude. Herschel puts his right elbow into the throat of the man closest to him, sending the bastard to his knees. Then there is general chaos. Fists and kicks swing wildly. The first Marine I get my hands on, I grab by the collar, and cram my left thumb into his right eye, crushing it into his skull.

"I was going to be a sniper," he screams.

"Not anymore," I reply.

Now it's the three of us against two.

I feel the anger swelling within me. The Earth calls out to my mind, saying, "Naomi, take my energy. Return to your path."

I resist because we easily pummel the remaining two.

But then, the larger Marine gets back on his feet. He grabs me with both hands and lifts me up against the wall by my shirt.

Nate and Claude are on my right, and Herschel is on my left. As they close in, Herschel sees my left hand glowing bright white.

"Step back," he screams at both of them!

Knowing exactly what Herschel means, Nate grabs Claude and pulls him away.

I reach up with my glowing white hand and light the man's entire right arm on fire. Wailing in pain, he falls back. I focus my energy on the wall behind him. The bricks disappear as I bring forth a stone archway that opens up to the night sky I saw in my dream of Frieda. Swiftly, I move toward the man, kicking him in the chest. He falls backward through the passageway. I catch a glimpse of the creature from before as it gallops by on its spindly, dagger-tipped legs. It releases a shriek that echoes out into the alleyway as it grabs the man off his feet with its long dark claws, fleeing with him toward the woods.

I pull my hand away and the portal closes.

The other men flee.

Herschel, Nate, and Claude look aghast at what they just witnessed. I, on the other hand, feel as though I have taken a deep breath at the ocean's surface after a long free dive.

I hear Frieda's voice telling me, "This is who you are meant to be."

4

"Come with us, Claude," I say.

"No, no, I can't. I have to go," Claude replies as he flees through the alley toward the church.

I pull out my flip phone and call Tiffany.

She answers, voice trembling, "Hello?"

"We need to go right now. Meet us at the car."

"What happened?"

"I'll explain later. Just hurry."

In the car, I run Tiffany through the chain of horrible events as she drives us home.

"Won't they go to the police?" she asks, panicked.

"They could, but I'm having a difficult time imagining the police, or their commanding officer will buy it."

"What about Claude?"

"I don't know, baby. He's scared. I can't blame him."

"Was that hell?" Herschel asks.

"In a way. It's more complicated than that. Don't worry, Herschel, it's far away from where you're going to end up."

"Those are the eerie fucking words I'm going to hear in my head right before I die. Thanks, Naomi."

"You're welcome, Herschel," I say with a less-than-insignificant level of authenticity.

"How exactly do you know that?" Nate asks.

"Thanks, buddy," Herschel says, jokingly to Nate.

"Frieda told me."

All mouths fall silent. Tiff turns to look at me in the passenger seat, taking her eyes off the road momentarily.

"Who, baby?" Tiff sputters as she looks ahead again.

"I thought it was a dream. It wasn't."

I explain what fragments I understand about the very structure of our reality based on the brief conversation I had with some lady who calls herself a Ceraphirian, in what I assumed to be a nightmare.

"I would believe you, Naomi, even if had not just seen it myself," Nate interjects.

This makes me smile slightly.

"Do you have Claude's number, Nate?" Tiffany asks.

"Yes."

"Perhaps you should call him?"

Nate dials the number. He sits there with the phone against his ear, waiting. Then I hear the slight mumble of an answering system and a beep.

"Claude, this is Nate. Give me a call when you can. We need to talk."

By this time, we are arriving back at our house. Tiff parks Herschel's car in our driveway, and we head up the side staircase.

Once inside, Herschel and Tiff step out onto the balcony to share a joint. Nate and I take a seat at the bar.

"I'm worried about Claude," Nate says.

"I don't know if explaining it to him will make it better or worse."

"Still, we owe him an explanation."

"How do you explain something like that?"

"The truth," Nate replies.

"Perhaps one where you leave out my true identity?"

"That is a reasonable proposition. I believe it is a good night to break out the brown stuff."

I retrieve a fine Irish whiskey I set aside after it was gifted to me by Diane last Christmas.

Holding my glass up, I say "Here's to Diane, may that feisty bitch live forever."

We clink our glasses together and proceed to get right fucked up. Herschel doesn't drink anything else, but he and Tiff smoke until we can hear them cackling like witches from the porch. At what? I don't know. I try to savor her laugh each time I hear it. She was away from me for so long.

My vision is getting blurry and the urge to sleep drapes itself over me. I don't hear the voices. I feel as though I can truly rest.

It's ten in the morning, the day after my birthday, and I feel like shit.

'Serves me right,' I think to myself. 'I need to stop hating myself,' I think immediately after.

I make a pot of coffee and head upstairs. There, I pass Herschel faceplanted into the sectional, snoring. Nate is already up, waiting on the deck.

"Claude isn't answering his phone," Nate says immediately after I open the sliding glass door.

"Maybe he's still asleep?"

"Perhaps, but I think we should go check on him. I know where he lives."

"We can go after they wake up."

I don't rush Herschel or Tiffany. Claude is likely in a similar state from the night before. Both of them rise from their THC coma around eleven-thirty. While they get themselves together, Nate and I sit on the sectional. I turn on the local noon news. Nothing, not a goddamn thing about what happened the night before.

"I figured there would have been a story about soldiers being assaulted," I say to Nate.

"I wonder if the lot of them went AWOL? Regardless, no one in their command, nor would any detective, believe them," Nate replies.

The four of us load up into Herschel's giant, black BMW. Nate drives us back to the mainland and into Wilmington proper. Claude lives in a long-established neighborhood off Oleander Drive. It's primarily modest-sized cottages, engulfed by lingering pines and imposing oak trees, whose generous canopies blot out the sun. This is by design, as most of the structures existed before air-conditioning.

Claude's place is meant to have a white exterior. Over the years, tannins from the pine straw, along with moss, have demonstrated conflicting aesthetic opinions. These days, it's a dingy yellow, with patches of thick moss growing on the roof.

I rap on the glass of the front door, trying to make the rhythm and intensity as loud as reasonably possible, without sounding like a cop.

Nothing.

My feet crunch over old leaves, crispy on packed, sandy ground, as we walk counterclockwise around Claude's bungalow. There, I find a short set of concrete stairs leading up to the back door. Resting upon the steps are shards of broken glass. Someone busted out the window on the door and stuck their hand through to open it from the inside.

There's a faint blood streak across the black-and-white checkered vinyl floor, directly adjacent to the wall leading to the back door.

"That's blood," I say, pointing.

"The person who broke the window could have cut themselves," Herschel states.

"But there's no blood on the glass," Nate interjects.

"I think it's Claude's blood," Tiff says, bewildered. "See how it makes a small puddle, then another. Someone may have hit him in the temple. This might be the blood trail left behind as Claude's head bobbed back and forth while he was dragged by his legs, unconscious toward the back door."

"Fuck," Nate says matter-of-factly.

"Can you call him?" Herschel asks.

Nate takes out his phone and dials Claude's number. Seconds later, we hear the phone buzzing. This leads us under the couch where it rattles against the hardwood floor. Nate picks it up and slides the phone into his left pocket.

"Maybe they'll call," he says.

The four of us return to our house to regroup.

"Hair of the dog?" Herschel queries, as he walks toward the bar.

"No, I need to focus."

Herschel calls his mother, Diane, and informs her of what has happened, and that he and Nate will be staying here while we sort it out. We can't exactly inform the police about Claude's disappearance. He is estranged from his parents, so they won't be stopping by. Eventually, his other friends will. They'll report the break-in, and perhaps they will issue a missing person's report. Sadly, the police down here don't generally put a lot of effort into finding men like Claude. Hell, a lot of the cops go to churches like the one across the street from Spectrum. Given the choice, many would rather pledge an oath to the Bible than the Constitution.

The day fades into night with no word from Claude, no voices, and no visions.

By midnight, we all return to bed, hoping tomorrow will bring answers.

———

At three-thirty in the morning, I hear Frieda's voice scream in my ear, "Wake up!"

I sense the heavy boot-fall of a large person in my living room. Leaving Tiff asleep, I move quietly toward the door. Cracking it open, I peek through to see the shadowy outline of a large man holding a pistol in his right hand. I think to reach into my closet and retrieve my 30 Hart, scoped hunting rifle, but the figure begins walking quicker toward our bedroom.

I reach down into the Earth and flash-heat the beach sand underneath the house, turning it into glass. I quickly pull up a two-foot-long, jagged, crystalized spear that blasts through the floor and lodges itself in the assailant's right forearm, causing him to drop the pistol and emit a piercing squeal. He begins to run, but I snatch up another, larger, glass shard, this time with back-facing barbs. I only allow it to go partway through the floor, and into his left foot. This pins him, causing the man to fall, which sends a resounding thud through the house. I reach down with my left hand and pick up the pistol. Racking the slide partway, I see a round in the chamber. The racket has woken everyone. Nate and Herschel bound down the stairs as Tiff opens the bedroom door.

The large man continues to scream.

I say, "If you don't shut the fuck up, I'm going to shoot you right behind the ear."

Tiff turns on the living room light. This allows me to get a good look at the inscription on the side of the pistol.

"A Glock nineteen," I say.

"Thank you for the gift. I lost my last one," referring to the gun I shot Vernon with as a child. I dropped it as I swam through an aquifer hidden in the secret caverns below Solid Rock.

The man is humongous. His brown hair is worn in a close-cropped buzzcut, allowing me to see the ripples of fat across the back of his skull. His body is like one giant rectangle of brawn. My guess is he's six-foot-eight and roughly three hundred and fifty pounds. He appears to be in his mid-twenties, has white skin, round features, and dark-rimmed, plastic glasses. He's wearing black pants and a black shirt. It's almost as though he got all of his ideas about covert ops from made-for-TV movies.

Unexpectedly, this behemoth begins to bawl like a toddler, snot and all.

"I'm Franklin. Frank," he moans.

"Well, hello there, Franklin. You must be in the wrong house," I say with maniacal sarcasm.

As he sobs, I realize what I'm looking at is some kind of Sunday school wannabe assassin, not the real thing.

"Before you were sent, did they not explain what I am?"

"What are you?" he asks, in severe pain.

"Divergent."

Nate, Herschel, and Tiffany stand in the periphery, quiet.

"I'm going to need to know a few things before I can let you go."

Now believing that I don't have the will to kill him, courage wells up inside the man as he states, "I ain't tellin' you anything."

Now that there are two spear-sized holes in the floor of our house, I can smell the timber it pierced. I begin to draw fine, fibrous strands of the shattered wood toward his leg. Dozens of them work their way into his ankles and begin creeping and weaving underneath the skin of Franklin's legs like wooden veins. He muffles a scream. As the fibers reach his groin, Franklin sputters, "Pa-Pastor Joseph! Please, Jesus, stop."

"And where is the good pastor?" I ask.

"Oak Island. Fort Caswell."

"Who is Pastor Joseph to you, exactly?"

"He's the prophet," Franklin groans.

"What!?" I snap. "Tell me his full name."

"His name is Pastor Joseph Proffit."

All of my neurons chant their furor in unison.

"And he sent you to kill me?"

"Yes," Franklin responds, weeping.

"How did you find me?" I say, gritting my teeth.

"The Prophet insists we keep holy sentries at our satellite church in Wilmington. It's the First Baptist across from Spectrum. Our man saw the incident. The sentry got into his car and followed Claude as he ran down the street. A few blocks away, Claude caught a taxi. Our guy tailed them. Later that night, I paid Claude a visit."

"Where is he now," I demand.

"He's locked up at Fort Caswell."

Franklin pauses for a second.

Tears run down his face, partially because of the pain, but also from fear, and the realization that his cowardice has made him a traitor.

Quivering, Franklin says, "I told you the truth. Please, let me go!"

"You know I can't do that, Franklin. But, since you've been cooperative, I'll make it fast."

He cries uncontrollably as I approach from behind. Placing my right hand on top of his head, I quickly pull all the moisture from his body, brain first, killing him instantly. Franklin becomes a withered shell, taking on the appearance of a Pompeii victim. The movement of me backing away shakes the floor just enough to cause the desiccated thing that used to be a human being to disintegrate into a cloud of flakey dust.

Without saying a word, I walk up the iron spiral staircase and onto the second-floor balcony. There, I release a cloud of mist from my hand that disperses across the harbor.

I turn to see my two best friends and Tiffany standing behind me, confounded.

Directing my statement to Herschel, I say, "Call your mom. Tell her to arm herself."

"Nate, phone Zeke and Beverley. Tell them to bring cleaning supplies and tools. I know Zeke doesn't like carrying a gun, but it's time."

I put the Glock in Nate's hand and say, "Stay here. Protect Tiffany."

I walk into Tiff's and my closet, retrieve my 30 Hart rifle, plus a box of cartridges, and hand them to Herschel, stating, "We need to go get your mom right now!"

5

"Mom, don't leave the house, barricade the doors, and arm yourself," Herschel says over the cell phone as I drive.

"Why?" I hear faintly through the receiver.

"I can't discuss it over the phone. We're on our way," Herschel replies as he hangs up.

We drive north through Jacksonville, into the Croatan National Forest, past New Bern, arriving in Little Washington just as the sun is coming up.

Today, Diane is a wholly different woman than when I first met her. Her blond hair, which is kept short, has returned. She's put on weight, her skin is healthy, and she exudes life.

"What the fuck's wrong now?" Diane says as she opens the door with one hand while holding a Browning A-5 in the other.

She sees me eye the shotgun and says, "It was dad's favorite. He used it to dove hunt when I was a little girl."

The thought of Diane with her father makes me smile ever so slightly.

"The motherfuckers kidnapped Nate's friend and sent someone to kill us," Herschel says.

"Are you okay?"

"Are you kidding? I was with Naomi. Their house is going to need a bit of repair, though."

I'm standing on a lower stair, so Diane and I are eye-to-eye. She leans in, kisses me on the forehead, and says, "Thank you, dear."

"Always," I respond.

"Naomi interrogated him. It sounds a lot like Solid Rock, only it's not."

I interject, "We don't fully understand, but the rube had a rough idea of who I am. He referenced a man named Joseph Proffit as their leader. He could be a relative or maybe it's more like a title. But what we do know is where they're keeping Claude. We have to be quick. They're going to get curious when their man doesn't show back up, and they'll eventually send someone else, or maybe even kill Claude."

Herschel says, "Zeke and Beverly are on their way to pick you up from my house. We have a bit of cleaning and fixing to do, so y'all won't be leaving until tonight. We aren't sure if they know where you live, but it's safer if we're all together."

"Naomi, will you stay here with mom while I go pack up Nate's and my things?"

"I'd love to."

Herschel returns to his BMW and drives three blocks to their house while I slip through the front door at Diane's. I don't worry much about him being on his own anymore. He was a pure savage the other night.

The inside of Diane's home smells like cannabis smoke. The ashtray on her kitchen table still has a joint smoldering on its edge.

"Tea?" Diane asks as she locks the door behind her, still holding the shotgun.

"Sure."

Diane drinks as much green tea as her bladder will withstand since going into remission.

After putting the water on to boil, she asks, "What do you think?"

"It's possible that this is just coincidental, but I doubt it."

"Why am I going with Zeke and Beverly?"

"Zeke is likely the one of us they know the least about. And, since they operate out of Oak Island, we figured getting you further away is preferable."

"Have you seen Mara again?"

"No. I think she's gone for good, but I've had other visions."

After explaining them to Diane, she says, "Frieda sounds a lot like a witch."

"Or maybe what we might call a witch," I respond.

"True," Diane concedes. "How many of our words are just humans putting a name to something we can't comprehend, then applying a value judgment?"

"Quite a few, it seems."

We each have our tea with a touch of honey while Diane continues to smoke her joint.

Herschel returns an hour later with two suitcases and two backpacks filled with their hiking gear.

The drive back is uneventful, except for the fact that Diane forces Herschel to play much better music. I'm one My Chemical Romance song away from strangling him.

I arrive to find Zeke repairing the floor. After I saved Herschel and Nate from the Mace brothers, when we first met, Zeke cleaned the blood out of Herschel's car with bleach and industrial-strength hydrogen peroxide. It's a rather strong odor, but the DNA evidence Franklin left behind will have been eliminated.

Zeke was able to patch the subfloor and replace a few planks of hardwood. The stain he applied is a bit off, but fuck it.

As much as I despise my friends being in harm's way, I haven't felt this well in two years. After we save Claude, I don't know if I can return to a normal life.

As the seven of us join up, I realize there is silence as everyone looks at me, assuming that somehow I know what to do.

"Zeke, do you have a sidearm?"

Zeke lifts his shirt to display a SIG Sauer nine-millimeter, tucked into a concealed waistband holster.

"I hate carrying this thing," Zeke says.

"I know, but I need you and Beverely to take Diane and Tiffany back up to y'all's place. Nate, Herschel, and I are going to take my boat to the southern tip of Oak Island and rescue Claude."

"What?" Tiffany says.

"Please don't be contrary with me, baby. I can't leave him to die. I'd rather you be pissed off at me momentarily than him gone permanently. Take my rifle with you. You're a damn good shot."

I kiss Tiffany on the lips right before she, Zeke, Beverly, and Diane load up into Beverly's chardonnay-colored Volvo four-door sedan. When he's at home, Zeke still drives a seventies model, white Chevy truck. But it's not practical for transporting three people and luggage.

It's dark when the four of them leave for Asheville.

"Make sure no one follows you," I advise Zeke.

First thing the next morning, we load up my dive boat and head south through the Intracoastal Waterway. After an hour and a half, we're sitting off the southern tip of Oak Island.

Fort Caswell occupies the entire southern portion of the island, forming a comma shape whose outer curve points into the sea. It's only connected to the rest of the island by a thin strip of land that hosts the one road into the compound.

Fort Caswell itself was built in the nineteenth century as the newly formed United States Government began to build up its defenses. The fort was captured by the Confederacy, twice. Throughout its history, somehow, Caswell was never directly attacked from the sea. The fort shut down a few years after the end of World War I, after which it was sold off to the Baptist State Convention. I spent a week there when I was twelve for church camp. Since then, there have been drastic changes.

Looking through binoculars, the most notable addition I see is a thick masonry wall, at least ten feet in height, going across the entirety of the island, separating itself off as a fort against what was on the land, as well as the sea.

I can see men standing near where the wall stops at the beach on both sides. They're wearing uniforms and seem to be guarding against outside access. Men in similar garb walk on top of the wall. Others patrol the beach in sets of two.

"It's like their own micro-country," I remark.

"The fuck you will," Herschel says, knowing what I'm thinking. "You'd have to swim a goddamn long way in the dark. We're at the mouth of a large river, which is exactly where bull sharks congregate. And, as you well know, the night is when they hunt. And if you miss the island, you'll drift out to sea through the inlet."

"How long do you think Claude has left? Worse yet, what if they move him to another facility?"

In silent acknowledgment, Herschel nods in agreement.

"Can't you use your abilities on them from the boat," Nate asks.

"I can only affect the environment within fifty feet around me.

Though, I can feel down much further into the Earth. From the boat, I'm useless."

We return to my house, making a stop for fuel along the way.

———————

All I need is time to get my thoughts together, everything else is superfluous.

———————

We leave around ten o'clock in the evening and arrive at midnight. The trip takes longer in the dark.

Nate throws anchor about a half-mile north of the island. I plan on letting the river's outflow push me along. I've donned a black, three-millimeter wetsuit, with a nice pair of thick-bottomed dives boots inside a set of fins. I'm also equipped with a mask, snorkel, and a belt where I clip my dive light. I keep a dive knife in a holster attached to my left calf.

"Once I have Claude, I'll signal you with my flashlight so you can pick us up off the beach."

With confidence, Nate replies, "We'll see you on the other side."

"It's like old times," I say to them as I plummet backward off the port gunwale of the boat.

I snorkel with my mask half out of the water to keep my eyes on the upcoming island. Herschel's words about bull sharks jangle around in my head. The scientist in me runs the raw numbers past my lizard brain, which, it seems, doesn't understand either facts or figures.

All goes without incident, and I wash ashore at the very southern tip of Oak Island.

6

The southern tip of the island is an open beach backed by thick, almost desert-like, scrub brush. All the modern structures were built on the better-protected western side of the island. North of my position is a retired six-inch gun battery. The gun was removed by the military, but it could be a lookout point. The only road into the compound runs along the western basin. It's lined with cottages. South of the road is an abandoned, fortified battery built into the dunes.

I sit on the beach and quickly remove my fins and mask, ready to make my way into the brush and wait. Before I can, I'm faced with a creature's eyes glowing in the dark, no more than twenty feet down the western beach.

I expect to hear the bark of a guard dog, but instead, it releases shrieks that sound like a possessed, screeching toddler. As it gets closer, I can see that the thing's eyes are glowing indigo. I hear the footsteps of two large men in the procession behind it. This is no dog.

It has brown, leathery skin and a long, conical gray beak, which parts in half as it releases that God-awful haunting call. Contained within it are two rows of pointy teeth, two up top, and two on the bottom. The four upper canines are so long that there are corresponding holes for them to protrude through in the lower beak. Its indigo eyes are recessed inside the head, facing forward. The pupils dance wildly as it scans the surroundings. Across its back are black chevrons that appear to be sharp obsidian, forming a kind of mohawk. They proceed down a lizard-like tail, which it lashes around violently. Its four legs are hinged backward, supported by feet bearing black claws, no shorter than six inches. From its head to the tip of the tail, it's six feet in length, and easily weighs two hundred pounds.

Now in range, I heat the sand, like before, and pull multiple spikes of glass up underneath the three of them. The two me let out momentary, high-pitched screams that extinguish as soon as their lungs are pierced. In death, the shards continue holding them upright.

The glass, however, breaks upon striking the thick skin of the monster's underbelly. Every hit creates an indigo static ripple effect from each impact point, much like a stone dropped into water. Its eyes spark. There are no pupils. They're like empty black marbles with tiny zigzags of electricity bouncing inside of them.

It's no more than twenty feet from me now. I reach into the Earth and push down on the mantle below the advancing beast, causing it to plunge into a newly formed sinkhole that begins to fill with ocean water. It stops moving and sinks.

North of me, two more men run in my direction. I create a new sinkhole under them in case they were in pursuit along with a similar companion. The men disappear into the sea.

But I hear that horrid scream again. Out of the bramble-ridden hill behind me leaps an identical beast. I heat my left hand white hot. As it lands on top of me, I attempt to burn my way through its chest to rip its heart out. Nothing happens.

The ghoulish thing reeks of sulfur and rotting meat.

Instinctively, I reach down to my calf, unsheath my dive knife and stab the monster in the left side of its gut. Just before plunging it in, I see the blade shimmering and sparking just like the eyes of the beast. The creature releases one last shriek and then dissolves into dust that rains down over me. Now, my knife appears normal again.

Another figure appears in front of me, holding a familiar lantern. It's Frieda.

"They're beasts of lamentation."

"Where?" I say.

"You know the place. It's the dark woods that birthed the spindly monster."

"The light, it protected me then. Tonight, it did nothing."

"It protects you from them when they're behaving by the rules and staying where they belong. That's the danger of having the beasts of lamentation crossing over into your world; they can't be killed by conventional means. The rules of physics are completely different in all three planes. So when something is out of place, it's impervious to the laws of science. How they're calling beasts forth, and controlling them without the light of a Ceraphirian, I cannot say. It is your path to discover how."

"How did I kill them?"

"There are only two ways we are aware of. First, there's no water in the Woods of Lamentation. They don't so much drown as shut down. They can get wet, but not fully submerged. And secondly, the lamentation blade.

"I have a normal knife. It's stainless steel so that it doesn't rust in saltwater."

"A lamentation blade isn't an individual weapon. It can only be produced by a human bearing the light of a Ceraphirian. Instead of pulling energy out of the Earth, you transferred fragments of reality from the Woods of Lamentation into the steel of the knife. That momentary transformation made it so the injury is dealt with matter from their existence."

"How did I open the doorway between our world the other night in the alleyway?"

"The primary emotion driving your abilities is anger, and rightfully so. The sudden burst of energy fueled by your rage gave you the ability momentarily. Eventually, you'll tame it."

"You're here. You're out of place."

"I'm not actually here. I'm a projection in your mind. My light gives me domain over consciousness. Only one of us has ever entered your plane. The Ceraphirian believe it's her light that you carry. Because you now hold it, we are certain that she is dead. Perhaps the transition between planes killed her. No one else has followed in her footsteps to test the hypothesis."

"I'm not sure if I can create a lamentation blade again," I say, holding the knife out in front of me, exerting maximum effort. "See, nothing."

"It will come when needed."

With that, she is gone.

"Goddamn, she's annoying," I say under my breath.

After fifteen minutes, no one else shows up. I step back onto the beach and approach the bodies of the men still being held in place by the shards of crystallized glass. They're wearing gray, police-like uniforms. Their badges are inscribed with the letters 'ACH'. Their clothes appear to be covered in a layer of indigo substance. I sink their bodies into the sand to be consumed by hungry crabs and sea worms, then fill in the sinkholes, repairing the damage I'd done. It's not the island's fault that vile men have desecrated it over the centuries.

I weigh my options on which structure to investigate first. If I head toward the gun battery, they'll see me coming from a distance. Perhaps I could get close enough to level it, but doing so might trigger them to kill Claude. The fortified battery to the south offers a similar set of circumstances. I can't walk down the beach in either direction without being spotted. However, now that the tide has begun to come in, I should be able to swim north with the current.

For half an hour, I snorkel my way around the northern part of the compound, and into the shallow bay behind the cottages. There's a dock to my left with several midsized craft and a couple of flat-bottomed riverboats. A path leads from it toward the cottages on the main road.

I tread water while scouting for potential danger. I think about the marine I blinded while defending my friends.

'If only I could take their vision,' I think.

It's then that I see the electric line suspended over the wall. It splits off from there and is routed to each building. It's a single point of failure. I focus on the ground below the pole closest to me and gradually shift it to one side. Slowly, it lays down on the ground like a tired dog. The tugging on the line exerts enough force to bend the pole on either side down, damaging their connections. Darkness.

Still treading water, I hear indistinguishable voices near the pole. They don't seem excited or angry, just irritated.

I swim toward the shoreline of the bay until my fins hit the mud. I reach down and pull them off. I crawl up onto a small strip of sand along the bay, stashing my mask, snorkel, and fins in its tall grass.

I place my hand on the ground and begin to feel for Claude. It's faint. They aren't screams of terror, but rather, moans of acceptance, as though life is draining out of him. I think it's coming from the fortified outpost building that's built into the southern dune.

I stay crouched in the grass as I wait for the small gathering near the light pole to disperse. One by one, I hear their voices disappear over the course of ten minutes. Then, only two remain. I advance forward, then stop and crouch behind the house closest to the downed line. When the speaking stops, I hear both parties walking in opposite directions. I move along the side of the house quickly. When I reach the front, I weigh my options. Who to follow? I decide to pursue the man to my left, as he's walking away from the wall.

He's small, five-foot-five, and quite pudgy. By the moonlight, I can tell he isn't dressed in a uniform. Rather, he's in a pair of blue pajama pants, a white t-shirt that has seen better days, and brown slippers.

Large oaks, planted along the street years ago, have since created a vast network of roots. I try to feel through the Earth itself and sense myself almost merging with it. I feel as though I'm lying under the soil, predicting his footsteps. I seep further into the root system. Not only am I controlling them, but it feels so much like a part of me that I'm no longer aware of my own body. I'm able to command the roots to free themselves from the ground and wrap around his feet. They form what looks like a giant boot made of root material whose surface is hardening into bark just as I approach. The man begins to scream for help. Just before he can, he feels my dive knife under his chin.

"Be quiet. I want to show you something," I whisper into his ear.

I begin to pull a lava tube under his feet but don't bring it all the way to the surface. As heat reaches the soles of his slippers, water in the ground and roots begins to steam. He squeals. I force it to recede, providing the man some relief.

"Do you know what that was?"

"No," a meek voice answers.

"That's where you're going if you disobey me."

"Are you an angel? Supposedly, they're terrifying," he says with a quivering voice.

"No, you stupid motherfucker, I'm here for Claude."

His demeanor turns to pure fear.

I begin to call the roots further up his body. I stop at his knees. Again, bark begins to form on the exterior after I stop.

He whimpers, "Are you a demon?"

Exasperated, I walk around his left side. Quickly, I switch the knife from my left hand to my right, so I can keep it against his throat as I face him. He's a clean-shaven white man with short brown hair.

"Your hand," he says.

"Yeah, it has a knife to your throat, dipshit."

"No, your left hand."

I pull the vines up midway up his thigh.

"Where is Claude," I ask angrily.

"The bunk. It's buried behind the southern battery. There's a door in the deepest part that leads to a short tunnel, then to a steel door. It opens to a shipping container we buried. Claude's in there."

I force the roots to swiftly crawl up and encase the man's entire body before he can scream. I tighten them around him until I hear the muffled sound of bones breaking through the wooden body cast.

I command the roots to pull him under the soil, so the tree can feed on him as its reward. Approaching the same tree, I compel it to articulate a limb down to me, sit, and ride it back up, twenty-five feet above the ground. I look toward the southern battery. It's a three-hundred-foot-long masonry structure built into a hill with portholes for cannons and muskets on the opposite side, pointing toward the ocean.

7

There doesn't seem to be any auxiliary lighting, but I'm close enough that I can see some movement by moonlight. There appear to be men coming up a set of stairs from within the far right of the structure. Each stands on either side of the staircase as they ascend. I can see that each has a rifle strapped across their chest as though they're in a warzone. I think of Frieda's words, "war is exactly what they want." Unfortunately, I'm too far away to take the fight to them with my abilities.

I see someone walking toward both men. He's in what appears to be a cloak charged with indigo sparks similar to those in the eyes of the beasts that greeted me on the beach.

As the man in the cloak passes between them, they turn and follow him down the staircase. I wait a few minutes longer. There's no movement from within, nor has anyone approached the structure. I have the limb I'm sitting on gradually lower my body down. I go for it and sprint toward the staircase the three of them just descended.

I expect to hear rifle fire at any moment but there's nothing. When I reach the stairs, I crouch and gradually work my way down until I reach a stone floor.

I place my hand against the cold wall and feel for the lifeforms inside. Mycelium courses through the soil surrounding the battery and into the crevices between stones.

Most people think of mushrooms as a singular organism. But it's only a fruiting body. Most of the critter's biomass lives underground, creating a matrix of interlacing fibers that work ceaselessly to digest rotting material. One network can span over thousands of acres and live to be equally as old in years. They use chemical and electrical signals to communicate and even play host to nutrient exchange between trees.

I see the mycelium light up all around me. They illuminate from within the walls, floors, and ceiling appearing as thin strips of white filament webbing, expanding in all directions. The hallway glows with a dim white hue. There's an obvious dead end to my right, so I proceed left. The wall curves inward, toward the island, making it so I'm not able to see very far ahead of me.

I sense the men. The mycelium touching their feet tells me their location. They're no more than twenty feet around the bend. I inch ever forward.

I see them bathed in light. They each wear an illuminated headlamp, which makes me realize that it's still dark to them. The mycelium isn't actually illuminating them, rather it's merged with my nervous system, allowing me to sense as they do.

I send my mind through the organic threads, arriving behind the men. I send the mycelium out through the mortar between each stone and encase both of them in white cocoons. Neither has time to scream.

I feel through the substrate for Claude. He's there but is growing weak.

Sensing no one else, I walk directly up to the chrysalises that were once men, now struggling through their transition. I hurry things along by removing the moisture from their bodies, leaving behind mummies wrapped in white casings.

There's a heavy plate steel door behind them. I melt it, then walk down the short, earthen hallway. After twenty feet, I'm faced with an equally thick plate-steel door, affixed to the buried storage container. The glow of electric lighting is bleeding out from around it. There must be backup batteries powering the bunker. Whatever is behind this door must be very important to them.

Waiting and listening, I hear a low moaning accompanied by gibberish, as a person attempts to speak Hebrew, poorly.

I pull heat from the Earth and force it into the door until it becomes molten red, then drops to the ground.

As it falls, I reach out my right hand and release the moisture from the bodies of the guards into the enclosed space, obscuring myself.

I can see electric indigo flashes emanating from the man's robe outlining him through the fog. The electrified shroud begins moving in my direction. I can't disturb the Earth under us without collapsing the container. The mycelium can't grow through metal, and roots piercing the walls would damage the structural integrity. Nor can I see Claude now, and I don't want to inadvertently harm him. I'm going to have to do this old school.

I take a couple of steps into the room, then allow the figure to make its way toward me. I unleash a left hook directly toward his temple, only to impact what feels like a stiff but pliable bubble, throwing indigo-colored sparks. No harm comes to the man nor my hand.

I swing my fist at the target again, to the same effect. We come eye to eye as the cloud empties out of the room like water down a drain, exposing the man.

He appears to be in his mid-thirties, five-foot-ten, with sandy-blond hair. His face is framed with a beard of the same shade. He has a robust, triangular nose, high cheekbones, and brown eyes. He would be considered traditionally handsome, almost pretty. I expected a ghoul like Vernon, but the man looks like someone I would see dancing at Spectrum.

The thought of Spectrum is fleeting, but I realize it's there because of a subconscious association. I've seen his face glancing at me from across the room at the club several times over the past two years.

"Motherfucker," I shout in shock at the revelation.

Then I look over his right shoulder to see Claude suspended upside down by ropes around his ankles, with his back against the left shipping container wall. His arms are extended toward the ground, each restrained by ropes affixed to two loops welded to the floor. I look around and notice there are more tie-down points lining the entire interior of the container. That means they have had, or intend to have, more than one victim at a time.

There is a needle piercing the left side of Claude's neck. It runs down into a clear tube, across a poured concrete floor, and to the center of the shipping container. There, it empties, drop by drop, into a pile of silty, white dust arranged into the shape of a bowl in the center of the makeshift room.

The only other objects in the room are a large glass container suspended from the ceiling holding a clear liquid. It drips down an identical tube, at the same methodical rate, also completing its journey into the same white dust.

Each time the drops combine, the dust emits a faint plume of steam. Suspended over it is what looks like a large, upside-down, martini glass with a diameter of three feet. At the interior peak is a cone that points down like a stalactite. Four glass loops surround the base of the stalactite, which are used to affix four strands of baling wire down past the tip. They hold up a coaster-sized piece of aluminum, with a Petri dish resting on it. As the mist collects at the top, it cools, then runs down the tip of the stalactite and staples as a shiny substance that is best described as having the consistency and appearance of old, crumbly indigo eye shadow.

I rush the man again in an attempt to tackle him to the ground, only to be repelled with such force that I stumble over backward. I move toward Claude, but the man just stands in my way. I pull my dive knife off my calf and attempt to ignite it into a lamentation blade, but there's nothing. I slash at him and only feel the blade rumble and skitter across whatever it is protecting him while throwing indigo sparks. I am helpless.

8

"Naomi," The man says in a middling tone over a southern Appalachian drawl.

"How do you know that name," I respond indignantly.

"There's not much I don't know."

The level of conviction in his voice sickens my stomach.

"I reckon you turned the lights out? And my guards? I assume they're dead?"

I say nothing.

"I've watched you for two years. I was on the ridge above you the night Sheriff Morton was killed. I saw that thing throw him more than fifty yards into the ravine."

"I had gone up there to buy a jar of moonshine from the Price brothers for my daddy. And, I'm ashamed to say, I also bought meth from them, and had parked to smoke."

"Once you sped away in Sheriff Morton's patrol Jeep, I drove down to have a look. I shined a flashlight into the passenger section of your van and caught a glimpse of fresh blood sprayed across the center console. I returned to the ridge and waited for your return. When you did, I saw you destroy the Jeep by crumbling it into bits just by touching it. When you left, I followed behind you at a distance the entire way."

"After you arrived at the church in Rocky Mount, I kept going, found gas, and returned to sit on the edge of the road with my lights out, waiting."

"At this point, I still wasn't sure if what I saw was real or part of a drug-induced hallucination. But I felt that somehow I was destined to bear witness."

"What I didn't know at the time is that you had Pastor Vernon Proffit inside the back of your van. I followed you all the way to your house in Wrightsville Beach. After, I watched two young men drive the van away from your house. Hours passed, and I assumed you had accomplished what you had your heart set on, and returned home. Later, when the tragedy of Vernon Proffit's kidnapping was uncovered, I realized what I had watched. I assume he's at the bottom of the Atlantic?"

"When I brought this to the congregation, the folks at Solid Rock wanted your scalp. I told them going after you was impossible because of what I witnessed you do. After they saw the remnants of the patrol Jeep, with Sherriff Morton's mummified hands still clutching the steering wheel, they conceded."

"Lost without Vernon, the church members turned to the man who first made the prophecy, Abraham."

"Centuries before Europeans used their God-given right of manifest destiny to tame the Americas, legend told of a witch with white skin living in the caverns running under Solid Rock. The night after Abraham learned of this story, he played host to a prophetic dream."

"Upon awaking, he wrote down these words, 'The witch shall call forth the one who will bring the end. She will be sired by

Vernon Proffit through a virgin girl, less than one year since her first menstruation. The child will present with a cloven left hand that will cause the world to tremble.'"

"His original name was Abraham Melvin. He's so devoted to Vernon, he gave up his own surname to become Abraham Proffit. I too have done the same."

"Vernon slashed your hand like that as a tribute to Abraham's prophecy."

"Abraham spread the gospel of Vernon's divine role, with little success outside of Yancey County. That is, until Vernon's disappearance, and the happening at Narrow Path Baptist in Rocky Mount."

"There, you recorded Vernon confessing to killing five young women while sitting in front of their rotting corpses. He, and the youth pastor, Brad Kershaw, were quite ingeniously castrated. Brad drowned in the baptismal pool while restrained to an upside-down cross. Both he and Vernon's testicles were left in jars on the altar, along with the confession tape, remaining under the silent gaze of five putrid cadavers."

"You might reckon the first thing the church staff would do when walking into such a grizzly scene would be to call the police. But secretly, the church elders knew about his predilection for young boys. They didn't care as long as it didn't get out. That's why news of what transpired never did. The tape and the rotten bodies of the five girls were burned out back. Narrow Path Baptist canceled their service that morning, citing an 'emergency plumbing issue'. The next day, Brad Kershaw's body was discovered floating in the Tar River. His red kayak was subsequently recovered downstream."

"I know this because a few weeks after Vernon's disappearance, we reached out to Narrow Path Baptist in Rocky Mount. This confirmed what we most feared, Vernon Proffit was dead."

"When forensic evidence from the Jeep, investigated by Sheriff Morton's own deputies, matched up with my eyewitness statement, people at the church perked up. Other pieces were put together. There's the anomalous stone cleave jutting from the ground in front of the Proffit's house that wasn't there before, complete with a bullet ricochet indentation on it. A deep vein of new volcanic rock appeared in their yard from right where the rifle would have been fired. Neither Vernon's wife Patty nor her rifle were ever found. I assume they were sucked underground."

"True belief has grown, expanding from Solid Rock Baptist in remote Yancey County, across other communities in North Carolina. Today, we are the 'Apostles of the Cloven Hand'. There are twelve of us who have been chosen to take up the title of Proffit."

"Each apostle has their own safe-keep province, strategically placed around the state. Abraham Proffit's money runs all the way back to the Carolina Gold Rush of the early nineteenth century. His family ingeniously hid their gold stores in the same caverns running below Solid Rock to save it from the tyranny of northern aggression during the Civil War."

"It was Abraham's money that originally bought up all the land around the old Solid Rock church, funded the school, and built Vernon's house on top of the cavern entrance. Abraham always wanted Vernon to have access at any hour to go down and pray."

"After Vernon's disappearance, he said that the prophecy must have been interrupted. The witch's light was to be passed on to the child Vernon would sire. Instead, it was mistakenly transferred to you. And now, the coming forth of an eternal age of happiness cannot happen because, without it, there can be no Armageddon."

"After going through Vernon's records and statements from church members, Abraham determined it all went wrong when Charles and you escaped, specifically the place where Charles died. He has studied many ancient texts and told us about the ritual of creating a Golem in the Talmud. That's what Abraham believes I saw accompanying you the night Vernon disappeared. Everything leads back to you."

"The dust piled up on the center of the floor is ground-up stone from the spot where Charles perished. The water is collected directly from the dripping stalactites. We, the twelve apostles, have been getting shipments of dust and water weekly to our respective provinces for a year. We've worked on recreating your happening. I was the one chosen by God to unlock its secrets. I'm the only one who knows the method. Soon, the light will belong to me and you will be burning in hell."

"Vernon's papers revealed your name. I couldn't be sure until your response to it a moment ago. We've tried water, blood, and countless prayers, but when our sentry saw what you did to those men in the alley, I knew we had to have the blood of at least one person who was nearby. I figured the light that shone upon those when the portal opened would affect their bodies, much like exposure to radiation. Perhaps just being in your presence may have the same effect? That's why we're collecting your acquaintances who fled back to Asheville. It was stupid, really. We're much stronger there."

"Our boy, Franklin, was no hitman. He had one job, to draw you out. It was the most that could have been made of his life. He was a fool, but in death, he can be a martyr for the prophecy."

"Franklin isn't much different from the man who died when we created the beasts a few days ago. They started as stray dogs. We fed them the first bits of the indigo powder. The transformation was long and torturous. After their metamorphosis was complete, they instinctively began attacking the nearest human. The man watching over them in his garage was torn apart, consumed, and defecated within the two hours his wife spent visiting her mother.

"I had the idea to rub the substance we've been referring to as 'indigo' into my clothes. Doing so, made the beasts follow my mental commands. I've taken most of it, though, and sewn it into this cloak. The higher amount allows me to do things, much like the sphere of light does for you."

I hear more men coming. I turn toward the door and collapse the tunnel leading to the bunker. Not satisfied, I bring down as much of the battery as my abilities allow, which is significant enough destruction to make it feel as though we're experiencing a small earthquake. This kills the men pursuing me instantly.

The overhead lights flicker, and the air fills with dust.

Coughing, I say, "Unless you can do that, Joseph, you're fucked."

Frieda was right when she said the primary emotion driving my abilities is anger. A serene, white-hot cold sensation overcomes me.

I sidestep to the left and place my hand on the metal wall of the cargo container. Fearful, Joseph walks backward, all the way to the other end of the fifty-foot-long bunker. I bring up three thick pillars of granite through the floor, stopping them at the top of the makeshift bunker. I think to bring shards of sharp metal from the container toward Joseph in the form of lamentation blades, but I'm unable to charge the metal into a blade. Even if I can't kill Joseph, I can trap him. I begin to melt the metal above Joseph, causing the structural integrity of the bunker to weaken. It groans under the stress of several tons of dirt. Right before it falls, Joseph places his right hand on the wall behind him and conjures a stone archway, like the one I made in the alley. But instead of the Woods of Lamentation, I see what looks like a giant, modern cathedral. He steps backward through it. The passage closes right as the dirt pours down.

9

Through the dust, I make my way toward Claude. When I reach him, I feel his carotid artery for a pulse. Claude's skin is cold. He's gone. I pull the needle out of his neck and cut his body down, then cradle him in my arms, as a mother would her child, and weep.

The thought of Joseph getting his hands on Tiffany consumes my mind. I'm overwrought with rage. Laying Claude's body down, I step toward the collapsed pile of rubble that lies where Joseph stood just moments before. I kneel and place my hands on the concrete floor. Focusing, I exert a small seismic wave that thrusts the dirt and debris upward through the hole at the top of the underground shipping container. Seconds later, I hear clumps of dirt pelting the ground above.

Left behind is an earthen ramp that allows me to climb to the surface while cradling Claude's limp body in my arms.

I systematically begin collapsing the entire battery as I carry his body back to the southern beach. Rumbling earth, falling stones, and debris awaken the entire island. I hear the occupants outside of their cottages milling around. But, because the lights are out, they cannot see me, or tell yet what I have done.

I'm exhausted by the time I get to the beach. I lay Claude in the sand. While still on my knees, I pull the flashlight from my belt and signal three quick flashes toward the ocean. Seconds later, Herschel replies with a duplicate signal from his flashlight.

With the navigation lights extinguished, Nate and Herschel approach the shore. At first, I can only hear the twin outboards. As they get closer, the moonlight exposes them. I see Nate at the helm, and Herschel approaching the portside gunwale. They idle ten feet from the beach. I put my arms under Claude's armpits and drag him backward into the light surf. I kick my way through the water with Claude on my chest until reaching the U-shaped swim platform around the outboards. I'm greeted by Herschel, who is unaware that I am carrying a corpse rather than an injured person. It is the severe whiteness of Claude's skin that exposes the truth.

Herschel reaches down and pulls Claude's body on board. I arrive on deck a few seconds later. That's when Nate realizes what he's seeing is a lifeless body. He runs toward us, leaving the boat without a pilot. Herschel jumps up and points the boat out to sea, ensuring we don't run aground.

I make my way up to the helm and say, "We have to get out of here. There are several boats in the bay. They're going to dispatch them eventually. I'll take over. Nate needs you right now. Go to him."

At full throttle, I plane out in no time. I head southeast for five miles before stopping. Herschel and Nate are sitting on the floor of the boat, their backs against the transom. Claude's body lies between them.

I cut the engine so Nate and Herschel can hear me. The water out this way is very shallow, and often quite placid, as it is tonight.

"We have to call and warn everyone before we get too far offshore for cell reception," I say.

I explain that the church is after Diane, Tiffany, Beverly, and Zeke. I don't have time to go into full detail, but that's really all that matters right now. Nate hands his flip phone to me and I dial Zeke's home phone instead of Tiff's cell. I'm afraid she'll hear the fear in my voice and become overwhelmed.

He answers after three excruciating rings.

I don't allow Zeke to get a word in edgewise, "Zeke, the church has been following you and likely knows where you live. They'll probably hesitate to approach your house because you live in a well-populated neighborhood. But, they mean to kidnap you all. Do not leave the house. Barricade the doors. Keep everyone on the second floor. If someone forces their way in, don't hesitate, kill them all."

"Jesus Christ," he says.

In the background, I hear Tiffany's voice. She asks, "What is it?" fearfully.

Shit. I upset her anyway.

"Do it now, Zeke. We'll be there as soon as we can."

I can't bear being so far away from Tiffany right now. I console myself, knowing that three of the four of them are armed. Beverley and Zeke hate guns, but Zeke has owned a pistol since being kidnaped by members of Odin's Oath, just in case. His pacifist stance has waned a bit, but never actually disappeared. Ironically, he's damn good at gunsmithing and a better-than-average shot.

Although he's competent, I'm expecting Diane to step to the front if shit goes down. I trust her as I did my adopted mother, Milly. Tiffany killed her first deer with my rifle last fall, but it's not the kind of gun meant to be used up close. It's more of a precaution, just in case someone gets past Zeke and Diane.

I explain to Nate and Herschel what happened inside the

compound. Then comes the horrible question of what to do with Claude's body.

"We have to bury Claude at sea," I say.

"His family should know," Herschel replies.

"Claude's family disowned him years ago," Nate states through tears.

"Both of you know this can't come back on us. It's the only way."

They reluctantly agree.

"I'll have to go further out; at least fifteen miles. The current should carry him to the Gulf Stream."

"Now Claude's life will be defined by him being a statistic, another dead or disappeared gay man," Nate says.

"This is the only way we can protect our family."

I realize that this is the first time I've referred to us as a family. Stressful times are the litmus test of human bonds; either they fray or become stronger. I want to believe it's more often the latter, but I'm not completely sure.

With the throttle wide open, we make the distance in about thirty minutes.

All of us stand over his body. Still and pale, he barely registers as the same entity I knew as Claude.

Nate says a short eulogy. "His name was Claude Basset. He was a friend and a lover. I only knew him for the final two years of his life. But I know this, no matter how his parents treated him, Claude was loved by me, his friends, and the community. He will be sorrowfully missed."

Remorsefully, we surrender Claude's remains to the sea.

We make our way north, through the Frying Pan Shoals back to the Masonboro inlet, then north to my house.

We secure the boat on its lift and head inside to pack up, ever watchful. They haven't played their hand yet because they're still afraid of me. If Joseph keeps getting stronger, I'm not sure how much longer that will last. Joseph is weaker than me because his abilities are like a mirror. He's reflecting the power of my light, extracted and distilled into indigo. Joseph has been vigilant in developing his abilities. He created a doorway at will and vanished. I can't do that. What else will he discover that I've missed while ignoring my gift? Where did he go? It looked like a modern-day cathedral. It very well could be some kind of a megachurch. If so, this problem is worse than I thought.

I drive my Jeep inland while Herschel and Nate follow in the BMW. The trip takes six hours.

We arrive at Zeke and Beverly's house at first light, fully aware the Apostles have likely been watching our every move. I wrap my arms around Tiffany, emotionally exhausted from worry. We all head upstairs.

"I'll stay up," I say. "There's no way I'm sleeping anyhow."

There are two guest rooms upstairs. We let Beverly and Zeke take one, and Diane the other. The four of us camp out on the thick carpet of the upstairs foyer. If you didn't know better, one could almost mistake it for a slumber party.

10

I sit on the top step of the staircase at Zeke and Beverly's house. Once upon a time, this entire area was a clandestine cannabis grow.

The sun has already filled the downstairs windows. I feel a hand on my right shoulder. It's Diane.

"Honey, you need to get some sleep."

"I can't."

"You will. I promise. I'll sit right here with my daddy's shotgun while you and Tiffany crawl into my bed and get some rest. You can't shoulder every burden. We will be just fine."

"Don't go downstairs. Wake me immediately if anything happens."

"Of course."

My knees and back pop as I stand. I walk over and nudge Tiff. She jumps.

"It's me," I say.

Tiffany picks her red-framed glasses off the floor and puts them on.

"Diane said for us to go sleep in her room."

"That sound lovely," she mumbles, half awake.

We shut the door and settle into a cool, cozy bed. I feel a brief sensation of privacy.

I will rest well knowing there's a mama with five shells of double-aught buck standing between us and the Apostles.

Tiff and I strip down to our underwear, then crawl in between the bed's gray cotton sheets. We both lay on our left sides. I wrap my right arm around her and close my eyes. I recollect that doing this seemed unimaginable a few years ago. And despite our present circumstances, I find a moment to feel thankful.

Explaining in words what it's like to wake up in another reality is impossible. The edges of everything seem fuzzy with electricity. Mara looked like this momentarily when she appeared to me on the golf course directly after my escape from Solid Rock.

My ears feel as though they'll pop. It's not like a dream. Instead of being ethereal, I feel my body as though is really here. I begin to wonder, 'How can I exist in two places if my consciousness weren't in itself able to disconnect from my body? Do I have different bodies in both locations? Or is our material reality not so material after all?'

Again, I'm in jeans, a greenish-black flannel, and boots. I stand, but don't leave the tracks this time. Frieda walks down them toward me, as she did before.

"Are you the one causing me to come here?"

"No, you come when you need to. We don't make those decisions. We have no idea why they are made. Ceraphirian do not experience time like humans. I'm just here, as I am everywhere else I've ever been, all at once. Only here, in the divide between worlds, can I know time as you do."

"Would you say your choices are predetermined, then," I ask?

"The choices are what they must be."

"Really?"

I hear the train coming. In a way, I feel as though I called it to me. Frieda instinctively steps off the tracks, toward the Ceraphirian side. I don't move.

Frieda, who has been unsettlingly poised during our two previous meetings, shows a faint tinge of concern. Standing her ground, she continues to stare as though she's expecting me to do something.

She's becoming visibly tense. I don't budge.

She begins to nudge forward.

"What do you think will happen, Frieda? Will I go back to my world, stay here, or be cast into the Woods of Lamentation?

"You're not supposed to," Frieda says, seemingly to herself, right before leaping in my direction. She pushes me out of the way using her whole body. I fall backward. Frieda lands on top of me. Rolling over, we see the train as it passes by.

Underneath its roar, Frieda says, "I shouldn't be over here. Why did you do that?"

"I wanted to show you how it feels to experience reality the way humans do."

The woods behind us begin to move as the train continues. We both become laser-focused on the tree line. Frieda is shaking with a fear that vibrates the air around me. I sense her as though we're both submerged in a thick substance, and she's receiving an electrical shock that is faintly tickling me like carpet static. I reach my right hand out to her left and clasp it.

"Have you ever been afraid before?" I question.

"There is no such thing as, 'ever'," she says. "Time is the plane we live on, like the floor of a house. It shouldn't change."

"The best I can figure is, y'all look at time as though it's a completed painting. For humans, we ride each brushstroke, terrified, not knowing where we're going, ever concerned about how the picture will end."

"Is it always this bad?"

"No, but the terror is constant, like faint white noise in the next room."

I see a familiar sight, an oblong-shaped head belonging to the spindly-legged creature I encountered my first time here. It releases a roar, causing Frieda to tremble even more. With our backs to the moving train, we have nowhere to go.

Four long legs, with spear-like feet, propel it toward us, in a semi-mechanical way, with its claws extended.

As it accelerates, I tell Frieda, "Stand behind me."

Its eyeless sockets home in on my person. I hold my left palm up in its direction. A small sphere of light begins to float there. I cause a tiny bit of it, the size of a marble, to fly in the beast's direction. As the speck of light enters its head, the creature immediately stops and kneels as one does in the presence of royalty. In a state of rest, it breathes heavily, like an old Labrador retriever taking a nap.

As I begin to walk toward it, Frieda shouts, "Don't!"

"Shhh, you'll frighten him," I say.

"Him?"

"Yes, him."

"It's like when I met Mara, I just knew. While beasts of lamentation don't have secondary sexual traits, they're programmed with basic identities, which can include gender."

"He's not the one who should be frightened. No Ceraphirian has ever been this close to a beast of lamentation. It's not just me I'm worried about. If he were to kill us here, our lights would become unbound. It's never happened before, but that kind of power let loose in between planes could be catastrophic."

"You'll be safe. The light put a mental lease on him. Mara

was different. The light was in her, guided by another force, autonomously, but Svangi won't act without my permission."

"It has a name?"

"Yes, of course."

"I've never seen anything like this before."

"Why couldn't I control the creatures Joseph created with the indigo?"

"Because they were mistreated dogs. True beasts of lamentation are the opposite of the Ceraphirian. Instead of light, inside them dwells true darkness. It's not the kind you experience at night. Within them is nothingness. As a human with a Ceraphirian light, you're able to control him because you can force a portion of your light into the creature's internal void. Ceraphirian are made of light. If any of it leaves us, we die."

I approach the still-kneeling creature and place my left hand on top of his oblong head.

"Svangi, it's so nice to finally meet you."

The train passes but Frieda, in shock and curiosity, doesn't budge. I back away, hold out my left hand, and say, "Go home, boy."

Svangi rises up onto his four legs. I see that his sharp feet are stained with a crusty, dark red substance.

"I thought there was no Water in the woods of Lamentation? Blood is mostly water."

"The bodies of those cast into lamentation are not like they were in life. They are devoid of water. Their insides feel as though they are made of sand, and they are infinitely thirsty. It's a crumbly dry matter left where blood should be."

"How did Mara survive in water?"

"She existed in all three planes simultaneously. Mara was a beast of lamentation tied to a human, animated by the light of a Ceraphirian."

"How do you know all of this?"

"Because we always have."

"But you're not sure what would happen if a Ceraphirian crossed into my world or what would happen if your light became unbound outside of Ceraphiria?"

Frieda returns to the Ceraphirian side of the track while answering, "Because you're the first human to hold a Ceraphirian light, the events based on your choices are blind to us. Knowing might cause the arc of time to bend, throwing everything into chaos."

"I'll try not to fuck up," I say, right before waking up.

I wake at five past one in the afternoon to an empty bed. I get dressed while listening to Nate and Tiff arguing about what happened to Ester Greenwood at the end of *The Bell Jar*, through the closed door.

I walk out into the fray. The second bedroom is open. Diane and Beverly are both sitting on the bed, cross-legged, having a quiet discussion. I can't make out what they're saying. Zeke is perched at the top of the stairs with Diane's shotgun.

I make eye contact with Herschel, who is staring at Nate and Tiffany, obviously confused and bored.

"Again," I say to Herschel.

"Yep," he says, making a popping noise when pronouncing the 'p' to emphasize how disinterested he is.

"I have an idea how we can shake them," Zeke says out of the blue.

"They can follow us in a car, but not on an airplane. Because of nine-eleven, they can no longer tail us on foot, directly to the gate. That means they won't know our destination. We leave the state, not to run away, but to formulate a counterattack for when we return. We have to go after them. Eventually, one of their beasts will escape, or worse. We don't know what else Joseph will learn to do, or how many they'll murder if we don't put a stop to it."

"Where to?" I question.

"D.C. It's out of their reach, but still close. We stay downtown where there's heavy surveillance."

All eyes train on me for my response.

"He's right. There are so many flights leaving Asheville Regional that they'll never be able to pin down where we went. Zeke, you'll need to kill what's left of your cannabis grow. We'll have to leave our guns and phones here."

I've never been on an airplane. I know Tiffany flew to California a few times as a child to visit relatives. Nate and Herschel have traveled to Key West together, twice. Diane and Beverly flew to Britain when they were teenagers to visit long-lost cousins. Zeke has been to the Cannabis Cup in Amsterdam numerous times. Me? I haven't left North Carolina since nineteen-eighty-nine when my parents took me to Williamsburg. There, my father got the opportunity to beat me in front of people wearing colonial-period clothes.

I have to admit that I'm terrified of this prospect. Not just flying, but spending time in a large city. I'd much rather come face to face with an eight-hundred-pound black bear in the woods of Yancey County, or a tiger shark lurking near a shipwreck.

Zeke uses a small, white MacBook to order seven tickets from Asheville Regional to Reagan International, leaving this evening. With such short notice, the tickets were very expensive. Lodging was arranged at the Hotel Lombardy, on First and Pennsylvania Avenue, five blocks from the White House. We book four rooms on the ninth floor for two weeks.

Zeke chops down the six plants he had growing, then cuts each into small pieces and flushes them down the toilet bit by bit.

Normally he composts them, but outside is off limits. We lock our firearms in the large floor safe Zeke once used to store one-pound bags and cash.

We arrange to have two mini-van cabs drive us to the airport. A silver Honda Accord follows us the entire way, then circles around and leaves when we enter the airport parking lot. I'm never able to get a look at the driver's face.

Tiffany insists that I sit next to the window. She takes the aisle seat to my right. As the airplane accelerates, then lifts off the ground, she holds my hand tightly. The higher we ascend, the fainter my connection to the Earth feels. It's a curious feeling, like suddenly losing sight in one eye, but experiencing it as a relief.

We layover in Newark for two hours, then fly south to Washington D.C. The second time we take off, I hold Tiffany's hand again, but only because I want to. By the time we reach our cruising altitude, I find myself fascinated by the ground sliding along below us.

We board a large Chevrolet Suburban, painted yellow and put into service as a taxi. Along the way, our driver explains that, before nine-eleven, he could have driven us past the White House. However, since then that section of Pennsylvania Avenue is barricaded.

To get to the ninth floor, we board an elevator with a metal cage door and an operator wearing a suit. He's a gentleman in his late seventies to early eighties, wearing a golden nametag with 'Charles' embossed in black. The sight gives me shivers momentarily.

Our rooms are small but very well-appointed. Each of the four has a king-size bed and white tiled bathrooms stocked with soaps and lotions imported from London. Zeke and Beverly are in one, Diane is by herself, Tiff and myself are in another, and Herschel and Zeke are in the fourth.

We spent the first weekend sequestered on the ninth floor, living off of room service.

On the morning of Monday, July thirty-first, Herschel and I go for a walk. Typically, I'm in the sun daily. After spending days without it, my field of vision fills with bright spots. These fade within two minutes. We cross First Street, which leads to a triangular island containing a small park. Each bench has what appears to be several armrests. I mention this to Herschel. He points out that they're made that way so people who don't have homes can't sleep on them. I feel somewhat naive, but I've never seen that before. It's shockingly callous.

After crossing Pennsylvania Avenue, we come to a small strip mall with a cozy little bagel shop. We each order a plain bagel with coffee, then take a seat at a two-top table next to the window.

"What now?" Herschel asks.

"We wait. I think Zeke was right. They've lost the trail. They probably believe we've run away for good."

"Without the indigo, what's their next move?"

"Joseph will want to make more beasts. He can't stay awake at all hours to control them, so his guards will need a constant supply of indigo for their clothes. Joseph will take from the only place he can, the cavities sewn into his cloak. He won't dare remove too much, so he'll make due. This will slowly degrade his abilities. Perhaps, the longer we wait, the weaker he becomes."

"Or, Joseph becomes more skilled and efficient with his abilities, meaning he'll require less indigo. All the while, he could be creating an army of beasts."

"Joseph might be tempted to make a few more, but I don't think he'll create an entire army. Math isn't in his favor when it comes to indigo supply. He needs enough to not only create but to also control. It all depends on whether he errs on the side of logical caution or fanaticism. We have no way of knowing until we scout. But, we aren't going to start at Oak Island. We show up where they least expect us, Solid Rock. While they may have ten other keeps whose locations we don't know, the ground-up rock and water come from the cave underneath the church compound. If we hold the cave, they can't make any more indigo."

"We don't have much to go on, otherwise."

"Right now we focus on seizing two of the three ingredients. After that, they'll become even weaker. Then, we kill Joseph. The knowledge of how to manufacture indigo dies with him."

"I've already booked us for two additional weeks," Herschel says, "It's taken care of."

"Thank you," I reply graciously at his generosity."

———

For the next three weeks, there's no sign of the Apostles. We eventually wander out, always sticking together, and acquire prepaid phones, just in case.

We visit several Smithsonian museums, the National Aquarium, and the Museums of Natural Sciences. The last one twice, because of my nerdy insistence.

12

It's Tuesday, October thirty-first, two-thousand-six; Halloween. I'm standing inside the doorway of a four-bedroom home in Tysons Corner, Virginia waiting for trick-or-treaters. It's been three months since we fled North Carolina.

Our stay at the Hotel Lombardy had become far too expensive to be reasonable long-term. To shield our identities, Herschel incorporated a business called 'Fisher and Sons Flooring' located at an empty office in a rundown building with little parking or access to public transit. Fisher and Sons Flooring, in turn, hired a real estate attorney as a nominee to sign for our purchase of the house whose door I'm standing in. All bills associated with the home were created using the company name. The house is located in a densely populated suburb with lots of prying eyes, which is exactly what we want.

The house was exorbitantly priced, but it's large enough for all seven of us. Herschel floated most of the cash for the purchase. We also acquired two used cars: a two-tone green and gray Subaru Outback and a blue Honda CR-V.

It's nice here, but this isn't our home.

The ghoulish costumes parading by take my mind to Joseph.

I contemplate the creatures he's creating, beast and human alike.

I'm living a life in suspended animation, waiting. On what? I do not know. I feel as though everyone in our family believes in me too much. They secretly expect that I'll come up with a miraculous solution. One has yet to come to mental fruition. Rather, I spend my days going for runs, waving at my neighbors as I go, and occasionally stopping to pet their dogs yet making no genuine conversation. It's difficult to be one of a handful of people who realize what reality-bending horrors are brewing only three-hundred hundred miles south of us.

It's not as though anyone would believe it anyhow. Even if they were proven to exist, many would lament, 'That's down there, it's not going to affect us.'

Bullets won't stop them. Once they're out, there will only be so much I can do. My abilities are finite.

As darkness falls, happy children with full jack-o-lantern pails skitter home. I turn out the front porch light and lock up for the night. The interior of our home is mostly painted in a dull off-white that could be rightly named 'modern American suburbia.' The floors are lightly stained pine. The foyer leads directly into our kitchen. There's a doorway on the left to a formal dining area we rarely use. To the right is a walk-in-pantry. The kitchen is small for such a large home. It exists in the space directly after the foyer. There are oak cabinets on both sides. The sink and fridge are to my left. On the right is a gas stove and additional counter space. As I walk through, I come to a large open living space with a twenty-foot ceiling. To the right is the primary bedroom, which Herschel and Nate share. It has a substantial bathroom and a walk-in closet. There's a brown sectional couch facing a large flat-screen tv in the far corner next to an unused fireplace. The rear double glass doors lead to a deck and a fenced-in backyard. To the left of the living space is a short hallway leading to a full bath at the end, and the bedroom Tiff and I share on the right. On the left, directly across from our bedroom is a guest room. Circling back toward the dining area leads to the stairs along the front wall. There's a walkway when you reach the top. To the left is the bedroom Zeke and Beverly share, which has its own private bath. Going to the right takes you to Diane's bedroom, which is a mirror image.

Despite how progressive the community likes to tout itself as being, I can tell they're doing the social calculus in their heads concerning what our relationships are with one another.

Even in the most mundane of circumstances, all people walk cultural tightropes. We pretend to be what the world wants to see but protect what we really are, afraid that revealing our true selves will cause us to be cut off from acceptance and opportunity.

In the living room, I find Nate, Herschel, and Tiff playing Monopoly on the coffee table. Herschel and Nate sit on the sectional, while Tiffany sits cross-legged on the floor across the table from them. That's one of her habits. She often will sit on the floor with her back on the couch when we watch television. As kids, she'd do the same when we played NES in my bedroom. Of course, I would join her. Tiffany always tries to buy up the railroads, Herschel Park Avenue, and Boardwalk. Nate thinks money is stupid but likes his friends, so he plays along. I don't, I'd rather watch. At the kitchen table, Diane, Zeke, and Beverly share a joint. In the background, their music plays on an all-in-one stereo. Momentarily, it's "Diamond Dogs" by David Bowie.

I sit on the couch next to Nate. His pretend cash lays neatly in a row, with the bills in ascending order from right to left. Herschel keeps his in a stack, and Tiffany spreads hers out like a handheld fan.

As I observe the game, a plan begins percolating in my mind. I realize that no matter how tough Herschel has become, how stoic Nate portrays himself, or how creative Zeke is, they were not made for what must be done. Rather than risk their lives, I should strike out alone and engineer the fall of Solid Rock's safe-keep single-handily. It won't bring down the Apostles, but it will stunt their future growth. If my plan goes horribly wrong, I'll only be responsible for my own death.

This thought grows over the next few days. I contemplate the best time to make my move. Then Charles's and my escape crosses my mind. It was when the school was empty for Christmas break. But how can I approach without being detected? I can't simply drive into town. Much of the congregation were around during my time there and will still recognize me. That includes law enforcement. I had hoped that after Mara pitched Sheriff Morton into the ravine like a shotput, the position might have fallen out of the hands of a Solid Rock congregate. Instead, they formed themselves into the Apostles of the Cloven Hand and dug in deeper. Some people are so attached to their hatred that even after their fallacy is exposed, they'll redefine their prejudice and clutch it like a rancid security blanket.

A web search reveals Yancey County's rudimentary website, which indicates that Clarence Hope is the current Sheriff. I'm not familiar with the name. If he has risen to the office of Sheriff, though, he must have been one of the deputies there the day Al was murdered and his cabin burnt to the ground.

At four in the morning, Saturday, December ninth, two-thousand six, I depart our new home in Tysons Corner without telling anyone. I take with me several changes of clothes and toiletries. I dress exactly as I appear each time I meet Frieda. I wear jeans, a greenish-black flannel, a heavy great jacket, and a new pair of tan-colored Asolo hiking boots, women's size twelve. Before walking out the door, I leave a handwritten note that reads as follows:

To my family,

I have made the decision to set forth with the intention of destroying Solid Rock, cutting off the Apostles' ability to create indigo. This is something I have to do on my own. I refuse to risk your lives in what may very well be a foolish endeavor. My gift provides me with an advantage none of you possess. While I have an edge, I can't guarantee the safety of anyone joining me.

If you do not hear from me by February, assume that I failed, and likely have perished. Do not attempt to follow or intervene. Continue living your lives, and be glad that I died following my path.

Zeke,

If the worst happens, please begin the construction of an underground bunker. Stock it with water, and two years' worth of shelf-stable food. I don't give a good goddamn what the city has to say about it. By the time they intervene, the Apostles' beasts may very well be running loose, making their injunctions written on flimsy paper moot.

Herschel and Nate,

Know you are my best friends. If I fall, I did so fighting for what I thought was right.

Diane, Zeke, and Beverly,

The three of you have become like surrogate parents to me, Tiffany, and Nate. I would not have become the person I am without your influence.

Tiffany, my love,

Do not be angry with me. Though you might not see it, what I am doing, I do for us. I can no longer stand idly by, knowing what horrors will inevitably come your way. If I had the chance to stop it, and didn't, I'd never forgive myself. If I do not return, please marry again. I wish for nothing else in this

I leave my cell phone sitting on the table next to the letter before locking up and driving away in our Subaru.

13

I stop at a little dinner north of Richmond called Evalyn's. It shares a parking lot with a truck stop. I'm greeted by a cheerful lady in her mid-sixties with an angelic southern accent that rings genuine when she addresses me as darlin'.

The entire place has a design motif centered around the use of tan and orange. There's a wall-to-wall tile floor in expectation of foods and liquids accidentally being dropped. High-top seats sit at a counter where they are serviced by one waitress who is also responsible for running the cash register.

I'm seated at a two-person booth against one of the front windows. The sun is just coming up over highway ninety-five. It's not stunning, but I'll take it. I order scrambled eggs, two thick pieces of sausage, grits, toast, and a black coffee. Few take mind of me, as there has been an uptick in the number of women who drive big rigs over the past decade.

I have two additional cups of coffee as I watch it become daytime. My destination is only a few miles away, but I'm too early. In my front-right pocket is a tan leather wallet containing ten-thousand dollars that I withdrew from our savings account yesterday afternoon. It's not the large pile of cash you might imagine. It's only one-hundred paper slips. It's a stiff fit, but it's tenable.

At nine in the morning, I enter the local raceway for the quarter-annual Richmond gun and knife show. I chose the route for my purchases because the private sale exemption allows me to bypass federal background checks. I hand the gray-haired, bearded man upfront ten dollars in cash for admission and enter the building. It's a vast interior space filled with every imaginable firearm. Most customers are in search of an inexpensive hunting rifle to put meat on their tables, or a shotgun for home defense. There's an undercurrent, though. Flowing between them are those who peddle weapons of war and conspiracy. It's a deadly mixture of fear, gullibility, and lethality.

I buy a very nice thirty-aught-six with a polymer stock, scope, and a threaded muzzle for an included suppressor. This will lower the rifle's resound and eliminate muzzle flash. Unlike in the movies, the sound is not whisper-quiet. It's just quiet enough to not make my ears ring. Luckily, I originally learned to shoot a long gun right-handed. I haven't seen a single left-handed rifle since I've been here.

From the same vendor, I purchase a leather sling and a range finder, which is a handheld scope housing a laser whose beam bounces back and displays the distance to a target in yards. This allows the shooter to adjust the clicks on her scope to compensate for the bullet's drop due to the Earth's gravitational pull. The man throws in two complimentary boxes of fifty cartridges and a shell catcher. The catcher will retain any ejected casings in a mesh net, preventing me from leaving them behind as forensic evidence.

I also inquire about incendiary rounds, which are quasi-legal and could be subject to unwanted attention. Phosphorus on the tip of the bullet ignites upon hitting a target, generating molten temperatures. He sells me ten for an obnoxious price.

At a survivalist vendor, I acquire a camo backpacking pack with a heavily padded rifle insert. The rifle is slid in through the top, muzzle down, and rests directly on the wearer's back, behind the pack itself. I fill it with a one-person camo backpacking tent, black paracord, a camp stove, three weeks' worth of freeze-dried food, binoculars, a hand-pumped water filter, two plastic bottles to hold water, a handheld GPS, a windproof butane lighter, a headlamp, a small flashlight, a metal match, a compass, a zero-degree rated tall sleeping bag, a camp stove, silicon plates, reusable utensils, and a lightweight frying pan with a removable handle.

At an outfitter's booth, I pick up several pairs of synthetic long johns and a nice set of coveralls in a tan camo print, with matching tactical gloves and balaclava. This will let me blend perfectly into the background. I notice a paperback book published ten years ago named *Into the Wild*. I take one of those with me as well.

I leave around one o'clock in the afternoon with a fully stuffed, yet somewhat disorganized, backpack in tow. It's heavy, nearly forty-five pounds. I've been working out regularly with Herschel and have a robust one-hundred and seventy-five pounds of lean muscle on my six-foot frame. While this makes it easier, the weight is certainly noticeable.

I load it all into the back of the Subaru's cargo compartment and head west on highway sixty. Two hours later, I stop at another truck stop where I fill up the gas tank and have a cheeseburger with French fries that I dip in mayonnaise. Tiffany would be displeased with my diet. She worries about my health. But I often wonder how long I actually want to live. At the moment, though, I feel refreshingly invigorated. I am going to war soon. Tomorrow I march. Today, I need to rest.

I make a stop at a small ABC store and purchase a fifth of Jack

Daniels, then at a convenience store for a two-liter bottle of Coca-Cola. On the outskirts of Roanoke, I check into a place called The Starlight Motel, just before the winter's early sunset.

It's one of those places where one can drive directly up to their room, all of which are ground level. The sign outside has a teal-green background with a shooting star created with yellow neon lighting. The lettering underneath states there are vacancies, complimentary HBO, and a pool. It's obviously too cold for swimming and I don't much go in for television. After paying for one night in cash, I settle in. I make sure to take my newly purchased pack inside. I fill the room's ice bucket a few doors down at the motel's automated dispenser. I then mix up a Jack and Coke in one of this fine establishment's styrofoam cups.

I put my iPod earbuds in and crank up Bad Brains, followed by The Gits, Tilt, The Clash, Des Ark, then Siouxsie and the Banshees. After four more such beverages, I'm fully immersed in a world of hazy music lulling me to an altered state of consciousness. In a moment of clarity, I take a look at the phone and consider calling home. I force myself to avoid the pangs of remorse and longing for Tiff and my family. I know very well that I'm in deep shit no matter what.

The sounds of guitars being shredded lull me to sleep while I hold the evening's eighth Jack and Coke in my hand. I wake up around three in the morning with it still balanced perfectly on my stomach, my left hand faithfully gripping it. I chug the warm, flat elixir before tending to the reason for my consciousness, the urgent need to take a piss. The cold seat is momentarily disruptive to my mellow, but it passes. I brush my teeth and return to the warm cocoon of rough sheets, cradled by a thin mattress lined with crinkly plastic.

I wake up at eight the next morning to the sound of church bells.

It's Sunday, December tenth. I'm so thirsty that I'm compelled to drink voraciously out of the bathroom sink before relieving myself. My head hurts a little.

I pack up the car and head southwest on highway eighty-one. An hour into my drive, I stop at a small diner for another round of unhealthy food. I arrive at my destination, Damascus, Virginia, specifically the public library. Across from this shrine to books is a small parking lot reserved for Appalachian Trail hikers. The trail itself runs directly behind the library and quickly disappears into a thick forest. Being in front of a municipal building means the car will eventually be spotted. The authorities will run the plate which will indicate the car belongs to Fisher and Son as a company car. Herschel will answer the burner phone listed as the business number. He and Nate will come and retrieve the Subaru. There's no use hiding my tracks. They know where I'm going. It will all be over by the time they find it.

By my math, if I can keep up a pace of eight to ten miles a day, I will make the one-hundred miles to Solid Rock by Wednesday, December twentieth. Solid Rock will be on Christmas break, eliminating the chance that my attack will inadvertently harm a student. Eighty miles of the journey will be on the Appalachian Trail, far away from the Apostle's prying eyes. I'll follow it to the Jones Branch Road parking area, where I'll encounter the Nolichucky River. Following it south for five miles will bring me to the junction where it flows into the Toe River. Then it's another five miles south until the river meets Highway nineteen East, the same road I met Herschel and Nate on when hitchhiking. Once on the other side of the road, I'll cross-country hike the final ten miles through Pisgah Forest. The handheld GPS will take me directly to the coordinates. Without it, I'd have to rely on my map and compass.

14

For the first time in three days, I experience silence, unbothered by other humans. Most people hike the trail during the summer. I pitch camp at twilight and break camp not long after dawn. I boil filtered water on my camp stove, then pour it into waterproof bags filled with dehydrated food, mostly chilis of various types. I'm careful to wash them out to diminish the scent of food. Even though bears hibernate this time of year, they're vigilant sleepers. I fold each used bag and stow it away in a small plastic bag to be discarded later.

At the end of each day, my feet, calves, thighs, butt, and back all ache. No matter my abilities or physical strength, I'm irrevocably human. Each night, I read through several chapters of *Into the Wild*. It recounts tales of people who, over the years, have struck off into the wilderness to escape the modern world. I certainly understand the appeal. Most were never seen alive again. The wilderness does not care about your ideology.

I was quite content during my time isolated with the Sillmans, but that was because of who I was with, not because I was cut off from society. I was engaged either physically or academically during every waking hour. I slept better then than I ever have since.

But to live that way forever would become like an over-tightened bowstring, eventually resulting in a snap. No one can truly hide from the world.

On the night of Wednesday, December fourteenth, the Geminid meteor shower begins. I view them through a small opening in the forest canopy.

The next day, Thursday, December fourteenth, begins like the previous three. It's quiet, lonely, and cold. Around midday, I stop and climb onto a boulder that's eight feet tall. There, I sit down and begin to boil water for lunch. It's then that I hear what sounds like a banshee screaming. I've heard the call before, but from further away. Al told me it's the sound of a mountain lion. He said that, despite rarely being seen, a small population still roams these hills. I never doubted him.

It's then that I see two young women running north screaming. One has brown skin, curly hair, and glasses. The other is shorter, and pale, with brunette hair tied into a bun. They're terrified. Within five seconds, I see why. There is an adult mountain lion pursuing them both. Seeing the form of a tan-colored cat gives me a fleeting moment of calm because it's not a beast of lamentation. I think to pull up a slab of granite in front of it. Running into rock would stun, but hopefully not severely injure, the cat. Then I realize the girls know nothing of my abilities and the fewer people who do, the better. I retrieve the thirty-aught-six from the pack laying at my feet. The suppressor isn't installed because, with it on, the rifle would not fit. Quickly, I chamber a round, then fire it into the air. Stunned by the sound, the large cat jumps straight up, kicks, and takes off into the woods. Both girls stop and slowly turn to see me standing on the boulder above them holding the rifle in my right hand.

"Come this way," I shout, "It might come back!"

Both quickly run in my direction. When they stop in front of the boulder, they're panting from exhaustion.

"Please tell me you both dropped your packs running and aren't out here without supplies."

"Yeah," the young woman with brown skin says. "They're lying in the trail a few yards south. It would have eaten us if you hadn't been here.

"I'm glad I was."

I slurp down the rest of my lunch, clean out the bag, pack up, and meet them down on the trail. I make sure to keep my rifle in hand, just in case. It's not until I get to the ground that I can see how gripped by fear they are. The brunette girl with white skin is crying and shivering. I don't blame her.

"Next time," I say, "don't run, fight. Fleeing animals set off a predator's instinct to chase. If it's confused about whether or not you're food. Running will convince it that you are."

"I'm Rebecca," the young woman with curly hair says. "This is Ezra," she continues while pointing at her sobbing companion whose hair is somehow still neatly in a bun.

"I'm Hannah," I respond in kind.

"Thank you for not letting us die," Ezra says in a high-pitched voice."

"The day isn't over yet."

Ezra's face becomes pallid.

"Why would you say that?" she responds in obvious distress.

"You'll both be fine. Now, let's go find your packs."

They follow behind me like ducklings. We recover both of their backpacks less than fifty yards south of us.

Ezra's is bright yellow, and Rebecca's purple.

"What are y'all doing out here," I ask.

Rebecca responds, "We're seniors at Appalachian State. The two of us decided to spend Christmas break hiking the trail through the North Carolina stretch."

"Don't you have families?"

"Not really," Rebecca says. "We grew up in foster care down in Fayetteville. You could say we're sisters. We've roomed together our entire time at Appalachian. But during breaks, the school shuts down and we have to leave, so instead of sleeping in our car, we hike trails and live out of a tent."

"Where do you stay during the summer?"

Ezra says, as her eyes dry, "We've worked at a motel called Linville Pines for the past three summers. Part of the pay is in room and board, along with meals in their restaurant. The owners are okay, I guess. It's hard work. We clean rooms and cook seven days a week for the entire summer. At least we have a door to lock behind us when we go to sleep, unlike on the street or couch surfing."

Rebecca asks, "What exactly are you doing out here, Hannah?"

"Clearing my head, I reckon. Lately, I've been under a lot of stress. I spend too much time drinking and not enough time talking. I feel as though I'm watching my family from the peripheries. I love them and they love me, but I had to go on this hike alone. They weren't ready to accept that."

Their faces are a bit bemused by the cryptic response. I pull the bolt back on my rifle slowly, so as not to sling the brass casing. Rather, I pull it gently away from the breech. I forward the next round into the chamber, click up the safety, then stow the spent casing in my front left pocket. With that, I begin hiking south again. They throw on their bags and follow. I'll keep the rifle at the ready for now.

"Why are you carrying a rifle," Rebecca asks.

"In case."

"If what just happened hadn't, I'd probably be asking, 'In case of what'," she says.

"Y'all just found out the fast way that the woods don't care who you are, everything is food."

"Cheerful," Ezra says in depressive self-realization.

"Honest," I respond.

"Who saw the cat first?"

"I did," Ezra responds. "He was waiting on a tree branch right above the trail. We both turned and ran, then the cat gave chase."

We hike in relative silence for the remainder of the afternoon. Rebecca is five-foot-five, and Ezra is five-foot-three. My stride makes it difficult for them to keep up. By dusk, both are exhausted. We set up camp directly off the trail. They pitch a three-person tent with a bright orange fly. It mildly irritates me. Most tents come in similar colors to make them easier to spot from the air in case of an emergency. For them, it makes sense. Me, however, I've been ducking into the woods twenty to thirty feet each night. I haven't been lighting fires, so as to not attract attention. That's pointless now, so I put together a campfire for us. I use a small piece of dried moss as tinder, then begin adding small twigs to it until I've built up a healthy fire. It's nice to have a lighter instead of a hand drill, which is subject to failure during high humidity. We three sit around the blaze, appreciating its warmth. Both of them hug their knees, obviously still shaken up. I sit cross-legged, holding my hands out to the warmth.

"What the fuck happened to your hand," Ezra says?

I'm a bit taken aback by her frankness.

"I fell out of a tree and onto barbed wire when I was a girl," I respond without a hitch.

That's been my go-to excuse for the scares on my left hand for the past two years.

"It's gruesome. Sorry, I'm not trying to be mean. Sometimes things just come out of my mouth."

"I appreciate the honesty. And yes, it was gruesome," I say, laughing slightly. Immediately, I pause and a few tears run from my eyes.

Both girls give me a sad look. I wipe the moisture on my cheek away and sniffle, then fake a laugh.

"There's rumored to be a cult around here whose leader mutilated his hand in a similar way," Ezra mentions.

Rebecca interjects, "They say he performs magic. But these are the same kind of people who handle rattlesnakes on Sunday mornings. They supposedly are building a megachurch south of Burnsville. That's the middle of nowhere. There aren't even enough people in the county to fill a church half that size."

Hearing this makes me feel so sick that I retire to my tent with no desire to watch the last night of the meteor shower. Tiff has probably convinced Nate and Herschel to stand in the backyard in an attempt to watch them through the light pollution, knowing that I'd likely be doing the same.

"I'm getting tired," I say.

Both nod in agreement. I shuffle myself feet first into my dark green, mummy sleeping bag, plump with down feathers. I leave my rifle beside me.

Wrapped up away from the cold, I feel cozy and safe. I think about how Tiffany and how afraid she must be, alone in our empty bed. I hate myself for hurting her. Tiffany's face is the last thing I see before falling asleep.

15

I wake just before the first light. My watch says it's seven o'clock. The date is Friday, December fifteenth, two-thousand-six. Dueling snores coming from the girl's tent. I open a pack of powdered eggs. They're a horrible facsimile of the genuine article, but they have protein. I'm able to cook a mess of it alongside some very bland grits.

I hear an audible, prolonged zipper sound. I see Rebecca emerge from their tent. She's wearing untied boots, a maroon beanie, and ragged, white long johns. Holding a heavy purple coat around her body like a cape, she walks off into the woods to pee. Upon returning, she sits on the ground beside me. I offer her some breakfast. We each proceed to eat our portions of the bland meal directly from the pan.

"How old were you when you met Ezra," I ask.

"Around five. Neither of us knew our parents. They were likely scared teenagers who gave us up for adoption. Often, I've found myself wishing that they had aborted my fetus. I was born to do what, sleep in the woods when I have nowhere else to go, and clean shit off the walls at Lineville Pines when some drunk tourist goes berserk? It's not much of a life."

"You're here now, what you think about your existence is completely up to you. I often don't care for it myself. When I had everything I ever wanted, I found myself restless, and unable to reciprocate love properly. Now that I'm away, all want is to be near her."

"Who?"

"My wife."

"I wondered about the ring."

Rebecca points to my plain, hammered-rose-gold wedding band. She doesn't flinch when she hears I'm married to another woman.

"How long have you been married?"

"Two-and-a-half years," I say, wiping a tear away.

"Whatever it is, she knows you believe you're doing the right thing."

I nod, unable to talk without overspilling with emotion. I take deep breaths, grit my teeth, and attempt to calm myself. If I live, I'm going to have to process these emotions one day. Unless I do, my heart will inevitably shatter with despair.

———

Rebecca continues, "Foster homes are semi-permanent. You can exist there for months or years. But you're always in a state of unease, not knowing when you might have your entire life hoisted from one place to another."

"Ezra and I met when we both lived with Ms. Berniece. There was another girl in the house with us named Margaret. She was ten. Being there was all I could remember at the time. I believed it was my home. But all things are temporary. When Ezra and I were seven, Ms. Bernice met her first boyfriend in years, Marshall. She wasn't a physically attractive woman by conventional standards. She was beautifully kind, but her heart was soft and easily malleable. And manipulate it he did."

"Marshall was a very small man, just a tad over five feet, and scrawny. But to me, at seven, he was a terrifying giant. At the time, he was roughly forty years old, completely bald, with tiny round features, sickly white skin, and brown eyes. His voice's high resonance still rings in my ears. A few months after he first started coming around, Margaret began wetting her bed, which she'd never done before. Mind you, she was twelve at this time. Margaret then started acting out aggressively at school. While at home, she withdrew into herself and refused to bathe. Eventually, she was referred to a school counselor and it all came pouring out like pus from a festering abscess. He was molesting her."

"Marshall denied everything and accused Margaret of lying. Ms. Bernice, blinded by the exhilaration of new love, took Marshall's side. Child protective services dragged their feet, and a month went by before Margaret was examined by a doctor. The exam was inconclusive because Marshall wasn't stupid enough to continue. The investigation was dropped and Margaret was sent away."

"When I was eight, he began molesting me. In the beginning, shame prevented me from talking about it. But one night, while Ezra and I played alone, she told me he was doing the same to her. Afraid that we'd be sent away too, neither of us said anything. He continued abusing us for two more years."

"At ten, my humiliation turned to anger when I caught him in our bedroom with Ezra. I looked directly into his eyes and said, 'If you ever do it again, I will kill you.' He laughed and exited the room. I wanted a weapon to protect myself. I thought to take a knife from the kitchen to keep under my pillow. But I knew Ms. Bernice would notice it missing, so I began asking around the school to see if anyone would sell me a pocket knife. A girl named Clarissa sold me her brother's for ten dollars. It was a Case brand with a textured black and tan handle. It had a two-inch-long blade on one side and a bottle opener on the other. It wasn't formidable, but having it made me feel safer. Before going to sleep, I'd extend the blade and placed it under my pillow. Then one night he came for me again."

"Typically, Marshall would get us when we were alone, and Ms. Bernice was out of the house. That night, I awoke with him laying on top of me nude. It was as though he was doing it with Ezra present to teach her a lesson. He had already pulled down my pajamas and began rubbing himself on the inside of my leg. Before he could put it in me, I reached under the pillow and grabbed the handle of the knife with my right hand, pulled it out, and plunged it into his naked abdomen. I then sliced to the left, cutting my hand in the process. The scream Marshall let forth was guttural and unlike anything I've heard since. He was mortally wounded and knew it. The gash was so deep and long that his small intestines began spilling out of his gut, even as Marshall tried desperately to hold them in. Warm, gooey snakes of human viscera fell onto my naked legs, then trailed across the floor as he ran toward the bedroom door. Marshall fell dead, facedown, in front of Ms. Bernice, who had woken up because of his agonizing howls."

"The rest of the night is a blur. I remember talking to the police and getting my hand stitched up. The following day, I met with a child psychologist."

"I wouldn't see Ezra again for six years. The reasoning for separating us was that we would talk about the abuse and re-traumatize ourselves. What I think they really want is for people like us to stuff our suffering deep down enough that it doesn't emerge again until we're adults and they're not responsible for picking up the pieces."

"We came back into each other's orbits again in eleventh grade, as we had aged out of the previous restrictions. We were both lucky to be placed in good foster homes, which allowed us the ability to do well academically. In our senior year of high school, we decided to go to Appalachian together. When you have no family, you piece one together."

———

"I know exactly what you mean," I reply.

It's then that Ezra's snores subside. I hear the zipper of her sleeping bag first, then the tent's as she crawls out into the new-day sun. Ezra walks into the woods to relieve herself. Upon returning, she eats the remainder of the breakfast quietly while staring off blankly.

"Are you okay," Rebecca inquires.

"Huh? Yeah. I'm okay. I had a nightmare is all."

"Don't dwell on it too much."

I see an empathetic, sad look flash across Rebecca's face. Quiet then blankets the three of us as we break camp and begin to hike south again.

16

The sun scrubs the peaks this time of year. A shadowy veil of tree branches filters out the already dim daylight. Today is December the sixteenth. Rebecca and Ezra have been doing a better job keeping up. Even with them in tow, my goal is still the same, to reach Solid Rock by Wednesday the twentieth.

Since we haven't seen any signs of the cat, I decided to pack my rifle away. It's cumbersome to carry by hand for such long distances. If there is an immediate, existential problem, I'll handle it. It likely wouldn't be from the Apostles, Solid Rock is still sixty miles away.

"Do you see your parents often," Ezra asks mid-morning.

"No. I haven't spoken to them in more than a decade. The people who actually raised me are dead."

"Why?"

"Why are they dead, or why don't I speak to my biological parents?"

"Both."

"Ezra, that's rude," Rebecca interjects.

"I didn't mean to hurt your feelings," Ezra says.

"You didn't. I'm long past being hurt by questions about my parents. Even if I was, it wouldn't be your fault."

"Did you love your birth parents?"

"I thought I did. It turns out they only loved the idea of a daughter without considering she wouldn't be a doll come to life that they could program."

"What did they think you'd become?"

"I'm not sure. Not who I am. I reckon by now I should be married to a Christian man to whom they could cede decision-making authority over my life. Fuck that. They disowned me when I fell in love with my best friend because that friend happened to be a girl. They think I'm dead, and I plan on it staying that way. I think they prefer it."

"That's horrible," Ezra responds.

I change the subject.

"Are y'all dating anyone," I ask.

"Neither of us date. Boys are cute but dangerous. Maybe one day. Right now, I'm more interested in my education and not getting trapped," Ezra says.

"Smart girl," I say. "My two best friends are men. They are lovely people. The problem is that the bad men look just like the good ones. Sadly, people who are attracted to men have to calculate the probability their suitor will be their murderer."

"Women murder," Ezra responds.

"Sure, but in raw numbers, men kill many, many more."

"My point is, a woman can fight back if she knows how."

I realize that Ezra is talking about Rebecca's actions. I can tell she looks up to her. It's understandable. But because of this, Ezra seems mildly stunted, like a sapling struggling for sun under a taller sibling. The larger tree will shield the smaller one from harsh wind and hail, but the little one will struggle to gather enough light to grow to full size. Ezra speaks her mind but is rarely more than a few feet from Rebecca. Ezra is always on guard, scanning her surroundings. It may have saved their lives. After all, she was the one who spotted the mountain lion before it pounced.

I'm quiet most of the day, though the two of them rattle on. This afternoon is dedicated to the playful banter between the two about Ezra's love of purposefully bad horror movies. Throughout the day, when they aren't giving each other shit, Ezra casually attempts to catch a glimpse of the scars on my left hand.

After we make camp for the evening and set up around the campfire, she outright asks, "Did you really fall onto a barbed wire, or does that have something to do with the cult?"

"No, it has nothing to do with the Apostles.

"Then how do you know they're called the Apostles?"

"A lucky guess."

"No. I think you're on the run from them. Why else would you be so well-armed and out in the wilderness, alone in the bitter cold? I like it out here, but I'm betting Rebecca would agree that a warm bed would be preferable."

"Fuck yeah, I would," Rebecca interjects.

"Have you ever considered that they're on the run from me," I say, immediately regretting my momentary hubris.

"No, I didn't."

"These hills," Rebecca says, "were isolated for a long time. As the world crept in, what was hidden in the hollers for centuries also wriggled out, both the good and bad. Isolated infectious diseases can wreak havoc on the world at large once they escape their confines. As of late, backwoods prophecies have begun to be whispered about. A man named Joseph Proffit is said to perform miracles. Fringe zealots trickle in to see him. They call themselves the Apostles of the Cloven Hand. Supposedly, this Joseph fellow bisected his own left hand as a demonstration of faith."

"You haven't been tempted to see it for yourself," I ask Rebecca.

"I'm the wrong shade of human. It's a whites-only affair."

"No surprises there."

"Rumor is, he walks through walls and can control the weather. Supposedly they're trying to bring about the end of the world."

"Do you believe that?"

"No. They're fucking lunatics, but some people are susceptible. They, in turn, spread it to the weak-minded like a mental virus."

Ezra interjects, "They pat down everyone who comes to witness his supposed miracles. There's no recording equipment allowed. They want his magic tricks to be seen in real life so that they can't be dismissed as special effects. It's said that witnesses appear dumbfounded after."

"I'm sure it's an illusion," I reply.

"What if it isn't," Ezra asks.

"Then you have a lot of worry about," I respond, agitated.

With that, I retire to my one-person tent and zip myself up to slumber like a frigid mummy.

———

The following two days go similarly. They goof on each other and I give them a mild cold shoulder, but deep down, I am glad to be hiking with companions. On the evening of Sunday, the seventeenth, I announce that I'll be leaving the trail the following day.

"Where are you headed?" Ezra questions with a hint of sadness.

"My hike is over. That's all."

"I don't believe you," Rebecca says. "I think you're a former member of the Apostles who's come back to get square."

"I'm most certainly not a former member," I say with a raised, indignant tone.

The terseness of my response lays my deceit bare. Why else would I have such an emotional reaction if some of what Rebecca said weren't true?

"I believe you're heading off to do something rash. You realize that fact, but you're going anyway. And it involves that fucking cult. Whatever they did to you, hurting them won't make you feel any better," Rebecca says.

"Not in my experience," I say.

Both of them quickly lock their gaze on me when I say this. In most situations, that response would certainly be a joke. They don't laugh it off. They know. All I can do at this point is limit what I say and avoid specifics.

After a pause, Rebecca says, "I trust that you have valid reasons, but you seem like a good person, and we'd rather you not die needlessly. Why not just keep hiking with us?"

"That sounds lovely, but it's just my time to leave the trail.

"Okay," she says with a sigh.

The next morning is Monday, December eighteenth. I wake around five o'clock, two hours before sun-up. Quietly, I break my tent down, pack it, and my other belongings away, then hit the trail without breakfast.

After getting fifty yards south, I turn on my headlamp and begin jogging the best I can with forty-five pounds on my back. After fifteen minutes I slow down, having exhausted myself. It's my estimate that I've traveled a mile. I've never been an exceptionally fast runner. When I run unencumbered with Herschel, I typically put in a seven- to eight-minute mile. He can dip into the sub-seven range. Considering he's over two hundred pounds, it's extremely impressive. I remove my pack and sit on a log for a few minutes. I'm sweaty even though it's cold. If I weren't wearing synthetic long johns, I'd strip down and take off my bottom layer. But the fabric is designed to wick away moisture. This prevents my body temperature from lowering as I cool off. Revived, I don my backpack again and hike on.

17

I reach the Jones parking area around noon. It's really just a strip of gravel on the edge of the road for day hikers, but it intersects with the Nolichucky River. I'll track it downstream where the water will merge with the Toe River, whose southerly course will lead me directly to Solid Rock.

Hungry, I stop along the river's edge to boil water for lunch. The Nolichucky is calm on this end and shallow in most parts. In warm weather, the average person could walk across and not go much above their chest.

I throw the intake hose attached to my hand-pumped water filter behind a few large stones at the edge of the river. The lack of turbidity lets the water clear of sediment. Falling to the bottom, along with it, go little nasties that can cause unfortunate things to happen to one's stomach. A foam float at the intake of the hose keeps it near the surface. Despite being filtered and safe to drink, it is by no means tasty. The bacteria and silt may be gone, but tannins from rotting tree leaves and the slimy taste of algae still remain. I chug it out of necessity. Thankfully, when used to rehydrate freeze-dried foods, the foulness is overpowered by the flagrant use of inexpensive spices.

There are a few small homes along the river, but seeing as it's winter, most people will be hunkering down inside while they're home. For good measure, I brought along a gray hoodie that I slide on underneath my camouflage pattern coveralls. I wear it over my head to hide the features of my face. That, coupled with my height, will shield my gender. Being that it's deer season, the rifle will add a convincing air of normality. I make sure to wear my gloves now that I'm off the trail. Otherwise, I risk having my scar noticed. Most hunters would wear orange as a precaution, but I'm trying not to be seen.

With lunch finished, I follow the river downstream. For most of the five miles to the Toe River, I'm able to stay fairly close to the water. Occasionally, I have to step out onto the edge of a country road where few cars journey. Nevertheless, they can be heard from a distance as they cut through the serene calm native to the forest, thus avoided.

I make it another four miles before the sun begins to dim and my muscles twitch from exhaustion. A mile before reaching the convergence of the Nolichucky with the Toe, I make camp in the woods about twenty feet from the water's edge. Unlike when I was with Rebecca and Ezra, I don't light a campfire. Tonight is the first time on this journey that I am in very real danger.

Just before tucking myself in, I reach down into the Earth and pull granite up from underneath the ground in a circular pattern around my tent. I force it to continue upward, eventually encasing my tent in a dome made of rock, with walls a foot thick. Hand still on the forest floor, I release my consciousness into the mycelium, which sends a chemical signal to the surrounding trees. Roots sprout forth around the dome, completely covering it. They harden with new, healthy bark. I'm completely protected and hidden. Even though I'm thankful to be safe, I miss the faint moonlight leaking in under the bottom edge of my tent fly. I feel the Earth's heat further down. I could pull it up and warm the space, but I only ask for what I need, nothing more. I have a sleeping bag for head.

Feeling relaxed and safe, I stay up and read through the instruction for my blue, handheld GPS. I transcribe the coordinates I have written on the edge of my topographic map into the device. It won't connect to the satellites through the granite, but the data is there for when it's time. Satisfied, I turn it off and fall into a deep sleep.

———

When I wake, I unzip my bag partway and press the illumination button on my wristwatch. It's six-thirty in the morning, December nineteenth. I intend for today to be the last full day of travel.

By tomorrow afternoon, I should reach the ridge above the cavern entrance. It connects to the chamber where Charles died. He bled to death right outside of the cult's underground weapons stockpile. The room containing it is blocked off from the rest of the cave by a large steel door. At the time of his death, Charles and I opened it from the inside by removing a long four-by-four bracing it.

We initially got down there through a tunnel that begins in the floor of a large safe hidden inside the Proffit's bedroom. After lifting a heavy manhole cover off the entrance, we were able to climb down a metal ladder and into the weapons room.

There were heaps of M-16s, ammunition, rations, and water. Even before Joseph, they were preparing for war.

I've never seen the original mine entrance because I escaped out of an alternate passage only a starved child could wrangle through. My shoulders are broader today, and I've put on a lot of muscle since then. I could expand the hole with my abilities, but either way, gaining access would require swimming through a flooded, dark cave during the sub-freezing temperatures of December. It would zap a lot of energy out of me that I need for fighting.

Studying a topographic map before setting forth from my home has led me to believe I can locate the entrance.

Highway eighty is a spiraling road featuring stomach-churning hitch-backs and cliffs with sheer drop-offs dangerously close to the outside lane. It was the road Vernon used to take me up the mountain after my parents handed me over to him when I was fourteen.

What few people know is that just inside the woods, there's also an old cobblestone road. It winds a similar path as the modern one and often runs parallel. Today, it's hidden by trees and moss.

On the map, three-quarters of the way up the dilapidated road is a tiny dot with the name 'Severe Mine' next to it. My research shows that it was once a cavern that was only wide enough to allow access for one person at a time. Back then, the small tunnel would eventually lead to a cathedral of stalactites and stalagmites.

The Severe Mining Company was established during the Carolina Gold Rush of the early eighteen-hundreds. They invested money to expand the opening to allow equipment through. After several months of nothing, they realized the granite walls were empty of any precious metals. Luckily, their money ran out before they could destroy the entirety of the interior. A few days after the mine closed, in the summer of eighteen-twenty-five, Frederick Severe is said to have wandered off into the wilderness in a trance. He never returned.

The spot on the map showing the mine entrance indicates there's a ridge across a small valley, about three hundred yards away, and fifty feet higher in elevation. It appears the shaft runs directly underneath the modern roadway. I can't get close enough to use my abilities. I'd likely be spotted and shot. What I can do is reign terror down on them with my rifle.

I place my left hand on the ground and feel for the vibration of footsteps. I don't want to open my protective shell of granite and living branches in front of a witness. There are light, quick vibrations coming up from the ground. It's not human. I smile. Squirrels. Often, their frantic travels across the forest floor are louder than a deer's.

With my left hand still on the ground, I command the branches on the exterior of my granite shell to recede into the ground and return to their root form. I cause my protective dome to open from the top and force the rock back into the Earth. It's slightly rearranged, but basically the same as before. The first light of the day comes through my tent. I unzip it and enter the cold air outside. I used my stove to boil water. Running low on breakfast-like food, I settle on creamy fettuccine. I swear the flavoring in this shit is giving me headaches.

By nine, I reach the junction of the Toe and Nolichucky rivers. It's wider but has little more than minor rapids. Less than a mile in, I come to a familiar sight. It's a small, unnamed creek that leads back to Al and Milly's house. It was the boundary of my childhood range. Hardly anyone ever comes to the creek. It was my route of escape after Al was shot and killed by Vernon Proffit. Al's body was likely burned to nothing in the subsequent fires they set. I'd like to know if the graves of Milly and Hannah are intact. After all, it's Hannah Sillman's identity that gave me my new life.

18

I have the overwhelming urge to go home. Not back to Tysons Corner or Wilmington, but just up the path, to my real parents' house.

I want to run by the brook, take a right at the rocky outcrop, then dash down the hill and into Al's workshop.

I'd wrap my arms around him and say, "Thank you for my new life."

We would then go in to tell Milly that I was home. We'd catch up on things. I'd tell them about my marriage and new friends. They'd tell me about their winter garden and the bantam chicks Milly is hoping to hatch in the spring.

The compulsion draws me in, and I begin to follow the stream uphill. It's an hour's hike. I'm not delusional. However, I can't help but want a taste of home, even if it's just ash and dirt. I pass by where Milly's ramp patch will come up in the spring. It's downhill, between two oak trees. Before long, I reach the rocky outcrop where I hid while Vernon Proffit commanded their house and barn to be incinerated. At the time, he believed me to have burned alive while hiding in the barn's feed closet.

I turn right and descend the hill. Upon exiting the old path, I see how overgrown the property has become. I should be where the barn once stood. Instead, all that's left is the metal shell of Al's Allis-Chalmers tractor. Now, instead of it being red, every inch is covered in rust. Its tires melted in the fire, leaving the metal wheels resting on the ground. Blocks from the foundation surround it as though the tractor is still inside a phantom structure.

Through the thick grass, I find the house's perimeter outlined in the same manner. There's nothing more. Then I realize something else is missing: the massive, ancient oak tree Milly and Hannah were buried under. As I approach, I'm horrified to see that only its stump remains, now covered in crackly black ash. It's as though they wanted the Sillman family erased. At the adjacent gravesite, I find a recently dug hole. Hannah and Milly's bodies have been stolen. The gravesites weren't marked, so they had to dig a much larger cavity than they cared to fill back in. Brown dirt still sits in mounds beside the empty graves. There's no vegetation growing in it. That means it has been done since the weather turned cold. I feel searing heat behind my eyes. Holding back screams of fury, I feel exactly the way I did when Tiffany and I were ripped apart as children.

I turn away in disgust, no longer able to stand it. Right before entering the wood line, on my way back, I feel like Lot's wife, wanting to look back, but I don't. Any more rage will turn my heart into hardened salt.

I hike swiftly, keeping my eyes ahead to avoid seeing Milly's ramp patch. My tears feel like fire. I begin to hear tiny sizzles coming from the ground. It's the sound of leaves burning where the droplets have fallen. I'm inadvertently pulling heat up from the Earth's core.

"Fuck," I say, wiping my face.

I turn behind me to make sure the path isn't on fire. The leaves furthest from me have stopped steaming. Luckily, recent snowmelt has left everything damp.

My clothes don't seem damaged. Generally, anything attached to me is immune to the effects of my abilities. It's like the light forms a bubble around me where reality can conform to the rules of the Ceraphirian or Lamentation realm.

After a hike of just under an hour, I begin to hear the rushing water of the Toe River again. But there's something else. I sense vibrations through the Earth. They're the footsteps of two people walking through the forest. I hear them using raised voices to talk over the river's turbulence. Their footsteps don't resonate like that of two full-grown men. Rather, they're lighter. I can make out that their voices are of a higher pitch as well.

Then I realize what I'm hearing.

'Shit!' I yell in my mind. Rebecca and Ezra are standing where the nameless creek I'm following flows into the Toe River. My first instinct is to conceal myself and let them keep going, but I realize they're searching for me. If they hang around long enough, they're going to be spotted by the Apostles. I don't know what they'll do. They could just ignore them. I know Vernon kidnapped one runaway. He figured no one would miss her. Sadly, the bastard was right. Who's to say the Apostles, who lionize him as a prophet, haven't internalized Vernon's wretched behavior? Who else could those tormented voices I heard belong to? Young people, especially girls, disappear every day, and the law doesn't seem to give a shit about it. No one will come looking for them. 'They're just runaways,' they'll say. I find myself feeling the fear and anger of a parent whose child, after being told no, continues to reach for a hot stove.

I walk down the path toward them, obviously flustered with

their arrival. I make no attempt to step lightly. Before long, Ezra hears me coming.

"Someone's here," she says to Rebecca.

Through the trees, I see them walking in my direction to investigate. I step ten feet into the wood line and shield myself from view. After they walk past, I return to the trail and silently stalk them.

Now, only about six feet behind, I say, "What are you two looking for?" with a raised, abrupt voice.

Both jump and turn in fleeting, confused terror. They breathe deep sighs of relief upon realizing it's me.

"What the fuck are you both doing here?" I growl slowly.

"Looking for you, of course," Rebecca answers.

"The two of you are foolishly bumbling about a very perilous region. Turn around and head back to the Appalachian Trail, right now!"

"No," Ezra says. "You're up to something."

"I am not," I say indignantly.

"I think you're hunting. But I don't think it's deer you're after, instead, it's a person."

The two of them are sharp. I really can't think of a lie to tell that they won't see through. I try to speak but just mumble, "Well, I," and then go silent.

"Don't follow me. I won't stop what I've set out to do because of you two. I don't care if you're planning on reporting me to the police. Do what you have to.

"No," Rebecca says. "We want to join you."

"How did you find me in the first place?"

"The expensive boots you wear have an easily distinguishable pattern. No offense, but you have huge feet, which make your footprints easy to follow down a muddy riverside."

"I'm going to shoot both of you if you don't turn around right now and head back," I say clenching my teeth.

"No, you won't. You have a very different kind of conscience than most, but you have one. I realize you're trying to protect us, but you can't make our decisions."

"What I'm doing will very likely fail, and I will die, probably by gunshot. That's a quick death. But after I'm dead, they'll catch you both. You'll be imprisoned, tortured, and raped. This could go on for years. Inevitably, they'll murder you and bury your bodies face down in a shallow grave. I know, I was their hostage for a year and a half."

Rebecca's eyes open wide with my confession.

Exhausted, I clench my left hand into a fist and huff while turning around.

"Maybe you won't die because we come with you," Rebecca says optimistically, "There are a lot of women who wish they could get revenge on the men who hurt them. I have, and I want more."

"That well will never fill up," I tell her.

"My well has already been dug," Ezra interjects.

"You don't even have a weapon."

Rebecca proceeds to put her bag down on the ground. She opens it and begins digging. After half a minute, she pulls out a semi-automatic pistol in a black paddle holster.

"It's a forty caliber Taurus."

"Maybe if you had that holstered before, it would have come in handy when the mountain lion chased you," I say exasperated.

"It's illegal to carry a firearm in national parks. I never thought I'd need to use it on an animal. I keep it tucked between us at night. We figured you were brazenly skirting the law because what you're doing is more important than a fine or arrest."

I fear the Apostles and their beasts more than judicial repercussions.

"I can't stop you from stupidly following me, but don't get in my way. I hope you two like sleeping under the stars because your bright orange tent is a giant liability. Pitch it, and I'll cut it to pieces with my knife."

"We understand," Rebecca says.

"No, you don't."

19

Just past midday, we continue to follow the Toe River south. Rebecca and Ezra present me with the same problem I tried to avoid by striking out on my own, liability. I can't fight the cult effectively while simultaneously keeping two other people alive. At least Herschel and Nate can handle themselves. These two want-to-be vigilantes are completely naive. Rebecca has potential. Ezra, however, is a wilting flower who is subconsciously mirroring Rebecca.

Before they decided to tag along, I intended to cross highway nineteen at dusk. That would allow for enough cover but sufficient light to get a fair distance into the woods on the other side to pitch camp. Now, my best option will be to establish camp early, rest, and make it across right before dawn. It's always best to get shelter up before darkness falls, even if it means not traveling the distance you had planned.

I turn on my blue, handheld GPS. The pixilated screen indicates we are approximately one mile from highway nineteen. It's three o'clock. Not wanting to get any closer to the road, we stop hiking. I won't be able to encase myself in a granite cocoon tonight like I did the night before.

After eating, I explain my plan to cross highway nineteen in the early morning hours.

"Get some rest," I tell them.

They retire to their sleeping bags at four-thirty, half an hour before sunset. They're ten feet from the entrance of my tent. Rebecca zips the holstered pistol up into the sleeping bag with herself. After settling in, I quickly drift off to sleep as the final scraps of daylight slide through the creases of branches, like water running through loose fingers.

I'm jolted awake by the sound of a gunshot in the early morning hours of December twentieth. I grab my rifle as I unzip the tent fly and shine my flashlight out to see a man crumpled on top of Rebecca. He's moving despite the large exit wound out of the center of his back. The animating factor isn't the corpse, but a very alive Rebecca underneath. She's struggling to push him off with her hands still restrained inside the sleeping bag.

I stand up as the man's body falls in my direction. He's an obese, bearded white man with dark hair. He appears to be in his thirties. He's wearing overalls and a thick denim jacket. His face is riddled with pockmarks and scabs. Under his large nose is a mouth only half-filled with teeth, some of which are black with rot.

Rebecca unzips her sleeping bag. It now has a singular bullet hole through it and is smeared with blood. As her arms are freed, moonlight illuminates the Taurus pistol in her right hand. Just then, Ezra sits up.

Realizing he might not be alone, I quickly turn off my light. I step over the man, then kneel on my right knee behind the girls as they're still sitting.

"Be quiet," I whisper.

I'm holding the rifle, with the muzzle up, in my right hand and the extinguished flashlight in my left.

At the moment, I don't know if these men are members of the Apostles. I lay the flashlight down and place my left hand on the ground. I feel for the vibration of footsteps. There's nothing for ten seconds. I sense a stumble coming from behind a tree fifteen feet to our left. I raise my rifle in that direction while picking up my flashlight. I hold the light pointing outward in my left hand, while simultaneously supporting the stock of the rifle above it. I illuminate it, exposing a far more slender man, wearing a brown jacket with his pants down. I can see that he has brown hair and a mustache.

It becomes clear that these aren't cult members. The man who stumbled out from behind the tree was pleasuring himself to the show his now-dead companion was putting on. I pull the trigger without hesitation. The bullet enters his left eye and removes half of his skull.

I don't sense any other movement. I point my flashlight down at Rebecca's open sleeping bag.

"Pick up the spent casing and put it in your pocket."

While Rebecca does this, I slowly cycle the spent round from my rifle and do the same. Casings may have the fingerprints of the individual who loaded them into the weapon on them even after being fired. This dissipates with rapid firing because increased heat can cook the residual oils. Though, I won't risk it by handling my rounds bare-handed, I'm certain Rebecca has.

After I see Rebecca stow her spent casing, I switch off my flashlight and lay it down, then place my left hand against the ground again.

"There's no one else."

"How do you know that?" Ezra whispers.

My thoughts flash to Frieda, and I say, "Because I'm supposed to."

Ezra looks up at me with gratitude laced with confusion.

"What the hell should we do with them?" Rebecca asks.

"Nothing. We need to get out of here. Eventually, someone will come looking and we don't want to be here when they arrive."

In the backcountry, gunshots at night don't bring the police. These men likely have kin nearby who will come to investigate when they don't return. And they will be armed.

I quickly release the two aluminum rods that create the arched dome of my single-person tent. The elastic cord down the center allows them to break down quickly and fit into a small space. Once everything is in my pack, I hoist it up on my shoulders. The only thing not in it is my rifle. It rests in my arms, the suppressor now installed on the muzzle and two fresh rounds in the magazine, for a total of four. As we head out, I see that Rebecca has the pistol holstered on her right hip. Both follow behind me.

After getting forty-or-so feet away from the campsite, I kneel down to retie my boot. I place my left hand on the ground to steady myself. I reach down into the Earth, pinpointing the corpses of both men. I command the tree roots to pull them underground. I sense them wriggle over the dead men like snakes. They sink into the ground to be consumed. Ezra and Rebecca are focusing on the path in front of us, oblivious to what is happening to the bodies.

"It was too loose," I say.

Back on my feet, both continue to follow me.

By five in the morning, we reach an area where the river exits the woods into a meadow.

There, tall brown grass, three feet high, covers the ground. We duck down low as we travel the last few yards to highway nineteen. We stay in a crouched position, completely concealing our position, no more than fifty feet off the road.

"When we get across, we'll duck back into the forest on the other side. However, we will have to climb. You're going to burn a lot of calories, so you should take this opportunity to make a large breakfast."

They share a full pan of powdered eggs and grits. I eat a carb-heavy bag of dehydrated mac and cheese. We sit in a kind of triangle, legs crisscrossed, all facing one another with our two stoves in the center.

"If I weren't afraid people could be scouring the woods for the two men we just killed, I'd encourage y'all to head back once more. Now, you have no other choice but to climb up the ridge with me."

Angrily, I continue, pointing my finger at both of them, "If you don't die, what you see here will forever transform you, and not for the better."

For the first time since the mountain lion, there is genuine fear on Rebecca's face. I feel the mood reverberate from her into Ezra, who tried to mimic Rebecca's confidence but is actually ceaselessly terrified.

For about an hour after eating, we sit silently. At six-fifteen in the morning, I lead them, staying low in the grass, toward the road. With my hand covertly on the ground, I sense nothing. Dense fog drifts in from the west, pouring over the hills like an avalanche. I wait another fifteen minutes for it to envelope us. Still feeling nothing coming, I signal to the girls that it's time to cross. We continue running until we reach the wood line on the other side. The trees are sparse here, which is not good camouflage.

As daylight spreads, I begin leading the girls up a steep rocky slope that's damn near a forty-five-degree incline.

20

The ascent is physically strenuous, especially with the added weight of my pack. I've stowed my rifle. I had no choice; we have to crawl on our hands and knees. Above us is an extension of the same ridge that should eventually overlook the entrance to the cave system. The other end of that system emerges through a locked safe and into Vernon's Proffit's old home. The climb takes more than an hour, and despite the sub-freezing temperature, I'm sweating like it's a July afternoon back down east. I begin to worry about the girls because they're both wearing old-fashioned cotton thermals that will absorb their sweat, which will have a chilling effect when they cool down. Both are barehanded because their gloves are cumbersome and not suited to gripping rocks and tree roots.

At the top, we remove our packs and stop for a breather. Before long, both Ezra and Rebecca begin to shiver.

I try to subdue my panic before saying, "You both need to take off your long johns and get redressed in only your outer layer or you're going to become hypothermic."

"We'll freeze without an insulative layer," Rebecca replies.

"You'll freeze in wet, cold clothes faster."

Both strip down and place their long johns on a low-hanging

tree branch. They're still shivering after removing them.

"Huddle together for warmth," I instruct.

With their arms wrapped around one another, Ezra asks, "Why aren't you shivering?"

"I prepared for this with proper, modern gear. You came with me on a lark."

While they're preoccupied with their discomfort, I walk over to the soaked, off-white long johns. I raise my hand and pull moisture from the garments the way I did out of the would-be assassin, Franklin's body. Only, I'm judicious with it, and don't take out so much that they turn to dust. Rather, just enough to make them dry again.

I pick the long johns up and walk over to the girls saying, "The wind dried them out really fast."

I drop them in their laps. Rebecca looks at me confused, but Ezra is so cold, that the impossibility of it doesn't register. Both change again, and we're on our way.

I turn on the GPS. The saved coordinates come up. It begins to slowly link up to enough satellites to calculate our location. It indicates that we are nine-and-a-half miles from the overlook.

As the fog lifts, patches of daylight reach the forest floor. Around ten in the morning, we stumble across a flat rock wall, twenty feet in height. Water is weeping through its face and trickling down the drop-worn vertical ridges. There's a piece of rock jutting out of the wall at knee-height, that must have once been much larger. Countless millennia of erosion has taken a toll. But the payoff is that the water also hollowed out a large divot in the top surface of the jutting stone, creating a bowl that eternally overfills with clear spring water. We pour out our containers of river water and refill them with filtered spring water. We could likely get by without the precaution, but why take the risk? Years of traveling up from deep inside Earth's crust has filtered the water and added a pleasant mineral flavor. It tastes better than anything bottled and sold in a store.

By two in the afternoon, we are five miles from the ridge. Exhausted, the three of us break for lunch. While cleaning up, I begin to hear the moans of a distressed man. I am suspicious. Placing my hand on the ground, I don't feel the presence of another person. Despite this, the groans and screams are becoming impossible to ignore. I'm concerned that it's somehow a trap set by Joseph. I'm also overwhelmed with terror that it might be an escaped captive of the Apostles.

"Do you hear that?"

An always observant Ezra tilts her head to the right and listens carefully with her left ear by turning it, and herself, in all directions.

"No, I don't hear anything."

"I don't hear anything either," Rebecca says.

"It sounds like a man moaning in anguish."

Both look at me as though I've suddenly become insane. I realize that the sound isn't a part of their reality, only mine.

As we hoist our packs onto our backs again, I can tell they're bothered by my continued absence of mind, as I'm overwhelmed by what I'm hearing. I try to ignore it. After about ten minutes of hiking, we approach a rocky outcrop with a cave entrance just high enough for a person a tad over six feet tall to walk through standing upright. The voice is emanating from within.

"You can't hear sound coming from the cave," I say, pointing at the entrance.

"What cave?" Rebecca asks.

"Fuck," I say under my breath.

Even with the two of them here, I can't very well ignore this. The smooth wall of the rocky outcrop is huge, at least thirty feet.

Water gradually weeps from above. I watch several drops slowly trail down to the cave entrance. Just as each reaches a point where they should fall, the droplets disappear. My perception is skewed by my divergent realities. For anyone else viewing the wall, the water would have continued tumbling down the rock and to the forest floor instead. The illusion malfunctions when I see it because of the Ceraphirian light within me. It allows my mind to exist and perceive each reality simultaneously, the Woods of Lamentation, our Universe, and the Ceraphirian plane.

The girls both stop talking and stare at me. I begin walking toward the cave entrance. Upon reaching it, I hesitate. 'This could be a trap,' I think. How can I know what Joseph is capable of? But I also worry that he is doing harm to others. Unable to walk away, I unload my pack and dig around in it for a flashlight.

Illuminating it, I say, "Don't go anywhere," and then walk through the entrance. Once inside, I turn to see both of them petrified by what they saw, which would have been me walking through a solid rock wall. I stand and observe the cave entrance. Muffled sounds from the outside reach me. The view is distorted, as though I'm peering through dense glass molded into the shape of the exterior rock as everyone else sees it. Rebecca and Ezra walk up and touch it. I see their fingertips and palms flatten and spread slightly, like someone pressing their hands against a window from the opposite side.

Ezra bangs on the rock, shouting, "Hannah!"

I can vaguely make it out like a distant echo. I walk out, passing in between them.

"Stop shouting, you'll give our position away. I'll try not to take long."

"You'll try not to take long, where, inside the rocks?" Rebecca asks.

"Yes," I respond, as I head back inside, vanishing from their sight.

I shine my light through the interior. Twenty feet away, the cave appears to expand. Gingerly, I step forward, careful not to trod loudly. I hear droplets falling from the ceiling into standing water. It's slight and only occurs every few seconds.

Reaching the end, I see that most of the interior is hollow, with a tall ceiling. Every square inch of the walls shimmers with faint eclectic indigo. The light isn't bright enough to completely illuminate the space, but there is a significant background glow. An underground pond takes up most of the floor. I shine my light down into it. It's clear mountain water. The beam continues onward for what seems an infinite distance. It must be several hundred feet deep. As I move the beam of light up, I see a flat rock in the center of the water. Upon it rests a figure that looks like a person. They seem to be lying on their left side, with their back to me. Their clothes appear to be worn into rags. I can see what looks like the bottom of a set of bare white feet moving.

21

The moaning person on the flat rock shuffles when it hears my boots scuff the dirt across the cave floor. As they turn, I make out what appears to be a sickly, emaciated man with skin so pale that it's taken on the appearance of old glass. He's dressed in worn, brown rags that once were clothing. His shirt is half-torn open, exposing protruding ribs. He has long, unkempt, white hair, and a beard to match.

A toothless mouth mumbles and groans under a prominent, triangular nose. His eyebrows have grown to the length of cat whiskers.

"Is someone, there?" a weak voice says.

I'm reluctant to answer. The Apostles could be using him to draw me in. I see that there is a metal collar around his neck, attached to a chain affixed to the stone floor. It clinks ever so slightly with each of his movements. Even if it is the Apostles, there's no way I can leave him here in this condition.

As the beam of my flashlight hits his face, it shows me that his eyes have become milky-white like a blind cavefish.

"My name is Hannah," I say.

The strength of my voice causes an echo to reverberate across the cave walls.

Laying facing me, he says, "My name is Frederick Severe. I've been trapped here for what seems like an eternity. Truthfully, I'm not sure if I even understand the concept of time anymore. The only thing that breaks up the long drone of it all is when it comes. I used to see him, but I'm blind now. He looks as though he's created from shadow itself, but he's not a shadow. He's the void where space should be, pure emptiness. When this happens, a staircase made of purple light forms underneath the water in front of me. A walkway appears, then joins itself to my island. The vacant form wields a large hammer, which it uses to break every bone of my body, from my toes to my skull. I used to try and resist but it was pointless. I've been mortally wounded many times over, but somehow I heal. It's a slow, painful process. Eventually, the void comes back. Once it was gone for so long that I believed it had vanished. In other instances, it comes to break me again before I've finished healing. It never talks. It's only capable of walking and swinging a hammer."

"Frederick, you disappeared in eighteen-twenty-five."

"What year is it now?"

"Two-thousand-and-six. That would make you one-hundred-and-eighty-one years old."

Upon hearing this, Frederick begins to weep.

"Everyone I know is gone from this world," he wails.

I try to imagine finding out that all the people in my life are dead at once. It seems impossible.

I feel the earth underneath the cavern vibrate. Water ripples around the island in perfect synchrony, taking the appearance of tree rings that won't sit still. Breaking the surface, a staircase made of sparkling indigo light rises, just as Frederick described. A walkway forms from the stairs to the island.

Someone ascends the stairs, out of the water and into the open air. Upon reaching the top, I see a statuesque woman, about six-and-a-half feet in height. She has beautiful dark skin and striking red, curly hair down to her shoulders. Her eyes are a pale gray, making the contrast stunning. She has high cheekbones, and freckles underneath her eyes, framed by a perfectly symmetrical nose.

"I am Theta," the woman says.

When she speaks, her words are audibly underlined with the faint sound of rushing wind.

"Why are you here, Naomi?"

"Because I am meant to be."

"You sound like Frieda."

"How are you here? Shouldn't you be experiencing time differently?"

"In this world, the Ceraphirian light inside you creates something akin to a black hole. Since your species has no choice but to experience existence linearly, the light bends time around you when you enter another plane."

I look at Theta confused.

She continues, "You're no longer in the human world. This is a mid-point between Ceraphiria and your universe. Since you and Frederick can only experience time linearly, so must I when here. Though, this is my first time in this place. However, you are prohibited from going any further. Your presence would alter our existence permanently. Likewise, we are prohibited from ever fully entering yours."

"One did, though."

Upon realizing I know this, an irritated, Theta asks, "What is your business here, Naomi Pace?"

"Why do you have Frederick Severe chained to a rock? At one-hundred-eighty-one, you've unnaturally kept him alive. He's lived two lifetimes of suffering. If his sins are so great, shouldn't he be in the Woods of Lamentation?"

"This man's crime was desecrating the sacred tomb of Zelia, the only Ceraphirian to cross over into your plane. I prepared the nether space we currently occupy, then began whispering ideas on the breeze in his direction, eventually, driving Frederick mad. This led to him aimlessly wandering around the forest after his mining venture failed. He followed my voice all the way to this cave. Since then, Frederick has been my prisoner. What he did to the rocks of Zelia's tomb, I now have done to him."

"What about Solid Rock and the Apostles? They've set up shop right where Frederick left off."

"I have tried. It's as though their minds are locked. No matter how much effort I exert, I cannot influence them."

"I asked Frieda how I arrived on the tracks between the Woods of Lamentation and Ceraphiria, and she answered, 'We don't make those decisions.' Who's making the decisions in this nether space?"

"I do."

"Who controls it elsewhere?"

"It's all rather like an ever-shifting equation yearning to solve itself, but it never quite can."

"That begs the question, Theta. Who decides which humans end up in the Woods of Lamentation instead of a paradise world of their own?"

"We don't know," she responds begrudgingly."

"If all of reality operates on an ever-shifting, endless equation, why did you have to imprison Frederick? Is it because you know the math is in his favor? What was his life like before he began building the mine?"

"He was an honest man."

"You're torturing him for unintentional disrespect, not rape or murder. At worst, he's a fool. I thought the Ceraphirian were more enlightened than humans. It appears not."

"Release him, if you wish. I won't stop you, but he will not make it long back in your world."

Holding my left hand in front of me, I instinctively form a bridge similar to Theta's, extending from myself out to the island. She watches as I cross and kneel down to the withered body of Frederick Severe. I melt the chain holding the binding to his metal collar. What remains attached is the length of a necktie. His body is so light that it feels as though he has hollow bones."

"What are you going to do with him," Theta asks before I enter the smaller cavern leading back to the tunnel entrance.

"Balance an equation."

It doesn't take long before we reach the entryway. Thankfully, I see Rebecca and Ezra through the thick, glasslike barrier between this nowhere world and our universe. They've yet to see me coming because, to them, the entrance still appears as a cave wall.

As I walk through the barrier, Frederick lets out an audible gasp, just before disintegrating into dust. Now outside, all I'm left with is two handfuls of coarse gray matter and the metal collar and chain that were affixed to his neck. The rest of Fredericks's remains lay all around in a similar condition, slowly being scattered by a slight breeze. I force moisture into the metal of Fredericks former restraints, crumbling them into flaky rust particles.

22

I stand there and let the rust and the remaining bits of Frederick's remains precipitate toward the ground.

Ezra says, "You walked through a rock wall, just like Joseph Proffit. Can you control the weather too?"

"No," I respond, irked.

"What was all that dust?" Rebecca asks.

"The dust was a who, not a what."

"Who, then?"

"A very old man. I tried to save him but couldn't."

In a daze, I pick up my backpack and GPS, then head forward without another word. After walking for fifteen minutes, I realize that it is far later than I thought. I stop.

"How long was I gone?"

"You were gone for two-and-a-half hours," Ezra says.

I look down at my GPS screen again. I have to illuminate it with the backlight. It's four-thirty in the afternoon. The sun will go down in less than half an hour.

"We have to make camp."

"No shit," Rebecca says. "How long did you think you were gone?"

"No more than twenty minutes, maybe less."

"I'm worried about you," Rebecca says.

"Don't waste your time. Worry about yourselves instead."

I'm not hungry tonight. I'm disturbed by the day's events. My delusion of Ceraphirian wisdom and altruism has fallen away. No one has ever blamed humans for having much of either, though. In a way, this puts Frieda and me on even ground. I go to sleep expecting to see her but awake disappointed.

It's five-thirty in the morning, December twenty-first, two-thousand-six. It's a bit less than two hours until sunup. The girls are both snoring slightly. I exit my tent quietly so they can continue to rest, then head fifteen feet from camp to relieve myself. I return to my tent and read for an hour. I wonder if I too won't end up lost in the wilderness without a trace.

As Rebecca and Ezra wake, I begin to shuffle about and fire up my camp stove.

While eating, I say, "Y'all are probably wondering what you got yourselves into."

As Ezra pours herself a mug filled with unsweetened, instant coffee, she says, "You walked through a rock wall."

"In my defense, I'd never done that before yesterday."

"You don't seem to be shocked by it."

Flustered, I realize there's no point in continuing to lie.

"I'm here to kill Joseph Proffit. My destination is four miles away. It's a ridge overlooking the entrance to a cave system they control. When I was their prisoner, I escaped through one of its divergent veins and into the wilderness. Don't be surprised by anything you see from here on."

Rebecca and Ezra look ashen. I don't think the weight of their foolish choice had hit them until this very moment.

"Is it too late to go back?" Ezra asks.

Rebecca looks at her with slight irritation.

"Safely," I say. "Either way is a risk."

Rebecca says to Ezra, "If we go back, it's just the two of us and one pistol against those men's kin. If we stay with Hannah, there are three of us and two guns."

"Yeah," Ezra says softly, yielding to Rebecca's stronger character.

The problem isn't that Rebecca is wrong, it's that they shouldn't even be here.

We get going about ten after seven, just as the sun lifts away some of the darkness. The way forward begins to increase in gradient as we climb to an even higher elevation. This slows us. We don't arrive at the ridge until around eleven-thirty. I can see a significant window of light through the trees ahead. What we find is a shard of rock creating a flat platform out over the cliff's edge. It's six feet in length and ten in width. I retrieve my binoculars and get on all fours. I shimmy my way to the edge by lying on my stomach. Through the binoculars, I bring into focus what I believe to be the cavern entrance.

I can see the old cobbled road, shrouded by the shadow of a thick forest. While evergreens grow here, a significant portion of the trees are hardwoods that lose their leaves over the winter. I may not have noticed it during the summer, but I glimpse a flat wall of OD green. As I sharpen the image further, it becomes apparent that I'm looking at a sizable, reinforced metal door. They've laid new gravel on the ground in front of it and have removed the trees growing through the old cobblestone road. I can see what looks like fresh black tire marks on several rocks, as though a vehicle momentarily lost traction. For now, the road is empty, and the door is shut. Putting the binoculars down, I scoot back off the edge and go rummaging through my pack. After locating the range finder, I crawl back out and return to a prone position. Zeroing in on the door, it gives a reading of three-hundred-and-nine yards. At that distance, I barely have to adjust the elevation of my rifle scope. I keep watch for about half an hour but see no movement. I put away my binoculars and then join Rebecca and Ezra, who are sitting safely away from the cliff's edge.

"Nothing?" Rebecca asks.

"There's a large metal doorway painted green on the side of the mountain. If the tunnel behind it is the same size, it's large enough to drive a vehicle through."

I have Rebecca crawl out on the rock with me and point out the door. It takes her a minute, but once apparent, it's impossible not to see.

Rebecca motions for Ezra, and asks, "Do you want to have a look?" She offers to give up her spot next to me.

I can tell she's afraid. For the first time in her life, Ezra is realizing Rebecca's threshold for risk-taking far exceeds her own. No amount of pretending will change that. Until now, Ezra had been fooling herself because of how much she admired Rebecca. But watching Ezra's legs shake as she withdraws from the cliff's edge tells the entire story.

"Can you keep an eye out while I pitch camp and eat?" I ask Rebecca.

"Go ahead," she replies.

I pitch camp twenty-five feet from the edge to make certain we're out of the green door's line of sight. I sit across from Ezra as I begin boiling water on my small stove. She sits with her knees up, arms wrapped around them, in a semi-fetal position.

"It's okay to be afraid," I say.

"I just didn't expect it to turn into this. I usually just go along with Rebecca. She's like a big sister. I was too frightened to continue alone."

"Often, life is like the mountain lion that chased y'all. It didn't matter that you saw it ahead of time. The cat charged anyway. The question is, do you run away or fight? Neither is a good option. I'll do my best to make sure you and Rebecca are safe."

"Perhaps that will be the thing that keeps you from doing something utterly suicidal."

"For me, death is like a cold that everyone else seems to catch besides myself. I know I can die. I've had plenty of opportunities, but Death's sword always misses. Often, I feel like the Universe keeps me alive because it relishes my torture."

I hear, 'psst.' It's Rebecca trying to get my attention. I unpack my rifle and install the suppressor. I take one of the fifty-count boxes of bullets with me, and the ten incendiary rounds. I join Rebecca by sliding prone onto the rock, taking the space on her right.

Quietly, Rebecca says, "They just opened the door."

Through the binoculars, I see four men in gray uniforms, just like the ones worn by the security forces on Fort Caswell. I hear a faint, repeating beep. It's the sound of a large vehicle's backup warning system. Through the trees, I see something sizable heading down the old cobblestone road toward the cave entrance. As it approaches where the trees have been more thoroughly felled, I make out that it's a small white dump truck with a green bed. The driver does a three-point turn at the cave entrance, then backs inside until they're out of sight. The four other men go about shutting the large metal door.

"What are they doing," Rebecca whispers?"

"Mining for something that's not theirs."

"I don't understand."

"There's a substance in the rock that allows Joseph to perform his, so-called 'miracles.' The water too. He must harvest that using a different vehicle."

"Then how do you do it?"

"They're mining for residue. I have the source."

We watch until darkness falls. There's nothing more. Figuring that they're done for the evening, we retreat to our camp. After eating, we pack it in for the night and drift off to slumber in the frigid Appalachian air.

23

I awake at five-thirty the next morning. It's Friday, December twenty-second. Opening the zipper of my tent rouses Rebecca. She peels back the top of her sleeping bag to reveal the Taurus pistol grasped in her right hand.

The bullet hole through the front where she shot the man on top of her a few nights ago was letting cold air in. I was able to repair it by cutting a short length of my black paracord and unfurling the white fibers contained within. After, I sheared a thin piece of the striker off my metal match with a sharp stone. I used the tip of my knife to put a hole through the shiny metal fragment while holding it against a log. I filed down the other end against a weathered, oval-shaped rock the size of a soccer ball. Interlacing a single white fiber through it creates a make-shift needle and thread. I sewed up the hole, ensuring the stitches were contained on the inside of the bag so they were less likely to get caught on something. We washed the blood off the best we could with spring water.

It takes us a moment to realize that Ezra's sleeping bag is empty. Rebecca and I both fight the urge to scream out her name.

"She probably went to pee," Rebecca says.

We wait for fifteen minutes just in case she's having a bowel movement. Nobody wants to be snuck up on while doing that in the woods.

"What the fuck," Rebecca says with a quiver in her voice.

I see where leaf litter had been shuffled about. It appears she headed back down the way we came.

"Let's go," I say, after noticing this.

I take my rifle from the tent and use the sling to carry it on my left shoulder. Likewise, Rebecca slides her paddle holster onto her right side. Reluctantly, I shine my flashlight in a slow, sweeping motion trying to take note of everything.

A quarter-mile from camp, my light hits a figure thirty feet to our left, sitting on the ground. It's Ezra. Getting closer, I see that she's stripped down to her white bra and panties. It's below freezing. Around ten feet away, I realize what I'm actually looking at. Ezra isn't sitting on the ground at all. A single length of paracord is suspending her by the neck in a seated position. Her bottom is about a foot off the forest floor. Her underwear is stained yellow from where she urinated while strangling to death. Seconds after this comprehending this, I hear Rebecca scream.

"Be quiet, they might hear," I respond at a low volume.

Quickly, Rebecca pulls out her knife and cuts through the paracord in one swipe. Rebecca pulls the cord from around Ezra's neck and begins CPR, but her corpse is blue. Her lips and face are engorged with pooled blood. Ezra's brown eyes are now bulging from her head, framed by burst capillaries.

"She's cold, I say as I check the radial pulse on her right wrist, "Stop. She's been gone for hours."

If Rebecca hadn't already been on her knees attempting CPR,

she would have fallen to the ground. She covers her face and sobs uncontrollably.

"It's not your fault," I say, as I gently place my hand on her shoulder.

I realize this is a shitty platitude that makes no difference, but I felt like it was something Rebecca needed to hear.

"It is. I dragged her along because I wanted to feel the way I did when I gutted Marshal. All I accomplished was killing my best friend. Why did she take her clothes off?"

"Because if the paracord didn't kill her, she'd eventually succumb to exposure."

I immediately regret saying that.

Rebecca lays down on the right side of Ezra's cold body and holds her while weeping softly. I stand a few feet away and wait. After an hour, Rebecca sits up and wipes away tears with her coat sleeve.

"We have to bury her," Rebecca says.

"We don't have shovels. Even if we did, I won't leave behind any evidence. She could be dug up later."

"What the hell are you going to do then?"

"Cremate her."

"And you don't think the smoke won't attract the damn cult?"

"You don't understand," I say, "I can do more than just walk through walls. When you're ready to let Ezra go, I will show you."

After a few minutes of silence, Rebecca whispers, "Okay."

I kneel down at Ezra's side, directly across from Rebecca, who is still sitting on Ezra's right.

"You may not want to watch this," I say delicately.

"No. I want to."

I place my right hand on Ezra's chest and begin to withdraw the water from her body while simultaneously letting it exit the scar on my left hand as fog. Within a few seconds, all that's left of her is a crumbly, gray pile.

"Step back a few feet," I instruct Rebecca.

After doing so, I draw a small lava tube from the Earth's core. As it comes up, I cause it to spread out completely under Ezra's body. Barely giving off smoke, the shell turns into fine ash.

I look up to see Rebecca in shock, holding her hand over her mouth. "How?"

"It happened to me when my best friend, Charles, died. He and I were prisoners of the cult. They tortured and raped us. Sadly, while we were escaping, one of them sliced open Charles's leg. Charles eventually bled to death in the same cavern we've been watching. It's a holy place. There, I was granted a golem who protected me."

"Inside her, she kept this," I say, holding up my left-hand palm out, forming a small, bright white orb, floating directly in front of my hand.

"The light wouldn't be transferred to me until years later when I was finally ready to carry the burden. It looks like magic, but what you are actually seeing is something from another plane of reality intruding on our own. I can pull from two other worlds that have different physical laws than our own. But it's also like a leash. I can feel it attached to my chest. The other end is anchored to the Earth's core. I think that's why most of my abilities revolve around controlling the planet's elements."

"The Disciples of the Cloven Hand are mining the residue left over in the surrounding rocks near where the light was gifted to me years ago. That's what allows Joseph to do his tricks."

"What do they want?"

"They're a doomsday cult who think they must fulfill a prophecy that will bring forth the end of our world. According to them, only they will inherit a new, perfect one. Obviously, this is complete horseshit. What isn't, though, is that Joseph's abilities are growing. The creatures he's creating cannot be killed with conventional weapons. Joseph is arrogant and reckless. He'll lose control of them, and they will wash over the land like locusts. Instead of wheat, they'll feast on living humans, leaving everything else untouched."

"Creatures," Rebecca asks.

"Yes, real-life fucking monsters."

I can tell by Rebecca's eyes that she believes everything I'm telling her. She's quiet for a few seconds, in contemplation of what I said, then shudders involuntarily.

Rebecca asks, "How long before the sun comes up?"

"About thirty minutes."

"We have to get back to the lookout," she replies.

"Okay," I respond, reaching my right hand down to her. She clasps it, and I pull a determined Rebecca to her feet.

We eat in a state of quiet, shared loneliness. I, for my family, and Rebecca for Ezra. Now that she's gone, Rebecca has no one.

We perch on the rock as before, both on our stomachs. Rebecca on the left, and me on the right. All the ammunition I brought sits in boxes between us. I teach her how to use the range finder and explain the way to adjust the rifle's scope in clicks based on distance. Bullets only fly straight momentarily, but all matter surrenders to gravity, eventually. Sitting there, I think about how much I would have loved to have a younger sister, but I'm glad I didn't because I couldn't have protected her from my father.

We don't see movement until nine in the morning. The door opens and four men in uniform walk out of the entrance, two on either side. They have rifles on slings across their chests. I recognize the shape. They're the M-16s I and Charles saw locked away in the cavern during our escape. The men are waiting for something. Out of the enormous cavern entrance exits a white, two-door pick-up truck. There's only a driver inside the cab. Two members of the armed security patrol jump into the bed. The truck turns left on the old stone road, then comes to a stop. This puts its right side facing me. Next emerges the white dump truck, with a green bed from the day before. Inside the cab sits a driver and passenger. The dump truck pulls out directly behind the white pickup. The other uniformed security guards return to the cavern entrance and begin to shut the metal door. The trucks wait to proceed until it's fully closed and locked.

Seizing the opportunity, I remove all the traditional rounds from my rifle and load two incendiaries first followed by two of the conventional rounds on top of them. That makes it so the incendiary rounds will be the last two in the sequence of four. I line up my scope's crosshairs onto the chest of the white pickup truck's driver. Breathing out slowly, I pull the trigger.

24

The impact of the bullet paints the now spiderwebbed windshield of the white pickup truck red. I cycle the bolt, ejecting it into the mesh shell catcher, and chamber the next round. It's the last of the conventional cartridges. I quickly zero my scope onto the chest of the dump truck driver. With another muffled hiss of gas, his innards find themselves equally displayed on the glass like a microscope slide. The final two rounds in the rifle are incendiary.

Chaos erupts upon the realization of what has happened. The passenger of the dump truck opens his door and stumbles out covered in blood and viscera. There's no cellular service here, so, instead of being able to call for backup, the two men with M-16s across their chests, run toward the large steel door that leads back into the cavern. Next to it, they seem to be accessing an intercom that allows them to communicate with someone inside.

I take aim at the exposed metal fuel tank underneath the passenger side of the dump truck. Momentarily, I can see the third bullet's tracer line. Its disappearance is followed by a gas explosion emanating from the tank it just pierced. This isn't the high-velocity explosion of a munition. It's more akin to pouring a Mason jar of gasoline onto an open flame, dialed up exponentially.

The flames engulf the dump truck's passenger. Doused with a fine mist of ignited gasoline, he flails and kicks as he burns alive. The other two don't bother to help. One is now banging on the door while the other is still trying to contact someone inside through the intercom. The white pickup truck has now also caught on fire.

The large metal door in the cavern begins to open again. It's cracked only wide enough for one person to get through at a time. A guard from the inside foolishly steps out to see what's going on, and I sink an incendiary round into his torso. His chest glows white-hot for a millisecond, then he's down. Both of the men with rifles across their chests step over his body to get inside.

As I begin to reload, they disappear and pull the door shut. The fire rages until eventually the white truck's gasoline tank also explodes with another large whoosh. Black smoke fills the sky. I feel guilty for spreading acrid soot across such a pristine landscape. There's enough moisture on the ground and in the atmosphere that the fire doesn't spread. After a few hours, it putters out on its own. Once the smoke clears, I fire an incendiary round into the intercom, disabling it and causing the machinery to release smoke for a few minutes.

We watch the door for the remainder of the day. There is no more movement observable from our vantage point.

After the excitement, Rebecca spends the evening vacillating between disbelief and grief.

When darkness falls, we retreat back to our camp. There, Rebecca is confronted with Ezra's empty sleeping bag and gear.

Her mood turns to profound grief.

"Pack up Ezra's belongs. We'll take care of it when we're done. If it would make you more comfortable, I can keep her things in my tent so they're out of sight.

"No, it's just stuff. Proximity to it doesn't make me more or less sad. And your tent is too small."

I nod my head in agreement.

We sit face to face around our two ignited camp stoves.

"I don't have a family. I only had Ezra. I have a few friends at school, but she was my entire life. I don't even know why I should keep going."

"Because that's what survivors do. They move forward. I can't tell you how to feel about it. My grief manifested with anger. The people who murdered my loved ones paid for it. But this isn't the same. Depression is a circumstantial flaw of neurochemistry. It's not as though it's an entity with intent. It just exists."

"It doesn't stop me from being furious with Ezra."

"I'd feel the same way."

My thoughts turn to Nate. He really struggled with the aftermath of his parents' abuse and desertion. And now Claude is dead. I'm just glad he's with Herschel and Diane.

"If I hadn't been insistent on following you, she'd be alive and we would still be on the Appalachian Trial."

"You can't undo your decisions. It was foolish but not malicious."

Looking at Rebecca's face, I realize my words gutted her emotionally. I find myself wanting to take it back, but I make it a policy to never shy away from difficult truths, for myself or others.

She begins crying. I move over and wrap my arms around Rebecca. I attempt to soothe raw grief by rubbing her back and rocking her like a baby. This goes on for half an hour.

As she calms, Rebecca asks, "What do you think they're doing down there?"

"It's probably pandemonium. Likely they didn't hear the report of the suppressed rifle, or see a muzzle flash. They may as well have been magic bullets. Hell, they may assume that there was a bomb. The Apostles are not a professional militia. Most of them have no training. Skill is not required, just true belief."

"How long are you going to stay up here?"

"I don't know. Until it's over. Eventually, I'll start setting up a network of snares. The small game will keep us fed indefinitely. We'll wait. They'll have to clean up the mess so they can continue shipping the stone and water out. The cavern opening is too small on the other end. It would have to be hauled up vertically through a manhole. There's no choice if they want to keep up production."

"Of what?"

"They call it, 'indigo'. It's made from using rock and water from the cave, and well, blood."

"Jesus Christ," Rebecca exclaims.

"Joseph seems to think so."

"Whose blood are they using?"

"The last person I know of was a young man named Claude. He's dead. I don't know if they saved some of his or what they're doing. But based on the size of their dump truck, I'd say they still have some. It only works if the blood comes from a person exposed to my abilities. This puts you and my entire family at risk. That's also part of the reason we had to cremate Ezra's body."

Not long after our conversation, we tuck in for the night.

The next morning is Saturday, December twenty-third, two-thousand-six, the day before Christmas Eve. Rebecca and I continue our surveillance from the cliff's edge at seven, right before sunup. The trucks are blackened shells. It reminds me of Al's burnt tractor.

There's no movement until nine in the morning. The door

opens just enough for a person to pass through. Out slip two young men wearing camouflage overlaid with body armor and combat helmets. They have rifles like the men yesterday. These aren't the same figures. They're scrawny boys, no older than twenty. Then I see a tow truck backing down the old stone road toward the burnt-out dump truck from yesterday. On its right side, which is facing us, plate steel has been welded over the tires, the gas tank under the side-step, and the passenger side window. The driver, who appears to be a husky man with a white beard, is wearing thick tactical body armor. Even from this distance, I can tell the plate steel is not robust. It flexes slightly as the truck rumbles over the uneven stones. It's likely only a quarter-inch thick.

I use a similar load as yesterday, two incendiary rounds and two conventional. This time, though, the incendiaries will be fired first.

The younger men stop about ten feet from the dump truck wreckage. Slowly, they unwind a thick steel cable and wrap it around the exposed front axle. The blackened rubble makes a screeching noise as it scrapes over the smooth granite.

I fire an incendiary round at the under-step gas tank of the tow truck. The steel plate is left with a molten bullet hole. This time, there's no explosion.

"They drained the passenger side gas tank," I say to Rebecca. "All the fuel is on the driver's side."

I consider putting the second incendiary round into the tow truck driver's body armor but instead opt to shoot through the front grill. The round meets its mark, hitting the radiator. Toxic, green fluid runs out onto the ground. Without coolant, the truck is immobilized. The engine stops a few seconds later. A fire can be seen peeking out from under the hood. The driver hops out of the tow truck, and all three flee back to the large steel door. I pull the bolt back and chamber another round as I follow the figures through my rifle's scope. I don't bother firing a shot because the vulnerable areas around the armor are too small to hit on a moving target.

The last one through the door is one of the younger men. He pauses and looks in our direction. With it being an unusually bright winter day, I quickly realize he's seen the glint off of my scope or Rachel's binoculars. Aiming at his throat, I fire, but it's too late. I hear the ricochet of the bullet deflecting off the thick metal door echo across the valley.

25

"We've been made," I say to Rebecca. "The last one glimpsed purposefully in our direction. It was the reflection off of one of our lenses."

"We have to get out of here before they make it to our location. We're hemmed in against the cliff edge. There's nowhere to go but down, the way we came in," Rebecca replies, panicked.

"They may not have cell phone access, but there's likely a landline right inside the door if my incendiary round didn't destroy it when I took out their intercom. It's not just the men in uniform. Their cult has complimentary access to every able-bodied man in their congregation. Those men all have guns and the ones closest will likely begin climbing in our direction in less than fifteen minutes."

"Didn't you plan for this?"

"I intended on fighting to the death."

"Can't you use your abilities?"

"Yes, but only within a fifty-foot radius. If they come in great enough numbers, my fortune will inevitably run dry. I'm not bulletproof."

"I was kind of hoping you were."

"It'll take them until at least nightfall before the first ones reach us. Instead of waiting here with nothing but a cliff to our backs, why don't we head down and meet them on our own terms?"

With a stern face, Rebecca nods her head.

"Isn't there a way around them?"

"The ridge is, at most, half a mile wide. It rises to our elevation like a ramp, leaving two edges on each side. They are too steep to climb down. The Apostles will send enough people to spread out so they can cover the entire rock formation. The further from the cliffs we meet them, the more space we have to maneuver."

"Right," Rebecca responds.

"Start packing up your shit. Take the food out of Ezra's backpack, along with anything else that might be useful, and put it in your own."

Swiftly, I begin to break down my tent. I get it stowed away in my pack, along with my sleeping bag in just a few minutes. Meanwhile, Rebecca is on her knees pulling packs of freeze-dried food out of Ezra's bag, along with a water bottle and matches.

"Make sure to keep Ezra's sleeping bag. Yours has a hole in it."

Rebecca stuffs her old sleeping bag and Ezra's clothes into the backpack and places it on the ground.

Kneeling, I place my left hand on the bag and use my right to pull heat from the Earth's core, channel it through my body, and release it out of the scar on my left palm. The plastic in the bag's fabric begins to bubble right before it bursts into an aggressive, but short-lived fire. The initial flash was bright white. The flames to follow exhibit odd shades of blue and green as the synthetic materials are converted into a plume of noxious smoke. In a few seconds, only ash remains. I look up to see a few silent tears fall from Rebecca's eyes.

"Let's go," she says.

"Yeah."

As we descend the steep gradient, I step slowly, trying to disturb as little ground as I can. All the while, I reach out and attempt to feel the vibrations of their treading feet through the soles of my boots. It doesn't work as well as bare skin, but it's far too cold to walk barefoot. In all probability, they're still several miles away. We'll be traveling faster than them since they're coming uphill and we're going down.

Every few minutes, I stop and place my hand on the ground.

"What are you doing?"

"I'm feeling for footsteps. As people walk, it creates a slight percussive, circular ripple."

"And you can sense that?"

"Yes. Sometimes it's like the soil itself talks to me. Not in words, it's a faint electrical tingle. The Earth knows without thinking and acts without effort. I don't understand how, just like I don't really have to think about how to use my abilities. Bits and pieces of what I can do are being exposed slowly, like a sculpture emerging from stone. I shouldn't have ignored their calling for so long."

We walk for another hour. Abruptly, I feel something running in our direction. It's faster than a human and on four feet. Its rhythm is familiar. Then comes the sickening realization that the last time I saw the pattern instead of feeling its vibration. It's the quick stride of one of Joseph's beasts. Through the trees, I see flashes of its thick, leathery skin. We hear the creature's horrifying screech resonate across the forest.

"What the fuck is that?" Rebecca asks in a whisper.

"A beast of lamentation."

I hear Rebecca's respiration increase.

"Will it attack us?"

"That's its only purpose."

"Shoot it."

"Bullets won't hurt it."

I motion for Rebecca to kneel next to me on the ground, and I also kneel. I begin to pull granite from the ground to form a dome-like structure, as I did the first night in the cult's territory. Only this time, I make it much larger. It's oblong, and shaped kind of like a jelly bean. The light through the forest canopy dies away, blotted out by stone until it's reduced to a small opening, then total darkness. I ask the roots of the surrounding trees to weave themselves around our dome. The exposed rock quickly turns green with lichen, giving the structure the appearance of an ancient, worn boulder.

I hear the clicking sound of Rebecca's flashlight turning on. I'm then met with a bright light to the face.

"Sorry," she says, pointing the beam down.

Illuminated, the interior looks to be twenty feet long, and eight wide.

"What did you do?"

"I asked the Earth to move these cleaves of granite around us."

"Are we safe in here?"

"I don't know," I say, placing my right hand on the ground.

"The creature is frenzied and desperate to eat. To endlessly feed is its only driving force. Without continuous victims to chase, like its brethren in the Woods of Lamentation, it feels excruciating hunger pangs."

"How can you know that?"

"I've been told by someone I believe. And, in the recent past, I've learned to integrate my consciousness into trees and mycelium. They're quiet. Both are content just to exist and exchange nutrients, nothing more. With them, it's like moseying through a cozy unknown passage into a friend's garden. This beast, on the other hand, isn't passive. It strikes out, forcing what consciousness of the animal used to create it has left upon me."

"It's hunting you," Rebecca whispers.

"You're right," I say pulling my hand off the ground.

The signal grows fainter, but sustaining, like a tiny itch just out of reach.

"That'll slow it down. Eventually, that thing is going to search you out. Are we going to just live in here until then? We don't have enough water."

I place my scarred left hand against the stone. The granite begins to glow white. A patina of lichen spreads across the interior, much like bacteria on a petri dish. The lichen exude a deep, blue bioluminescent light, which illuminates the interior with a faint glow. Everything looks odd bathed in it. Using our flashlights returns whatever is placed under its beam back to a more natural hue.

In the center of the void, I pull a lava tube from deep within the earth. I stop it eight feet below us. The temperature noticeably warms. On one end of the structure, I pull a spring up to form a pool of water two feet in diameter. On the opposite end, I force a deep depression into the ground for us to use to relieve ourselves.

As we begin to take our coats off, Rebecca asks, "You could have done this the entire time? Instead, you've been filtering stream water and sleeping in a tent."

"I only ask it for what I need. Otherwise, I'm abusing it."

"I understand."

We settle in, rolling out our sleeping bags side by side in the center of our dome structure. I make an effort to keep my bare skin off the ground. I stay on top of my sleeping bag and make sure to wear my boots when I move around. At around four in the afternoon, I begin to feel the faint hint of about a dozen footsteps. After a while, they move on. This happens several more times as the evening wears on. Several parties are crisscrossing the ridge in search of us. Around ten in the evening, we both feel confident enough about our protective shell that we tuck ourselves away for the evening and doze lightly.

———

The next day is Christmas Eve. We experience a significant drop-off in walk-by traffic. It dwindles to nothing by evening. We begin to wonder if they won't eventually just give up.

26

Christmas morning goes by quietly, then around one in the afternoon, I sense a group of at least twenty. I feel a surge through the ground. It feels like when their beast was homing in on me, only sharper and more clever.

"He's here," I say to Rebecca.

"The creature?"

"No, Joseph."

We go quiet for a few minutes, so as to not attract attention. I expect them to continue on like the parties before, but this time they seem to be circling.

"They know we're in the area, somehow. Joseph can sense my proximity through the Earth if he's close enough. He's stopping every few feet and putting his hand on the ground to reach out. They're following me one ping at a time."

"Shouldn't the rock protect us?"

"In my experience, 'should' and 'will' are two very different concepts that don't often overlap."

Rebecca's face becomes still as the stone that surrounds us. She points up above my head. I quickly turn to see Joseph's left hand piercing through the rock from the outside, into our protective shell.

There are fresh scars resulting from his act of self-mutilation in an attempt to replicate the wound Vernon Proffit gave me. I pull the auto-knife from my jeans pocket. I press the release button. Anger takes over after I hear the metallic click of the blade opening. With little effort, I create a lamentation blade. Then, without hesitation, I stab Joseph's disembodied hand through the scar and quickly pull the knife down. I feel his screams vibrate the earth beneath us. As his hand retracts, it splashes blood across the walls and onto us.

Moments later, I sense the beast walking in from the periphery, guided by two men on either side. They give a command, and it bolts toward our location. We hear heavy scratching against the rock wall, directly outside of our position. Between the scraping noises, there's the distinct sound of stones falling to the ground.

"It's coming through. Grab what you can."

I hastily begin stuffing all I can into my pack. I try to rebuild the stone on the exterior wall, but the beast is crawling through the rock faster than I can replace it.

"We're not going to be able to run fast enough with our packs on," Rebecca says.

"There aren't going to be many of them left in a few seconds," I say placing my left hand on the rock wall of our shelter.

The dome around us begins to crack and shift. With a single thought, I cause the walls to shatter into thousands of pieces. They accelerate out in a three-hundred-sixty-degree pattern.

Rebecca instinctively ducks down and puts her arms over her head.

The sudden daylight temporarily blinds us. As it subsides, we find ourselves in a field of bodies that have been dashed into disordered, bloodied fragments. As my sight comes back, I see the beast charging at us from more than fifty feet away, which is where the last of the rocks lay. Its pointy gray beak opens, exposing four long canines.

Rebecca trembles.

"Don't run," I say.

She stands her ground, as do I.

I reach into my pack and retrieve the tent bag, dump it quickly and pull out one of the tent poles. The elastic band running through it allows the pole to extend to its full length of eight feet with ease. I hold it out in front of me. The hollow aluminum feels flimsy.

"What are you going to do?"

"You need to trust me."

"I do," she says, not budging an inch.

Just as it reaches us, I charge the tent pole into a lamentation blade and shove it into the beast's open, snarling mouth. Its body disperses into dust, which falls at our feet. It's then that I spot Joseph walking from the same direction, his left palm split open, leaving a trail of blood behind him.

I throw the pole down and hold my knife in a backhanded position, waiting to throw a punch that will slice open Joseph's face. After getting twenty-or-so feet from us, he stops when he catches a glimpse of the blade glowing in my hand.

Stepping no further, Joseph holds his bleeding left palm out in our direction and projects a tremendous gust of wind, which causes us both to stumble backward. We stand and he walks forward and does the same.

Off our feet again, I say, "He's injured. We can outrun him and hide. I'll climb a tree to get myself away from the ground so he can't locate me. But we're going to have to drop our bags."

"But all of or our…"

"We have no choice."

I drop my pack to the ground and pull my rifle out of it. I don't bother taking the time to install the suppressor. Stealth is pointless now.

"Shoot him," Rebecca whispers.

"It won't do any good. He's just like the beasts."

With that, we take off uphill, back toward our original camp at the cliff's edge. Both of us slow after about a mile and continue walking briskly. Eventually, the gradient is so steep we practically crawl. Joseph is long out of sight and unable to affect us with his abilities. He's haggardly plodding along, getting acquainted with his own weakness after a brief stint as a living god.

Before long, we're in the area where Ezra died. I approach a gigantic oak tree. Putting my hands against its bark, I instruct it to curve one of its highest and longest branches toward the ground. Rebecca watches, still in disbelief.

"Come, sit next to me," I say.

We each perch on either side of a sturdy branch. Myself on the left with the rifle across my lap and Rebecca to the right. I put my left hand on the branch and ask it to raise itself up again. We're thirty feet off the ground.

"Once he passes by us, we'll head down the mountain. Joseph will sense me, but he's not fast enough."

"Won't he have backup?"

"Maybe, but I can handle them."

"I've never seen so many dead people.

"You can get used to almost anything.

After an hour and a half, Joseph appears, treading slowly, obviously weakened. Not long after getting within a hundred feet of us, he stops. I can tell that he faintly senses me. After fifteen seconds, he continues toward the ridge's peak. Thirty minutes later, I ask the tree to return us to the ground. We step off and it slowly retracts its branch back into its regular position. We hurry down the incline as fast as we can without stumbling.

Before getting more than twenty feet, we see stones stacking themselves into an arched doorway, floating freely in space. When completed, the interior flashes indigo. I see Joseph on the other side. The edge of the cliff is behind him. He attempts to walk through, but the barrier flashes each time he touches it, shorting out like a defective old television having its rabbit ears adjusted. He runs toward it, breaking the barrier and falling to the ground just as the archway crumbles, just missing him. I pull my knife and charge him. Joseph stands, holds out his gory left hand, and pushes me back with a gust of wind that causes the trees around us to sway and crack as hurricanes do back east. On my feet again, I run back toward Rebecca, who is still on the ground from the wind burst. Before she can stand, he blasts us again and we roll across the ground like fleshy tumbleweeds. Small trees fall in our direction, just missing us as we stumble away. Both of us are barely able to stay on our feet. Before long, the edge of the cliff is visible.

"There must be a way down," Rebecca says.

I don't want to tell her the truth. We're both about to die.

As Joseph approaches, I try to pull a sinkhole under his feet, but nothing happens. He pushes us back again with a torrent of wind. He doesn't stop this time. We're on all fours trying to stay in place. Slowly, we begin sliding toward the ridge, no matter how low we crouch.

I pull a wall of granite up out of the ground to protect us. It's eight feet high, and fifteen wide. The wind subsides. Now Joseph will either have to walk through or around, putting me in striking distance. Wind whistles as it meets in eddies behind us. I'm beginning to question if the rock wall will continue standing. Before I can pull up more stone, the wind stops.

"I've come to take you home, Naomi," Joseph's soft,

disembodied voice echoes around our protective barrier.

Rebecca looks at me, confused. She knows me by my forged identity, Hannah Sillman.

I don't respond, not wanting to pinpoint my location.

"I'm walking around to your left. I expect you to behave," he says.

I step back a few feet from my side of the wall and wait for his next play. Lying, of course, Joseph walks directly through the stone. No more than six feet from us. I duck and roll in his direction, just as he raises his brutalized left hand.

The blast of wind pushes Rebecca even closer to the edge, while I avoid the brunt of it. Jumping to my feet, I charge the knife and deftly swing it backhanded, slicing a huge gash on the right side of Joseph's face. I swipe low, attempting to gut him, but miss and inadvertently cut off all four of his left fingers, leaving only a thumb attached to his bisected palm.

He shrieks in pain and crouches over. When I lunge to finish him off, Joseph pulls a pistol out of his waistband, points it at my chest, and pulls the trigger. I look down expecting a gushing bullet wound but instead see a large dart. I pull the projectile out and throw it to the ground.

"I never wanted you dead," he says coyly.

I drop my knife and stumble backward. Joseph pelts us with more wind. I can barely fight against it now. Rebecca is right on the edge of the cliff. I'm no more than five feet in front of her.

"I'm going to fall," she screams.

Joseph directs the next gust right at her. Rebecca disappears over the cliff, screaming. I dive toward the edge, on my chest, with both arms extending over in hopes of being able to miraculously catch her. Instead, I see Rebecca in freefall, accelerating toward the rocks below us. I reach out and open a doorway precisely underneath her. It goes to the one spot I have in my mind, the front door of my family's house in Tysons Corner. Just as Rebecca falls through, I catch a glimpse of our kitchen. I see Christmas lights flickering from within the living room. Then, narcotic-induced darkness begins closing in like a tunnel.

———

For Rebecca, it's as though the world turns ninety degrees. Her momentum is decelerated as she slides across the wooden floor with a loud squeal. Coming to a stop, she looks up to see a red-headed woman.

Both of them peer through the doorway to witness Naomi hanging over the cliff's edge. They make eye contact just before she goes unconscious and the passageway evaporates into a mist of indigo.

27

I can feel the railroad ties underneath my back. I'm at the small slice of ethereal real estate between our worlds. I sit up to find no Frieda, just strange stars above me, bearing no resemblance to the constellations that I'm familiar with. No Big Dipper or Orion. No Moon, either. The stars themselves seem normal, though, mirroring the celestial bodies I'm used to.

I sit up to see eternally straight tracks heading out into infinity both ways. I move off to my left, onto the side of the Woods of Lamentation.

A thought passes through my mind as I stare at its dark tree line. 'Somewhere in there, Vernon squeals in terror, forever.' This puts a smile on my face. Regardless, I am so tired. There's nothing more I can do now. I may not even be alive back in my universe.

I sit and wait for hours. There are rumbles and screams, the song of lamentation. This, though, isn't abnormal in any way. The beasts are in harmony with the woods, always well-fed and locked away from the rest of us. They're no more or less evil than a jellyfish who incidentally bumps into your leg while swimming in the ocean. They just function. The sound I've been waiting for perks up my ears. It's the train, heading up behind me. I tried to will it to come, but this place is stubborn. The locomotive releases a loud, deep horn in three blasts. I begin running beside it. I peer through the windows to see passengers sitting like blank statues of their former selves. No expressions, no emotions. Then I see her, Ezra.

She's being whisked away with the others who have committed suicide. It's not a punishment, but relief from thought. Frieda said, 'Tormented people run toward it.' When the train reaches its destination, they lose their sense of self and become engulfed by joy until that's all there is. No thought, no memory, pure rapture.

'It's not an unpleasant set of circumstances,' I say to myself.

I slow my pace, letting Ezra's car move off into the distance. I wait. Moments later, the freight cars appear. I begin running again. I keep pace with one. I'm able to grasp a handle and lift myself up into the car. Once my legs are over the edge, I feel relief. 'It's over now,' I think.

I roll over onto my back, sit up and push myself against the wall to the right of where I boarded. This places me facing in the direction the train is heading.

I begin settling in, confident in my choice because, despite loving her, I feel as though Tiffany would be better off without me.

It's after this thought that I realize I'm not alone. Pale gray eyes peer from the darkness, directly across from me, against the opposite wall of the train car. They then rise up. I get to my feet too, ready to engage my opponent. The eyes belong to a being taller than myself. As it comes closer, I make out the face of Theta above me.

"Giving up so easily, are we?"

"As if I have a choice. It's the honorable thing to do. I have failed."

"The only failure is to stop moving forward."

"How would you even understand the idea of moving forward, if your knowledge of time isn't linear?"

"I understood the concept. Having experienced it now, I can say it's like staring into a dark tunnel, unsure of what awaits you ahead. And when you peer far enough into the distance, it becomes a void. The existential fear of your species is understandable but unnecessary."

"How can I return to a world where the Apostles have won?"

"They will only succeed if you give up. My experience with Frederick Severe was transformative. Existing in the same plane while confronting you, I could feel the weight of time and the reality of what one-hundred-eighty-one years meant for him. That's when realized what I had done. It was hubris to believe I could circumvent the rules. That's why what comes next is so confounding. While I realize intellectually that I shouldn't repeat the same mistake I did with Frederick, I can't ignore the need to act on emotion again."

With that, Theta grabs both of my shoulders. I struggle against her but make no progress. I'm helpless against her strength. I try to harness my abilities but am unable. With little effort, Theta walks me to the open train door and tosses me out into the night.

My feet hit the ground first, then I roll down a short, grassy embankment, dusted with a light coating of snow. After coming to a stop, I sit up. It looks like the same spot where I arrived. The entire length of the track appears practically identical, making it difficult to tell. During the tumble, my body kicked fine, icy particles of snow into the air. It drifts in front of me, then stops. An outline begins to coalesce. It looks like a person. As its features begin to fill in, it becomes Frieda.

As her form completes, she says, "Dear Naomi, Don't be so quick to throw yourself away."

"I thought it was my choice," I scream, almost on the verge of tears.

When they come, each teardrop that hits the ground creates a faint sizzle as the snow sublimates into indigo vapor rising up into diminutive mushroom clouds.

"And that's what they want, to drain you. They're planning on keeping you alive, slowly leaching blood from your veins. Even if you had finished your train voyage, they're prepared to put your dead body on life support so your blood can keep flowing. If they couldn't, there's still at least another four quarts they could drain from your corpse. A drop of your blood is worth the entire volume of Claude's. It's enough to last their cult centuries. Then there's the conundrum over what happens upon your physical death. Will the light retreat back into the Earth, or can it be captured? We simply do not know. So no, it's not your choice anymore. You're playing with the lives of everyone, both on your plane and mine."

"Why was I chosen for this!?"

"You choose yourself the night you refused to die, even though you were supposed to. Instead, you defied your mortality's time limit. When you fought back, it diminished Vernon Proffitt, both to his followers and himself. He loved having his name on the lips of others, but Vernon wasn't a true believer. He knew himself to be a fraud. Joseph, on the other hand, believes. He never actually knew Vernon. Instead, Vernon is equal parts deity and legend in his eyes. Joseph has repackaged his memory as such. The Apostles have been fooled by his arrogance. A lot of people respond positively to this kind of trait in a leader. They want nothing more than to be 'right', damn the cost. Perfected by death, Vernon's legacy is a greater risk than the man himself."

"Am I even alive?"

"You are, but you are not well. Look for yourself," Frieda says before waving her left hand, transforming the space around us.

We're floating unnoticed, high above a hospital bed. But it's not in a hospital. No, it's resting on a smooth, wet, rocky surface. There's an unnatural blue light spectrum creating a stark image of the patient's face. It's me. My cheeks look sunken. I've obviously lost weight. I can't tell any more about my physical body through the loose hospital gown. Then I notice a ring of people kneeling around the bed. There are at least twenty. All speak independent flows of nonsensical words, supposedly from an unknowable language only spoken by God himself. It's a cacophony of lunacy. Both my hands appear to be cuffed to the bed on either side. They're not police-issue restraints. They appear to be rudimentarily fashioned irons. Each has a rusty patina that glimmers with specs of indigo. There's a feeding tube in my left nostril, and a bag of saline running into my right arm.

"It's been a month since you were captured. The Apostles have drained two quarts of blood from you since that time. They're praying for the light to leave you so the prophecy can be completed. Joseph believes the shackles and chains smelted with indigo will restrain your abilities. Just in case, they keep you sedated with ketamine. What they haven't taken into account is that they have to keep upping the dose gradually to counter your body's growing tolerance to the drug. Today, you wake up.

28

I expected the return to my body to be a sudden jolt, but it's akin to waking from a summer afternoon nap. I'm warm and placid under heavy blankets. My consciousness, while on the railroad tracks, wasn't affected by the ketamine, but here my brain is sloshing about in a chemical stew of dissociates.

I drink alcohol, but otherwise I've never done any other substances for recreation, not even Zeke's cannabis, so I'm having difficulty with this unusual sensation. I wouldn't describe myself as awake. Rather, I'm aware of the blur in my fore-vision that will morph into physical reality. It's far away, and I'm immobilized and sunken into a soft, deep hole lined with a singular hospital mattress, stretched beyond reason. As my body comes back online, I notice that I'm very hungry. When my tactile senses awaken, I feel that my arms and legs are smaller and weaker. Even so, because I had become so fit by training with Herschel, I'm not completely without muscle tone. But the anemia from losing too much blood makes me feel shaky. My hands and feet feel absurdly large.

Looking up, I see the ceiling of the cave shows damage where the stalactites have been smashed in the pursuit of rocks behind them. They've been ground into dust to create the indigo fueling

Joseph's growing empire. In their place are a series of fluorescent bulbs lighting the entire cavern.

The self-serving, blathering encircling me continues as it did in Frieda's vision.

My first conscious thought is, 'Goddamn, they're annoying'. They go on a while longer and eventually file out one after another. In their absence, I hear water dripping from the ceiling. Each drop point is a former stalactite that has already begun to rebuild. A while later, I begin to feel the presence of a large man walking toward me. He sits in a chair to my right.

I recognize his gruff voice as it splits the air. Amos Pace, my father. The last time I saw him was thirteen years ago. That ended with his fist hitting my face, knocking me unconscious, all because he found out about me and Tiffany. And well, that I broke her sister's arm in Tiff's defense. But Lesley had had it coming for a long time before then. Amos has believed me dead since I went missing from this same cave, eleven-and-a-half years ago.

He begins speaking to my still body, "Your mother wouldn't come. I don't blame her none. Everyone knowing we had a queer for a daughter hasn't been easy. Why you got it in your head to care so much about that stupid little redheaded cunt, I'll never understand. But at least something good will come of it. Your body can be used to serve Joseph and the fulfillment of Abraham's prophecy. After I ascend to heaven, I'll have forgotten you ever existed. Then I'll be free, and I can be happy again."

I'm long past the point in my life where I care what Amos thinks. The vile opinions of a man who would beat and abandon his own child mean nothing. But my seething rage over his words boils over in memories of abuse at his hands. He is a very violent, angry man. But that's not why he's shunned in their community.

Acrimony and assault may as well be a sacrament in their religion. It's because he sired a lesbian apostate. But to me, his insults about Tiffany are fighting words.

They cause my eyes to pop open. Amos immediately takes note of it.

"Awake, are we? Don't get no ideas. Them shackles won't let you extend those abilities beyond your own body. Goddamn girl, you look furious. It's the lines on your forehead that tell me. Figured I'd be disgusted at the sight of your face. But to see you helpless, there, being punished for all the crimes you done, makes me feel a little better about it."

As he's saying this, I reach out, but can't connect to the Earth to affect anything around me. My arms and legs tingle with electricity, as though the circulation has been cut off for some time. I physically struggle against the handcuffs, but it's of no use. Even if I weren't gaunt from starvation, my physical strength would be no match for the thick irons.

My father, Amos, stands above me now.

"You ruined our lives," he screams, slapping me across the face with his right hand.

I barely feel it through the narcotic haze. But what I do feel is fury over the indignity of it all. I pull my consciousness away from Amos's tantrum and abuse, letting it fade into the background as I focus on the light inside me. I feel it, but it's been disconnected from the environment. I can sense nothing, nor speak to the sentient lifeforms lurking on the peripheries of existence. Hidden behind the chaotic blur, the solution presents itself. The feeling of returning to my arms has left me with a singular realization, I'm still wearing a wedding band on my left ring finger.

I ignite the small circle of gold into a lamentation blade. Slyly, I ease it toward the chain attached to my shackles. It sounds like an acetylene torch cutting through iron, a sizzle followed by tiny metal shards shooting away from the reaction. I push myself up onto my right side. Facing Amos, I deliver a solid blow to his throat with a closed fist. It takes me immediately back to Biology 101. 'Hyoid,' I recite involuntarily to myself, as though the flashcard I made for it twelve years ago was in front of me again. There's a wet, dull thud, followed by gurgling and wheezing. Amos doubles over in pain, trying to breathe. He then falls to his knees and crumples over. His respiration imitates the sound of a very deep whistle played in spurts. There's not enough oxygen getting to his brain for him to remain conscious.

I take the opportunity to slice through the shackle on my right wrist with my wedding band. After, I remove a piece of the broken shackle. I charge it into a lamentation blade and cut through an identical shackle still around my left wrist. Free, I begin pulling the feeding tube out of my left nostril. I wince and cough as the bizarre plastic worm shimmies up my innards, through my throat, and out my nose. Finally, I pull the ketamine drip out of my right arm.

Slinging my legs over the left side at the foot of the bed, I brace to support my own weight. It feels like there are sharp pieces of glass embedded in my shin bones. Every vertebra in my back cracks as I unfurl into a standing position. My body moves with pops and clicks. The tendons feel like they're overtightened guitar strings. The racket my neck makes when I shift it from side to side is so loud that my ears ring.

I lift my light blue hospital gown to have a look at my stomach. I have no fat reserves left. I'm so thin that I can see my hipbones sticking out. My attention turns to the diaper underneath them. I check to find that I was lucky enough to have been recently changed.

Looking up, I see the metal door Charles and I escaped through back in nineteen-ninety-five. Behind it lays a room stocked with weapons of war, food, and supplies. They've had me laid up in a bed perched directly over the spot where he died.

'Fucking bastards,' I think.

Amos is still alive. His breathing seems to be raspy, but less constrained. Fully mobile now, I place my left hand under the mattress, and onto the circular tube making up the outside frame of the hospital bed. I heat it, causing the springs attached to it to pop off, making high-pitched pings. Red hot now, I break off a piece two-and-a-half feet in length. I transfer it to my right hand. I use my white-hot glowing left hand to shave off one end at an acute angle. This leaves me with something resembling a large hypodermic needle. I let it cool. The hot orange glow it casts across my face begins to dim as it solidifies into its new shape.

"What happened," I hear my father say in a gravelly voice as he lifts himself clumsily from his stomach into a seated position. Amos gets no further than laying on his right side before seeing me walk around the end of the bed, then toward him. I stop three feet from his head.

I kneel down, and look him in the eyes, saying, "You're supposed to keep the wolves from the front door, not invite her in."

I stand back up and place my left hand against the wall. I work my mind into the granite and begin to slowly fracture it until the cave wall, fifty feet away from us, begins crumbling. It starts slowly and quickly accelerates, setting off a chain reaction that collapses the tunnel all the way to the entrance where they drove the dump truck through. Dust billows out, thinning by the time it reaches us. We're now trapped in a small pocket of the cavern. The only way out is through the Apostle's weapons cache, up the same ladder Charles and I escaped down thirteen years ago, and out of a manhole in the large safe located inside Vernon Proffit's old house.

I look at my father and say, "How does it feel to be the weak one now?"

29

"What are you going to do with that," Amos shouts, referring to the sharpened metal rod in my hand.

"I'm going to stab Joseph through his goddamn heart!"

"He's a prophet sent to lead us after Vernon's passing. You can't kill him."

"You don't believe that. I think you're genuinely nervous that Joseph isn't holy. You're afraid that if I'm able to kill him, you'll have to deal with the conflict it will cause within yourself. You know the things I've done. Perhaps, unwittingly, your belief in me is stronger than your belief in him?"

"I believe you are a witch and a degenerate homosexual. You corrupted the divine prophecy with your wicked incantations."

"Corrupted what, y'all's sick lust for death? You only want Armageddon so the people the Bible told you were okay to hate will suffer for not thinking exactly like yourself. That's why it was so easy for you to throw me away and gift me to a child molester. I deserved it, right?"

"Vernon was doing you a favor. It's too bad receiving the communion from the body of a godly man didn't make you straight."

"I believe you mean rape, Amos," I reply with disdain.

Redirection the conversation, I say, "What exactly did you think I'd be doing at this age?"

"I figured, eventually you and that girl would drift apart. Then you'd get married to a godly man and be subservient to him, as the good book intended. You'd have his children and keep a home. Your mother and I would retire and spend our remaining years bouncing grandchildren off our knees."

"You got part of what you wanted. I did get married. But, it was to 'that girl', Tiffany," I say, holding my left hand up to display my wedding band charged as a glowing indigo lamentation blade.

"It's not a real marriage."

"Do you mean like the one you have with my mother, whom you beat? The same marriage that produced a child to whom you did the same? How exactly is hitting and choking little girls godly?"

"Children need guidance, some require harsher techniques. Pastor Howell approved it."

With that, I charge the sharpened rod in my hand with static electricity and discharge it directly into my father's left thigh with a large pop. followed by a waning crackle. He screams in anguish.

After catching his breath, Amos says, "Men will be here at any moment."

"They already are. I can sense their vibration through the granite. They feel clumsy, like a disjointed gaggle of unprepared boys, trouncing on a roof. They haven't come down the ladder because they're afraid.

"Joseph ain't afraid of you!"

"I can't say, but I know you are. Now, where are my clothes," I say, pointing the tip of the sharpened rod, sparking with arcs of electricity, in Amos's face as he stares up at me from the wet cave floor.

"In the weapons room," he says, pointing over his shoulder

with his right hand. "They dumped all your stuff in the corner, farthest from the ladder. It'll be on your left when you go through the door."

With the rod still in his face, I say, "If you do anything but lie right there, I will turn you into dust."

He nods his head to indicate that what I said was understood.

Cautiously, I approach the door, as I do when I relive my last minutes with Charles in my nightmares. But this is no dream. There is depth and temperature to this reality. It even exudes the smell of wet rock that I recall.

It's not like the inconsistent, thin farce of my ever-shifting, subconscious terrors, with interweaving plot schemas that shouldn't be present.

The light inside me becomes heavy in my chest. I feel its glow become stronger, as though someone has turned up the amperage.

'It likes being,' I think to myself.

The warm glow spreads until it feels as though lumens will stream out of my every pore. It's not painful. It's joy, almost as though the light is singing a song with one harmonizing tone that resonates within the very ground beneath us. This is why Joseph is so strong. This place was meant for the one gifted the light to return and study its nature. This is a holy place, just as Theta said. That's why they placed my hospital bed over it, to increase the potency of my blood.

I approach the thick metal door. On the other side is the weapons room. From there, I can escape up the ladder into Vernon's old house, where he kept me captive for a year and a half. There is a huge safe over the manhole leading through the floor, but I don't think it'll pose much of an obstacle. With my left hand on the thick metal door to the weapons room, I analyze the situation more closely using the vibration emanating from the men above. Then I feel and hear a large thud followed by the recognizable rhythm of one of Joseph's beasts. It's followed by two more identical crashes and subsequent skittering, then comes the beasts' high-pitched calls, imitating a toddler screeching in terror. The unnaturalness of their cry is unsettling because of the mismatch in stimuli. Your ears tell you to run toward a child that needs protection, while your eyes inform you of the terrible truth that you're being hunted.

Before they can reach the door, I place my hand upon it and charge the metal into what I think of as a lamentation shield. While I can't use it to kill them, this makes the passage impenetrable. But this traps me. If I take my hand off, they will inevitably get through.

I think back to my escape. I try to picture the room on the other side. I know there is a large four-by-four across the door, held in place by heavy iron braces attached to an equally robust metal frame. If I were to let the door open, it would create a small enclosed triangle between the open door and the granite wall. I hid there right after Charles died. Perhaps I can again?

I look back at my father and discharge the lamentation shield. There's a violent crash into the door. In under half a minute, they snap the piece of four-by-four bracing the door on their side. Seconds before it swings open wildly, I step into the crevice closest to the hinges and stand like a flag pole. When it flies open, the corner of the door smacks the rock wall so hard it breaks off small shards of granite. Falling bits of it sound like rice being spilled across a tiled kitchen floor. I'm now pinned right where I wanted, hidden behind the door with the rock wall to my back. Through a small crack, I watch my father's reaction to what I just did. He's still sitting on the floor, then I see terror flash across his gaze. He's gruff and strong but he screams like a child when he sees them.

They never stopped moving in his direction after the three of them burst through. He stands to run toward the already collapsed passage, his lizard brain's vestigial attempt to save himself, if only for a few seconds more. In less than five steps, they're on him. Wet sounds of flesh tearing and bones fracturing between ragged teeth echo. I hear my father's last vocalizations. The squeals sound like that of a swine. By the time my mind processes it, his vocal cords have already been consumed. I don't feel sad about it at all. I don't really feel anything at the moment, even fear.

The beasts begin sniffing the ground, much like dogs. The three head down toward the collapsed tunnel, likely because they can smell the blood of the men who were crushed by the ceiling I collapsed on them earlier. But soon the trio turns back, unfulfilled. Just as they come into view of the small crevice between the door and rock wall, the one in front begins smelling the ground where I had recently been. He looks up and locks his sight on me. It let out a scream that perks up the other two. They approach slowly, unsure of what to do about the door. I charge it into a lamentation shield. Still inspecting it, they appear troubled. Something about it must signal danger to them. The granite behind me is another thing. They burrow at the edges, using their claws to chip away the rock closest to the door. As they make headway, I pull the handle, closing the gap. But the space for my body has become smaller. If I don't do something, I will be crushed to death.

30

I feel calm about my impending death. All I have left to do is emancipate myself from the burden of life and drift away. Lost in that feeling, I realize it's not enlightenment but selfishness. Another emotion begins to come into focus through all the background noise: fury. Fury that the Apostles have beaten me, and fury at what they'll do to the helpless once I'm gone. With two quarts of my blood, they will be able to manufacture generations' worth of indigo. Then it hits me. They expected me to show up at some point. I fell into their trap. The men I killed were nothing more than live bait on a barbed hook.

I think to make a doorway behind me, taking me back home, just like Rebecca, but it doesn't come.

A voice enters my mind, it's Frieda.

"Naomi, by now you must know why you can't make a doorway for yourself?"

"Can't you see I'm busy dying," I scream aloud at an invisible Frieda?

"It's because your abilities are based on emotion. Your anger opened the doorway you kicked the marine through. With Rebecca, you were able to open one to your home. I believe when you love someone, that you're able to create a doorway to them, but you can't pass through because you hate yourself. There is no escaping this. You must fight."

I consider collapsing the floor beneath them, but I don't want to damage the chamber further, possibly leading to a total cave-in, killing me and leaving nothing of a site the Ceraphirian deem to be a holy place. I contemplate what Frieda said about our encounter with the five marines in the alley. I reach deep into myself and retrieve the engulfing anger I felt when I saw the largest of them attempt to assault Nate for the crime of being himself. I hear ringing in my ears and feel the sensation of cold liquid being poured across my synapses. With my left hand remaining on the metal door to keep it charged as a lamentation shield, I place my right on the rock wall behind me. Since I cannot see beyond the door, I send my consciousness into the granite until I reach the opposing wall. There, I create an arched doorway, revealing the night sky over the Woods of Lamentation. I hear a familiar scream echoing through. It's Svangi.

His four sharp, spear-like appendages click loudly, in a full gallop. Even through the thick metal door, Svangi's scream is painfully loud. The Apostles' beasts suddenly stop clawing at the wall. I realize what just happened. Svangi stabbed the two closest to me through their backs in one motion as he crashed down on each with one of his front two legs. I sense the third turn and run toward the caved-in section of the cavern. I push the door open gently, creating a larger and larger gap between it and the wall. Stepping out, I see two large piles of dust. They're remnants of the false beasts of lamentation. Svangi has the last of the Apostles' beasts cornered. It's inexorably outmatched.

The Apostles' beast lunges toward Svangi. Quickly lifting himself onto his two rear legs, Svangi is able to dodge. He smashes down his sharp legs on either side of the other beast. Svangi clutches him with long black claws extending from his hand-like, front appendages. Helpless, the creature is lifted into the air. Svangi tilts his head back and feeds it head-first into his gurgling, open maw.

Like all beasts of lamentation, Svangi's primary driver is to eat. After finishing, he walks back toward me. He kneels down and begins to suck up the dusty remains of the first two beasts he killed. I stand watching in awe of this thing whose purpose is to torture and consume the wicked act like a pet, eating peacefully by my side. Svangi's prominent veins begin glowing with an even brighter indigo color. I scratch his oblong, gray head, then make my way to the weapons room while he finishes.

Despite the frigid outside temperature, it's somewhere in the mid-fifties inside the cavern, likely much warmer than outside. The atmosphere this deep into the earth tends to be constant throughout the year. That's good for me because I'm still wearing a nightgown with an adult diaper for underwear.

I hear Svangi continue to feed in the background. It sounds a bit like a vacuum sucking sand out of a shag carpet, only deeper. I turn to my left to see that the last thing my father said to me wasn't a lie. My pack, clothes, and rifle are butted up in the corner furthest from the ladder in the Apostles' weapons room.

They were so damn certain that their drugs and bindings would hold that they foolishly left a room full of guns mere feet from my bed. They never even considered my ring to be a means to break the shackles because they only think in concrete terms. To them, a lamentation blade could only be a blade, nothing more. Their sloppiness gives me hope. Despite that, it stings me with embarrassment that they got the better of me. But I did save

Rebecca, kill a fuck-load of the Apostles' militia, and four of their beasts. Now they're terrified. I no longer sense them directly above me. There are dozens of them encircling Vernon's house, each at a distance of at least one hundred feet, which is out of my striking range. Every one of them will be armed, likely with rifles or shotguns since I'm down here with all their military-grade hardware.

I drop my hospital gown to the floor and begin getting dressed. I don't rush. Miffed as to what to do, they're waiting on my next move.

Once I'm tucked away in my coveralls, I begin stuffing their MREs into my pack. I leave what remains of my tent. I'm certain the earth will not mind creating shelter for me in my time of need. I do, however, pack my sleeping bag, despite my ability to harness heat from the earth. I'd rather rest with something between me and the ground, even if it's minimal insulation from Joseph's prying senses.

Next, I inspect my thirty-aught-six. I pull the bolt out slowly. Inside, there are four rounds stowed within the internal magazine. The suppressor is even lying on the ground beside it. I install it, then rack a round into the chamber. An unsuppressed blast from this monstrous rifle would be deafening inside a cave.

There are new items down here. There are now about fifty Glock nineteen pistols. Each shoots nine-millimeter rounds and holds fifteen in a magazine. I put a full magazine in one and rack the slide. It goes into my left pocket. In my right, I stow four more loaded magazines.

Something else catches my eye. Slews of OD green body armor vests. I don one. It has a black velcro patch across the front with the letters 'ACH' stitched in bright white. I rip the patch off and toss it to the floor.

There's a small shelf of random items: watches, jewelry, pocket knives, and other personal belongings. I realize what they are.

They're leftovers from the Apostles' rape and murder victims, likely young runaways they've kidnaped. These are the people whose cries were reaching out to me in my dreams. Something catches my eye. It's a tarnished pair of brass knuckles. I inspect them. Engraved inside the middle finger holes of each is the name, 'Vincent.' I slide one into each of my side pockets.

They're trying to emulate Vernon's behavior. These children and young adults are sacraments to them. Vincent and the others are likely already buried facedown in Hickory Hill cemetery. Charles's remains are still there. I haven't come up with a feasible solution to retrieve his body so that he can be interred with the respect he deserves.

I assumed that after Vernon was gone, the church would crumble and I'd be able to fetch Charles's body, but I was wrong. Instead, they dug their heels in harder and constructed a new lens to view their disproven prophecy through. In it, they're always virtuous and persecuted, which means that no matter what they do, it's justified.

Before I leave, there is the matter of Svangi. I don't have the energy to open a door home to the Woods of Lamentation. But maybe I don't need him to go. What I've done to the cave will certainly slow, the Apostles, but not halt them. However, they cannot defeat Svangi. Anything that comes down the manhole will be deftly consumed.

No matter how much indigo Joseph has stuffed into his cloak, Svangi won't care. That's because he's animated by a small portion of my light that I have transferred into him, instead of raw instinct. Since part of me exists on all three planes, it seems just that I task a Beast of Lamentation with protecting a Ceraphirian holy site. I walk back out into the cavern where Svangi is sucking up the remainder of his dry, powdery snack. Finishing, he kneels at my feet.

I stroke this horrifying monster's head and say, "Svangi, I need you to stay here and protect what is sacred."

He nods while letting out a long, deep sigh. Svangi doesn't have to eat to stay alive, but his instinct is to do so. In the Woods of Lamentation, meals come continuously. Here, his stomach will ache the entire time. Regardless, he must obey. As I walk away, I feel a small phantom pain in my left hand. It's like a sharp pinprick. I realize that the light I put into Svangi is signaling the beginnings of his physical distress to me. So long as he is locked away in this undeserved prison I have made for him, I'll have a continuous reminder of his suffering. The equation has to balance somehow.

31

Looking at the ladder ascending to the manhole-opening inside the safe feels suffocating. At the base of these rungs, in nineteen-ninety-five, I wanted nothing more than to flee. Now, I'm purposefully returning to a place of nightmares. I was on the property when I captured Vernon Proffit two years ago, but that took place outside. I haven't been inside this house since I was a frightened child.

I lay my pack on the floor and the rifle against the wall. I'll come back for them. Right now, I have a safe to deal with. Before ascending, I place my left hand against the wall. The men encircling me have moved even further out. I can barely feel them now.

They know I'm coming. What if it's a trap? Would they even have enough time to assemble one?

With the path clear, I climb. When I reach the top, I place my hand against the rock wall once more. I feel through my surroundings carefully. I sense an object affixed to the safe, just outside the door, about the size of an apple, but made of metal.

I know this shape. It's a fucking grenade.

Once the door opens far enough, the string attached to the loosened pin will pull it out of place, setting off an explosion.

The blast they've planned is intended to send shrapnel into the safe's opening and kill me.

I descend the ladder back to the floor of the underground weapon's room. I consider forcing heat up the wall and through the safe with enough intensity to ignite the grenade. But if I did that, the searing temperatures would start a structure fire in the path of my only escape route. The grenade blast itself would be less likely to create a blaze because the energy released occurs at a high velocity, insulated by a metal casing. It'll fuck the room up, but holes in drywall won't stop me. Also, if the house burns down, I forfeit cover.

I give thought to the collapsed portion of the cavern. Even with my abilities, it would be impossible to create a tunnel without the means to haul away rocks. I could create a void and steer the boulders around my body, but it would take so long, I'd likely starve to death before finishing. Even then, there would be guns pointing at me when I reached the former cavern opening. I'd be in the same spot as I would burning the damn house to the ground.

I begin thinking about how they would have attached the grenade and subsequent string and realize that it's unlikely they were able to do it well with what little time they had. It was probably achieved with the cure-all of repair, duct tape. If I heat the metal just enough around the grenade, I can melt the adhesive, causing it to fall, pulling out the pin, and igniting it outside the closed safe. The door is so thick that when Charles and I were children, it took both of us to move it. The robust metal should protect me from the blast.

I crawl up the ladder again. At the top, I push open the manhole. Even in my weakened state, I'm able to push it aside with relative ease. I think back to how heavy it was when I was young. If only all burdens of youth could be so easily lifted. With the large circular disc of old iron pushed into the back corner, I place my left hand against the interior of the safe, opposite the grenade. I begin pulling heat from the Earth and direct it through the metal, gradually warming it up, making it no hotter than a radiator. Within two minutes, I hear a fast, concussive thud come from outside. It rattles the safe so much that it feels like my head is inside a ringing bell. Before making my next move, I wait a few minutes just in case there's a subsequent blast. There isn't.

I push myself up, through the manhole, and into the safe. Placing my left hand on the spot where the bolt holding it closed is located, I heat it red hot, but not molten. I make sure to localize to a small area, so as to not start a fire. Taking my hand away, I give the door a swift kick. It budges a little, so I give it two more blows before I hear the sound of a large piece of metal groaning, then breaking. It's higher-pitched than you might imagine. The door budges an eighth of an inch. I pick up the metal tool used to open the manhole cover from the outside. It's a galvanized iron rod, two feet in length. The triangular handle has been formed into one end. The other end of the rod is bent at a right angle. The bit after the bend is three inches in length. I use it to push open the safe door six inches, still wary of another booby trap. With that done, I retreat back down the ladder and wait. Grabbing my gear, I run back to the cavern.

Svangi has already begun to prowl. He's about halfway between the door and the caved-in portion. We're linked together by the speck of light I placed in him. Because of this, he instinctively acts on my intention. Svangi gallops ahead, beating me to the rubble at the end furthest from the weapons room, a bit more than forty feet. In front of it are boulders that have rolled off the main pile. One is especially large, twelve feet long and six high. Svangi joins me behind it, squatting to stay out of sight. I feel men drawing in from all directions. After fifteen minutes, they find the courage to send someone down. But why not dispatch another beast? Did they only have three left? It seems Joseph hasn't allowed his malignant narcissism to get in the way of good sense. He knows the Apostles don't have enough resources to keep more than a few at a time. He's likely the only one allowed to have them. They're not easily handled and require constant monitoring and fail-safes.

With no more creatures, they shift to the old playbook, which involves sending the least senior but most fanatical down first. It's two young men. They move slowly and timidly. Each is armed with a hunting rifle, too inexperienced to even bother trying to operate the M-16s.

After they make it three-quarters of the way to our position, I can hear their conversation. One has the squeaky voice of a late-blooming young man, and the other is quite nasally.

The nasally one says, "Do you think she'd been killed?"

"I reckon, wherin' else would they be?"

"There weren't no blood in the safe."

"Prophet Joseph said she might been dissolved."

And with that, these titans of military strategy decided to give themselves marching orders back to the exit to let the others know it was 'all clear'. This leads to an influx of men filing down the ladder. They gear up in the weapons room, stupidly never questioning their youthful comrades. From what I can sense, there are between forty and fifty men piled up in that room now, covered in Kevlar, and carrying automatic rifles.

The door opens and they rush in. Once they're all inside the cavern, I place my left hand against the ground and begin working my way through the granite. At times, my consciousness passes directly under their feet. As I do this, Svangi reveals himself, crawling directly over the large boulder, towering above all the men who are now unleashing an untold number of rounds into him. Each hit emits a puff of dust but does no damage. After most of the men have exhausted their first magazines, a chorus of screams, mixed with the sounds of flesh tearing, creates a symphony of death. He's eating them. Many go down alive, headfirst.

With my mind, finally, at the door, I cause a sheet of granite, three feet thick, to rise up from the floor, making the exit back into the weapons room impassable. Realizing they're trapped, the men spend the remainder of the ammunition pointlessly.

Once all the rifles are empty, they bang against the sturdy blockade of rock, crying for help. No one answers.

Task completed, I release my consciousness from its travels through the cave floor and stand on my tip-toes to have a peek over the rock. It's absolute carnage. There are men, half-eaten, crawling across the floor, bowels dragging in their wake. Others frantically attempt to tie makeshift tourniquets around the nubs left over after their own limbs had been severed. I watch two expire while doing so. There are so many that Svangi hasn't caught them all yet. They run in circular and figure-eight patterns between the cave walls. Many of them begin to sob like little boys. One lies down against the wall, folds himself into a fetal position, and rocks while he squeals, 'mama mama mama' repeatedly. Svangi decapitates him just as he is saying 'ma-' for a fourth time. Then comes the dry sucking sound of Svangi inhaling the head. When it passes into his throat, it makes a large popping noise.

Svangi runs toward the sealed-off weapons room and pins several men against the wall. One gets loose and makes a bee-line in my direction. I see him glance up and look me directly in the eye as I peek over the boulder's top.

"Fuck," I say. I switch the safety off of my rifle and prepare to fire. He's six feet away as he comes around the corner to my left. He no longer has a rifle with which to shoot me. After exhausting the rounds, it was nothing more than a worthless trinket to be thrown to the ground. I shoulder my thirty-aught-six, aim it at his neck and pull the trigger. The vest doesn't take the impact; rather, an indigo field appears around him as the bullet strikes, emitting sparks on impact. The field bends but doesn't break. The force pushes him off balance momentarily, but he doesn't fall. The Kevlar vests have indigo sewn into them. There's not enough to allow the Apostle's soldiers to possess the abilities of Joseph, but it protects them in the same manner. Svangi can break through it because he operates on the physics of the Woods of Lamentation. I can't harm the men without a lamentation blade. I won't risk the damage to my rifle's barrel by charging it, then swinging it at him. It would be cumbersome and put me at a disadvantage. Keeping my eyes on him, I prop the rifle against the large boulder to my right. I feel for the metal rod I sheered off the hospital bed, only to realize I must have dropped it during my sprint.

'Vincent', I think, sticking both my hands into the pockets of my coveralls. I find what I'm looking for, a set of brass knuckles.

32

The man is gargantuan, easily six-foot-five and two-hundred-seventy-five pounds. Starved for a month, I'm likely clocking in at a mere one-hundred-sixty pounds. Looking at his face, I can see that he believes that I am outmatched. This is his weakness. The brass knuckles exit my pockets simultaneously, both glowing with the indigo spark of a lamentation blade. He doesn't seem to take notice.

The brutish man seethes with anger underpinned by existential terror. Before inevitably being gorged on by Svangi, he wants to dispatch the enemy. Does he believe doing so will buy him God's favor, or does he just want to murder?

That becomes irrelevant when he throws a right hook. Still reeling from the effects of ketamine, I'm not fast enough to dodge it. He connects with my left temple, stunning me. I stagger but don't fall. For some reason the indigo-laced body armor I'm wearing doesn't provide me the same protection it does normal people. My light cancels the effects out. The man rushes in my direction and pushes me backward. I sail through the air, landing on my back. The momentum causes me to flip over onto my stomach before coming to a stop. I push myself onto my knees as he approaches. The man swings the tip of his right boot from the side, in the direction of my head. Just before it makes contact, I recharge Vincent's brass knuckles into lamentation blades and throw a hard right. It impacts the man's shin, eliciting a sickening, moist crack. He shrieks, grabbing his leg with both hands. He takes a long drop to the hard cave floor, landing on his back, and knocking the breath out of him. The oafish boor takes a gasping, lungful of air right before I'm on top of him.

He holds his hands up to block my left roundhouse punch, but it's too late. The brass knuckle fractures his left orbital socket, leaving it caved in. His eye bulges out, no longer fitting in its rightful home. The man's screams are cut short by a right hook to the jaw, shattering it. I rear my right fist back again and land a direct blow to his temple, rendering him unconscious. But I don't stop. I alternate, left to right, repeatedly, to a discordant melody of squishy thuds and crisp pops. Hot, warm blood is sprayed and aerosolized across my chest and face. I continue until Svangi rounds the corner. We lock onto each other's bloody faces. I step away from the mess I've made so that Svangi can eat. The joy of his company is that he doesn't judge me for my vile savagery.

Svangi continues back around the corner to finish off the stray body parts. I follow. He pauses briefly and shakes like a wet dog, sending the Apostle's spent rounds into the air like water droplets. They clatter across the ground. As he eats, I pick up my pack and rifle. I eject the spent casing slowly and stow it away in my pocket.

I walk back down the cavern, picking up my steel rod along the way. I come to a stop at the granite wall I had the Earth create to barricade the weapons room. I place my hand on the ground directly in front of it. There is no discernible movement in the room, so I command the sheath of rock to slide back into place, underground. I use my mind to call Svangi over to me. Upon reaching me, he kneels at my feet.

"I'm sorry, boy. I'll be back for you someday," I say petting his blood-slathered head.

I turn around and climb up the ladder leading into the safe inside Vernon's old house. With each rung up the old metal ladder, I feel more and more as though I'm going to suffocate. I didn't experience this before. As I reach the top, just below the open manhole, I realize why. It's the smell creeping down the now-open safe door. It's not a bad smell, just stale with a background hint of lemon-scented cleaner. The memory isn't of a specific moment. Instead, it's an emotion, as though the feeling of powerlessness is wafting on the breeze.

At the top, I pause momentarily and place my left hand against the cave wall directly underneath the manhole cover. I can't detect anyone. Three of Joesph's beasts and more than forty of his militiamen died and were eaten by Svangi in the cavern. Combined with the men and beast killed before I was captured, this constitutes an unprecedented blow to the Apostles' operation. It will be hours before more men arrive from other keeps. And probably at least a day for them to come in large numbers.

For now, Joseph has only a skeleton crew of dimwits. Anyone worth a damn, he already threw at me in desperation. He's scared now, and likely still healing from the gaping wound and amputated fingers that I dealt him.

I push my pack through the manhole first, then my rifle, and finally myself. The carpet is different. It's no longer the shitty Berber. The material is softer in texture, and a dark blue. Brent and Charles bled all over everything the day we escaped. There was no choice; it had to be replaced. Other than that, the bedroom looks exactly the same. The armoire around the safe, hiding it from plain sight, is in splinters. Many of those splinters are embedded in the bedroom walls. It appears as though Vernon and Patty still live here. It's been two years since I killed them. I figured someone might have moved in, possibly another pastor.

After exiting their door, there are two bedrooms on my right. The first one was Charles's, the second mine. To my left is the bathroom where Patty tried to drown me. I walk in and turn on the light. The blood that paints my bruised and swollen face has begun to coagulate. I wash off as much as I can in the sink using a bar of soap from the shower. I try not to think about my history in this room while I complete the task. I'd rather not take too long. Joseph is still out there, weighing his options.

The small twinge returns to my left hand. Svangi. Goddamn, I feel bad about that. But I can't have them getting back into the cave. Now that I'm on the surface, I feel as though the chamber itself wants me to return. Serendipitously, to the nascent consciousness of this place, my promise to Svangi assures that I will. I think the chamber's desire is for me to stay and learn. That's why I feel a pull in my chest sometimes. It's a silent call home.

After washing up, I go across the hall and peer into Charles's old room. It's exactly the same. I picture him lying there, eternally a teenager. 'If only I had gotten him out' is a thought that runs through my mind regularly. I know that Charles is at peace, but I can't help but run through scenarios where he could have survived. I keep them in a secret box hidden away in the messy storage closet of my mind's childhood. I don't even share its contents with Tiffany. She sees me staring off. When Tiff asks what I'm thinking, I usually tell her 'nothing'. She knows that's bullshit but never pressures me.

I approach my old bedroom door with trepidation. It has not

changed. Both bedrooms were designed to be austere as a means to strip away the resident's individuality.

The living room and kitchen look the same. The stove's clock says it's nine in the morning. I don't know what date, but I assume it's the end of January, two-thousand-seven. What's puzzling me is that it's completely dark outside. Is the clock wrong? I go to the front window and take a peek through the blinds. It's utterly dark, with no moon or stars. The stove clock could be wrong, but I've never seen this kind of darkness outside, and I've spent many nights offshore, far from humanity's artificial lights. No, something is wrong here.

I go to the garage door. Perhaps there's a car stowed away I can escape in? I crack it open. Through the glass of the storm door, I see nothing. Nervously, I flip the switch to the garage lights. It's empty, nothing but a smooth concrete floor. Cautiously, I make my way to the garage entrance. Digging around in my pack, I pull out my three D-cell Maglite, which puts off a substantial beam. I open the outside door and unlock the exterior, glass storm door. I push it open a few inches, and switch on the flashlight.

I'm inside the megachurch I saw Joseph transport himself to after Claude died.

33

My instinct is to go on the offensive, but as I sober up, I realize the inevitability of impending withdrawals. I've been on a twenty-four-hour drip of ketamine for the last month. I think about Tiffany's withdrawal from heroin. It was dreadful. If this is even a fraction of that, I'm not going to be fit to take on Joseph within a few hours. My best bet is to flee and consider the blow I dealt to the Apostles a victory in a longer war.

I need to kill Joseph. He's the only one who can manufacture indigo, but If I die trying, while I'm weak, no one else will be able to stop him. The other Apostles know what ingredients to use, but not the methodology. With Joseph's supply of two of the three cut off, it will slow him significantly, buying us time.

But, with the indigo he already has, Joseph will continue to garner followers because his abilities seem like miracles to those already prone to believe in them, even if they're now reduced. That will allow him to manufacture the most dangerous thing of all, the consent of a large group of people to be ruled over without question. That's why he's become Abraham Proffit's de facto right hand. Each has the other by the balls, one with his infinite finances, and the other with the powers of a demigod. Both are needed to push the Apostles forward.

The house has become some kind of memorial. It sits undisturbed, inside an auditorium. It's not a megachurch the size of ones in Charlotte and Atlanta, but it's a well-executed attempt. There's no way he has enough followers to necessitate these facilities, but he's damn sure confident that they're coming.

Shining my light through the auditorium, I momentarily flash over something small and hunching, skittering between the pews. My mind occupied with the fear of withdrawal sickness, I forgot to be vigilant in feeling for the vibrations of footsteps. Whatever this thing is, it's small. I immediately shut the door, lock it, and head back inside where I also lock the interior garage door leading into the house. I shudder. There's something terrifying about how it moves in a wriggling shuffle. The bit I could see appeared to be a gray, hunching back with protruding vertebrae. It moaned continuously, obviously in distress. There's something different about it, as though it were conscious, instead of acting on primal instinct. I back into the hallway and shut the bathroom and bedroom doors, providing me with some protection in case it decides to break through the windows in those rooms.

Then comes a high-pitched scratching on the front picture window. It sounds like a multitude of claws clattering and sheering off microlayers of glass. I place the rifle in the crook between the hallway wall and the left door frame of Vernon's old bedroom, then drop my pack to the floor. The only protection I have are Vincent's brass knuckles and the rod I stripped off my hospital bed. I charge all three items and they glow electric indigo, waiting for whatever comes.

Clawing on the glass becomes faster and heavier. Then it shatters. Large shards smash down onto the floor, then I hear footsteps coming from inside the house. Its claws click with each step across the hardwood floors. A hand with unnaturally thick and pointy nails quietly curls around the corner, not far off the ground. It's followed by a gray, circular head, the size of a ripe pumpkin. It's a humanoid figure, with pupilless black eyes the size of golf balls. When it opens its oblong mouth, two rows of long, pointy teeth are visible. There are two long nasal passages, much like slits, under a blunt, gray nose.

When the creature first became visible, it was on four legs. But now, it begins to stand. It's only four-and-a-half feet tall. Much of that body length is covered in gray, leathery scales that ripple, flashing indigo when it breathes. It releases a high-pitched noise that makes my ears ring. The thing charges, leaping at me from about four feet away. I drop to my knees and thrust the charged hospital rod upward, impaling it through the chest with the sharpened end. The beast dissolves into gray dust that gently rains down like toxic snow. I shake it out of my hair the best I can. The rest of me is pelted with the stuff. After taking a few steps, it begins to gradually slough off.

Dropping to the ground, I place my left hand against the wooden floor. There's a single set of footsteps. A glow through the windows lets me know that the interior of the church's auditorium has been illuminated. I hoist the pack onto my shoulders and pick up my rifle before heading back into the garage. There, I approach the problem as I did before. I crack open the wooden door a bit so that I can peek through the glass storm door. I see that the house is surrounded by a field of pews, housed inside a mammoth open space. There appears to be Astroturf surrounding it, as though it's staged as a historic site. Rifle-first, I step outside.

On either side of the church, there are two sets of pews with three smaller sections down in the front. The walls are white and the ceiling is made of dark, oak-stained wood. The stage is rounded and large enough for a rock concert. There's an altar in the center, then two sets of stairs that extend out the length of the stage on both sides. Behind the podium is a choir riser bigger than any I've ever seen. Even further back is a baptismal pool bolstered by thick polycarbonate, so large that it could be used for lap swimming.

I see a dull outline of indigo on the wall directly to the left of the stage. The figure becomes Joseph as he attempts to walk through the wall. He struggles, getting caught halfway, quickly jerking himself, and stumbling slightly. He looks like hammered shit, pale and skinny, left forearm in a cast. Amazingly, he's on two feet. Joseph leisurely walks up the stairs to the podium, as though he's about to give a sermon. Speakers amplify Joseph's voice as he begins to speak in his soft, droning style.

"Naomi, how pleasant to see you awake. You have caused an awful lot of trouble this morning. So many of my men wasted. For what? Your vanity? You believe yourself to be special, above prophecy. God sees you for what you are, a queer harlot."

"I seem to remember your lord being rather kind to people who were pushed to the fringes."

"Perhaps, but he's only the precursor to the one, true prophecy, born of our brother Abraham. Search your heart, and you will see that it is true. I know that you won't, so let me speak plainly. Naomi, you stole something from us, and we want it back."

"Not we, you. Cleverness has gotten you far, but you wouldn't care about the prophecy if there weren't something in it for yourself. You just like to be in charge of something. You force others to do as you say, even to the point of their deaths, merely for your gain or entertainment. Even I have lost count of how many souls I've liberated from your people."

We can wait you out. I have enough of your blood, stone, and water to last me for years to come. But you have to die someday. Afterward, the light inside you has to go somewhere. I suppose we'll see what happens then, however it comes."

"You look sick."

"Did you meet, little Albert?" he interrupts.

"That creature had a name?"

"It was a little boy. We wanted to see what would happen when a person ingested the indigo. Obviously, it didn't turn out as we'd hoped. Instead of becoming a god, Albert became a ghoul. Don't worry, he was just some transient. We found him and his mom sleeping in a run-down van by the Toe River. They'd been there for a few days, homeless, and taking advantage of our hospitality. We fed the mother to our beasts while the boy watched. He willingly ate the indigo after, having nothing else to live for."

My mind reeled upon becoming aware that I had killed what at least began as a child. Furious, I ignite the shaft of metal in my left hand, along with the brass knuckles.

Seeing this, Joseph replies, "You know very well that you're more valuable to me alive."

From behind, I hear the hiss of a dart gun. It must have been aimed for my neck but struck low, lodging itself into the back of my Kevlar vest. I turn to see the rifle that fired it sticking out of the projector booth, thirty feet behind me, perhaps twenty feet in the air. The rifle pulls away as the gunman loads another dart into the breach. I shoulder my rifle, simultaneously flipping down the safety. Aiming through the small, square hole meant for a projector lens, I watch for him to return. Just as I see the rifle begin to exit the window again, I take my shot. After the report, the gunman's rifle gradually slides back into the hole, pulled by gravity because the sniper who held it is now dead.

34

As he stands at the pulpit, speechless, a look of panic breaks Joseph's facade upon realizing his ruse has failed. Despite Joseph's intellect, I can't help but think again about how inept the Apostles are. It's just that there are so many of them, and I fear they're multiplying. When they see Joseph display the abilities indigo gives him, they wash their hands of any social norms that may have bolstered up any flimsy tolerance for others. Now, they're certain that they're infallibly right, and everyone else is wrong, laws be damned. He's opened up a spillway for the cult's members to act upon their basest desires for violence and sexual abuse.

Perhaps I can end that, right here?

Joseph holds out his casted left hand and attempts to send a fast gush of wind in my direction, as he has done before. It's hardly a breeze.

"Fine," Joseph says, pulling a blood-splattered aluminum baseball bat from underneath the podium.

Holding it up in his right hand, he screams, "This is what we use on apostates in this very chapel, nearly every Sunday!"

I wonder why no gun, and I realize it's because he can't pull metal through the wall. Subsequently, I notice that he has on no belt or watch. Joseph was so confident in his sniper that he disarmed himself just to make a dramatic entrance.

He walks casually down the right set of stairs, then through the aisle in my direction. Seeing Joseph holding the bat in his right hand, the left unable to grasp anything, I switch the metal rod to my right hand. This will give me an inside angle when he swings the bat at my head.

But instead of charging me head-on, Joseph throws the bat in my direction, striking me on the right hand. I drop the metal rod as my entire forearm goes numb. Despite this, my right-hand brass knuckle remains. I clutch my hand instinctively. The bat and metal rod clink over several pews, landing somewhere unseen. Joseph takes this opportunity to charge me. With my longer reach, I extend a left jab to his face, breaking out his front two teeth. He falls backward, holding his right hand across his mouth. His mouth bleeds profusely. Exhausted, and injured, I'm not able to mount a follow-up blow before Joseph is able to get to his feet and run away. He stumbles back through the exterior wall to my left.

With no easily accessible door, I'm reluctant to chase after him, wary of ambush. For some reason, my thoughts turn to Moses. I kneel, placing my left hand on the auditorium floor. I weave my consciousness through the rock below, then into the wood running up the walls, all the way to the ceiling. I begin to pull it apart, starting directly at the peak of the roof. The ground rumbles as it's shorn in two. The split lets in daylight, exposing a slice of blue sky. With all my effort, I'm able to break the building asunder, sending each side in opposing directions, leaving a pathway for myself in the rubble, as though it parted like the Red Sea.

The temperature drops precipitously once the structure collapses. Surrounding the island of rubble is a world made of pure, fluffy, white snow, damn near three feet deep. Leading away is a path through it mapping Joseph's frantic moves. Still spacey-headed, I'm torn between following him or fleeing. Without being at full strength, I'm wary of forcing more contact with him.

To my left is the short bridge crossing the Toe River, where Daisey Chambers was shot in the back and killed by Patty Proffit right in front of Charles and myself when we were children. I remember the steam rising from her body in the cold air as if it were her spirit escaping.

Looking behind me, I see Vernon's house demolished under the rubble of the now-flattened, smoldering megachurch. Not only have I escaped the same prison for a second time, but I have also finally destroyed it. The rut Joseph made in the snow is sprinkled with blood from his mouth. I follow it. When he reached the bridge, he continued straight. But I turn left and cross, leaving him to flee. Out in the open, I'm defenseless. I enter into Daisy's perspective, briefly living her final moments. Fear consumes me, but as I pass the spot where her body fell, I begin to feel as though I am on fire. Surging with adrenaline, I run as hard as I can against the mounds of snow and into the woods underneath the ridge where Rebecca fell and was transported to my home in Virginia.

Though not as steep, the incline is noticeable to my weakened calves and thighs. I push onward anyway. The day passes with the sun low in the sky. By three o'clock, I make the decision to stop. I place my hand on the ground and begin forming an elongated granite dome, covered with hardened roots encasing it, blending into the environment. A blue light slowly fills the ceiling and walls, caused by bioluminescent lichen. Lava heats the space, and a spring brings me water. There is a hole on the far end for relieving myself.

As I lie on top of my sleeping bag, I feel the first tremors of withdrawal. There's a headache that pulses lightly in the background, like a metronome ticking slowly until it becomes a spear piercing my skull. Every joint begins to ache, then shriek in sharp pain, as though they will explode. I retch bright yellow bile comingled with white mucus, leaving a deep bitter taste. Then the psychosis kicks in.

The Earth begins to breathe. My field of vision becomes blurred and choppy. The air seems to create a high-pitched 'wah-wah' sound. Despite the surrealness, I'm still linked to the physical world, where I continue to vomit uncontrollably. Now it's just one line of thick saliva dripping in strings from my bottom lip. A feeling of overwhelming sleepiness washes over me. My muscles begin to involuntarily relax and the last thing I remember before slipping into oblivion is the gritty feel of dirt on my face as it remains on the ground off the right side of my sleeping bag.

When I awake, I roll over onto my back. The glowing lichen leaves tracers of light in my field of vision that morph into a fractal pattern floating in mid-air. I begin to feel as though I'm defying gravity, pinned to a cavern ceiling, peering into empty space. Shaking my head, I'm able to snap back to objective reality. How long have I been asleep? Hell, what day is it? A thought about the blue, handheld GPS flashes through my consciousness. GPS has a built-in time function. The only problem is, is that the satellites won't link up through thick granite walls. Opening the door to the outside could put me at risk. But my want to know gets the better of me. I open the small zipper portion at the top of my bag and pull the gadget out. It lights up with a yellowish backlight. As a precaution, I palm the auto-knife tucked in next to it. The black, LCD map is frozen at the last location where it had been powered on. It's the cliff where I shot down upon the Apostles. A message flashes endlessly across the screen, 'linking to satellites'. Placing it aside, I put my left hand against the ground. I don't sense anything larger than a small herd of deer bedded down for the night. I make an archway in the wall to my left, four feet in height. Stooping through, I wade out into the snow, no more than three feet from safety. Gradually, an animation representing the Earth and satellites, shows each nearby linking up. The date and time flash on the screen. It's two-o-three in the morning, Thursday, January twenty-fifth. According to the map, I'm less than two miles from Highway Nineteen. If I get across it, I can follow the same path, up the Toe River, toward the Appalachian Trial, and out of the Apostle's territory.

It's then that I feel an excruciatingly sharp pain in my chest, coupled with the unmistakable sound of a pistol. I fall toward the door and scoot swiftly back inside on my butt. Quickly, I seal the thick protective wall. It's Joseph. I must be weakened to the point that I didn't sense his presence. Afraid, I reassure myself that he can only bring non-metal through, which means getting to me requires dropping the gun.

A guttural noise exits my lungs as I catch my breath. With each inhalation comes sharp pain where the bullet impacted the Kevlar. I undoubtedly have several broken ribs. I get to my feet and stand in the center of my shelter. I pull out my auto-knife and ignite it into a lamentation blade, along with Vincent's brass knuckles. Joseph walks through the wall in front of me and to the right. We are both haggard and weak. He has no weapons and is smaller. However, I feel unsteady on my feet. As Joseph steps in my direction, I swing the knife wildly, hitting nothing. Then I feel the cast on his left hand across my cheek, knocking me to the ground. My knife is flung from my hand and falls away. I land on my back, sit up, pull the Glock nineteen from my pocket and begin releasing round after round in his direction. While they can't break through the field created by the high concentration of indigo sewn into Joseph's coat, each shot knocks him back just a little, fending him off for a few seconds. I'm not even sure if the bullets are hitting him. All I can do is aim where I think he may be. After fifteen rounds, the magazine is empty. Quickly, I drop it, pull another from my pocket, and rack the round into the chamber. Firing with my right hand now, I reach back with my left and desperately try to open a portal. Slowly, an archway forms on the wall behind me. I can see inside the front door of my house. I catch a glimpse of Tiffany.

At least I'll see her once more before I die.

She screams something I can't hear. After emptying another magazine, I get up and make a run for the open doorway, only to hit it like a wall. Knocked to the ground, I bang against it with my right fist, to no avail.

I see Diane rush through our kitchen carrying a black, sawed-off, pump-action shotgun with a pistol grip. Nate and Herschel are directly behind her. She walks through the doorway and begins unloading shell after shell of buckshot over my head. Each blast strikes Joseph's protective indigo layer, pushing him back several times, and then he falls. As she stands over Joseph, still firing, each round prevents him from standing. I feel Nate and Herschel's hands slide under my armpits. Quickly, I grab my rifle as they drag me through the archway. Diane is the last one to return, still pointing the shotgun at Joseph as she walks backward. Exhausted, I release my connection. Just as the passageway closes, I see fury sear Joseph's face. None of that matters. I am home.

35

I've been in and out of consciousness. The few minutes of clarity I get often involve vomiting. Walls and inanimate objects appear to move on their own. Our newly refinished hardwood floors reflect a blurry version of my gaunt face. When visiting the bathroom in one of my waking moments, I get a good look in the mirror. My face is covered in purple bruises, as is most of my body, except for my feet, which were protected throughout the ordeal by thick boots. The worst bruise is just to the left of my center mass. There's a deep purple, almost black, wound directly behind where Joseph's bullet struck the body armor I was wearing. Its residual pattern is drawn across my flesh in expanding lines. The injury becomes less purple on my skin further from the bullseye. It appears almost like the radar image of a hurricane. With each breath, pain radiates from that point, throughout my chest. Several ribs are obviously broken.

The purest form of anger is that of an intimate partner furious that you put yourself in danger. It's akin to the anger we feel at a victim of suicide, only we have a living person to scream at. And Tiffany does, while crying. I hear all of this vibrating through the thin plastic of a small trashcan I'm puking into.

"I've been sick to my stomach for a month-and-a-half, not

knowing if you were alive or dead," Tiffany screams.

Tiffany's high-pitched voice is as loud as I've ever heard it.

"I know," I say, my head still hanging over the bucket.

"That's all you have to say for yourself?"

"I had to, and I'd do it again," I say retching.

I turn my head slightly. Tiffany is standing there with her cute freckled arms crossed, hands hidden away in her armpits. She looks terrified, as though she's protecting herself subconsciously from getting the awful news of my passing.

When I've finished emptying my stomach's remaining contents, I sit up. There's an inflatable mattress on the floor, about five feet away. I realize Tiffany put it here so she could keep a better eye on me while I'd been hanging over the bed's edge.

"My brain is still having difficulty believing you're real. I'm afraid if I turn away, perhaps you'll vanish like Charles, into dust."

"There was no choice. If I had taken Nate, Herschel, and Zeke, at least one of them would have died, perhaps all. But look at me. It appears the curse of my life is that it will be long."

"It seems in this long life, you brought someone back with you."

"Rebecca."

"How could you let those two girls follow you?"

"I ran away to shake them, but once they caught up with me it was too late. I even threatened to shoot them both. Neither believed me."

"Rebecca said essentially the same."

"Where is she?"

"Find Herschel and you'll find her," Tiff says, rolling her eyes.

"Fuck, how long did that take?"

"Two weeks. They're in that gross stage where everything about the other is perfect."

"I accept you for your sleep-farts," I quip at Tiffany.

She half grins involuntarily, then stiffen up, trying not to encourage my irreverence. Tiff secretly enjoys the minor annoyances I cause her because she knows that's how I flirt.

"Nate's taking it kind of hard. The boys have been tight since I've known them. While Nate and Herschel may not be a romantic couple, we'd be remiss to forget there is more than one type of intimacy."

"Isn't that the fucking truth."

"The thing everyone under this roof has in common is trauma. Though there are unspoken forays of affection or length of distance in any group. The way you and I are a pair within our family, Herschel was to Nate until just a month ago. I'm worried about Nate, actually. Herschel stopped sleeping in their bedroom. Instead, he spends each night with Rebecca in the guest room. Nate's mostly been hidden away in his bedroom since the night Herschel left his pillow bare. Herschel is so blinded by new love, he can think of no one but her. When Herschel realizes what he's done to Nate, it's going to sting. I don't even think Rebecca and him have been intimate, which in a way, makes it worse. Had there been the immediate draw of sex, Nate might have been able to deal with it better. All Nate sees is his best friend paying special attention to another and utterly ignoring him."

"It seems selfish."

"Somewhat, but I don't think it's on purpose. Rebecca and Herschel really are quite infatuated with one another."

"I know the feeling," I say, looking Tiff in her pale blue eyes."

That's all it takes to topple presumed anger. Tiffany breaks down into tears. Ultimately, it's all about fear of loss. She crawls into bed behind me, clutching the square tissue box on her bedside table.

"You look fucking terrible," she sobs.

"I'll be fine."

"I hope so because we can't take you to a hospital for this. Wounds resulting from gunfire have to be investigated. Emergency room staff certainly know what gunshots through Kevlar look like. If that happens, the Apostles will find you."

"They'd regret it."

"It didn't look that way to me. It looked like Diane and the boys saved your life."

"But I killed so many of them, Tiff."

"At what cost to yourself? To us?"

"It's my life to gamble," I say curtly.

"That's not fair," Tiffany sobs.

"It's not supposed to be fair. It's supposed to be reality. If I can't stop them, the Apostles will use their beasts as weapons. Many more will die, including yourselves. I was trying to save all of you, and who knows how many more. The blow I dealt the Apostles will debilitate them for some time."

Tiffany cries so hard that the mattress moves slightly. I reach my scarred left hand out to her right. She holds it briefly before needing it back to gracefully blow her tiny nose.

Eventually, the vomiting subsides. Of course, Diane kindly offered me some of her medical cannabis, but I turned her down. I subsist on Pepto, Nauzene, and chicken broth. I haven't left the house yet because my face and body are so badly bruised that one of my neighbors would rightly call the cops because they'd believe I'm being abused. No matter all the things I've done to balance the equation, I've never stopped feeling like a helpless little girl. Sometimes I examine myself in the mirror, unsure how I can be so large.

It seems as though everyone is filing into my room, like they would a wake, paying their respects, and shaking the departed's closest relative's hand, quietly stating platitudes about how they're in a better place, blah, blah. Tiff is that relative, and I'm playing the part of the corpse. The only exception is Diane, mother to the core. She's in and out of our room, assisting Tiffany. My chest hurts so much that I have difficulty getting in and out of bed myself. Both assist me with showers. I've been coughing up blood off and on because the hydrostatic shock of the impact likely ruptured the alveoli in my lungs.

Nate is the next to enter my sarcophagus, despite the fact he's been sequestered for the last few weeks. Nate's so overcome with emotion that he grabs my hand and weeps.

"I'm going to be okay," I say raspily, through my swollen face.

"How can you know that?"

"After everything I've survived, this ain't shit. Just some bruises and broken ribs. It's nothing time can't heal."

"I think we should get you to a hospital."

"Then everything I've done will be for nothing. We'll have to move and start over again. If I die, I can't risk having the Apostles attempt to track y'all down. They'll bleed each of you to death so they can create more indigo with your blood. Even my dead body is a risk. They may try to steal my corpse. They dug up Milly and Hannah's bodies. They probably ground them up in an attempt to eke out something usable. It's unlikely that worked. Hell, Hannah was never even in my presence while alive. If I perish, burn me."

The look of fear and sadness, mixed with love, pooling the tears in Nate's eyes breaks my heart. He crawls into bed next to me for a few minutes. He's ginger with his movements, so as to not inadvertently hurt me. When I awake, he's gone.

Shortly after, Zeke peaks around the corner with Beverly in tow.

"How are you doing, kiddo?" he asks, like a concerned uncle.

"I feel like shit."

"Fair enough."

"How many of those motherfuckers did you kill?" Beverly asks.

She's very much like her sister, Diane, that way; frank and rough around the edges. Just the kind of people I like.

"More than one hundred, including my own father and four of their beasts."

"Jesus-fucking-Christ!"

"I don't think he had anything to do with it," I reply.

In the evening, as the light dims outside, Herschel comes in with Rebecca.

Looking them both in the eye, I say, "What the hell did I do?"

"You saved my life," Rebecca says in a serious tone. "Not only that, you transformed it," she continues, staring coquettishly at Herschel.

Tiffany is right, they're at that gross stage of new love. Let them have at it. That's the kind of thing that makes the world worth saving.

36

Over the next month, I convalesce. It takes my ribs that long to heal enough that I feel as though I can leave the house. Even now, I'm in constant pain, but I can fake it. My face has healed to a point that it only shows a faint hue of purple. Having lost two quarts of blood in one month stressed my body further, making recuperation take longer.

Because I could only speak so long without severe pain, most of that time was spent quietly with Tiffany and Diane. After the perpetual vomiting subsided, Tiff joined me in our king-sized bed. I'm six feet tall and have PTSD-induced nightmares. We've found that it's best for her to have distance from my limbs while I sleep. The two of us learned this in the weeks after we were first reunited. While sleeping on a double mattress, I kicked and punched Tiff as I dreamed because I was fighting off a phantom Vernon in my sleep. I was more upset about it than Tiffany. After, I remained on the couch until we got a larger bed.

We have a new thirty-two-inch flat screen television in our room with cable and a DVD player. But there's only so much TV or movies one can watch. My obsession with nature documentaries and science fiction has worn on Tiffany, who'd much rather see arthouse films with subtitles. That's all well and good. I enjoy those as much as the next person, but no matter how brutal I am, I'm a nerd-girl to the core. I still eyeball every creek and ditch for lifeforms that intrigue me. Even though I know what to expect, I'm always in awe of the magnificence of life itself. Tiff, on the other hand, cares about how people interact with one another. The interworking of the human mind and our condition, existentially, are what fire up her intellectual steam engine. That's why today, she's out with Diane, Beverly, and Nate to see a movie. It's some romantic farce captured on film. No, thank you.

Around two in the afternoon, a feeling of isolation washes over me. Even though I've gotten out of the house a few times, I spend a lot of time in bed. It takes a bit of grunting, but I sit up, then step barefoot onto the cold floor. I put on a loose-fitting back t-shirt and slide on a light blue pair of pajama pants. I make my way out the bedroom door. The television is on. Rebecca and Herschel are curled up watching Jackass reruns. Both of them chuckle as grown men fly out of shopping carts and face-first into the pavement. I hear Zeke pounding away outside. He's been constructing a new workshop for himself. It's becoming apparent to me that he's settled on our living arrangements becoming permanent. Hell, he already has a small hydroponic pot-grow upstairs. The fact that no one has spoken up in opposition to him settling in means the sentiment is shared among the group. Maybe they're right?

It's not safe to return home, even though the Apostles are in a weakened state. The last shipment of rock from the Severe Mine was destroyed when I blew up their dump truck. Joseph likely has dust and water from the mine to continue making indigo, but he will inevitably run out. Some of the other Proffits may even deny him access to their supply, in a form of light mutiny. In the early days of a cult's reformation, everything is in flux. Establishing one's self as the eminent leader who stabilizes the group after a disaster is a relished spot. If a cult survives to become a religion, these are the people they name universities after.

"Hey," I say, approaching Herschel and Rebecca. I sit on the part of the sectional that puts them on my right; the television they're watching is to my left, directly across from their lines of sight. At our feet rests a large coffee table. It's the same one the boys and Tiff were playing Monopoly on the night I conjured the idea for my solo mission.

Rebecca mutes the sound and they both sit up in an attentive state.

"Can I get you anything?" Herschel asks.

"The only thing I need is y'all's company."

"How are the ribs?" he replies empathetically.

"Better. I'm able to breathe in deeper than before, but there's sharp pain with every inhalation. I don't think I'll be out running with you for a few more weeks."

"I'll be there when you can."

"So will I," Rebecca says."

"You know, it just dawned on me that you were only one semester away from graduating," I say to her, defeated.

"I can't collect my diploma if I'm dead."

"I wish you hadn't gotten yourself tangled up in my horseshit."

"I do, and I don't," Rebecca says, raising her left hand, which is intertwined with Herschel's right. I mourn Ezra, but why punish myself by missing out on love despite the circumstances?"

"You're right. Guilt won't bring her back. When something like that happens, you have to live the best life you can for two people, yourself and the one who fell too soon. I do that with Charles. Lately, I feel as though I'm failing him."

"Not at all," she replies.

"Charles was a pacifist. He would be disgusted with my choices."

"That doesn't mean they were wrong choices. The Apostles won't stop just because you ask nicely. You're in a position where you've had to make impossible decisions."

"I saw her while they had me sedated."

"Who?"

"Ezra."

"How?" Rebecca asks, covering her mouth in awe.

"Our reality slides through time, separating two other existences. We're like the axis that the hands of a clock turn on. Because of my light, I'm able to exist in a nether place between them. The internals of our cosmic timepiece appears like a train track to me. On the train, wayward souls are transported. Those who want to exit time voluntarily, like Ezra, are obliged to board. Natural deaths are sorted by an unquantifiable moral equation and are deposited where they belong separately. Ezra isn't suffering for her choice, she has been tucked away by time into such joy that she will eventually become it. But the consciousness you knew as Ezra is no more. I tried to join her. It didn't work out."

"Jesus-fucking-Christ," Herschel says, with sadness in his voice.

"There's a version of, 'the golden rule' in every human culture. Some actions present as axiomatically wrong because rudimentary empathy tells us as much. But most things are not so discrete. Suicide is one of the many nebulous ethical dilemmas. I think most people who kill themselves really just want to run but have nowhere to go, or any other way to escape. However, those who end their own lives to escape the punishment for horrendous actions are not provided such accommodating treatment. The equation is always in flux."

They both look at me with concerned stares. But behind their eyes, I can see them both rationalizing what I'm saying as people who have experienced reality-warping phenomena themselves.

"So, that's it? She's gone," Rebecca says as tears dribble from her lower lashes, onto her cheek.

She doesn't sob. It's just a stream of salty water as she speaks.

"Ezra didn't get much of a life. Twenty-one years, most of them hell. I just hoped, in some witless way, that somehow I'd see her again. To know that she's just gone is unfathomable. And yes, I'm still furious at her too, which I beat myself up about. I compulsively look for places where someone could hang themselves, then superimpose the mental image of Ezra's blue face framed by her bloodshot eyes as they bulged from her head."

"Did you have to say that?" Herschel asks?

"Yes. It's the truth."

For the first time since I've known him, Herschel raises his voice at me.

"What the fuck, Naomi," he shouts.

But before it can go any further, Rebecca squeezes his hand tightly and says, "Baby, she's right. Telling me the truth, regardless of how much it hurts, is respect because I'm not a child. Naomi understands that. So do you, but I don't need you to stand up for me. I'll do it myself when need be. But this isn't one of those occasions."

There is a long silence. Not only is this the first time Herschel has raised his voice at me, but it's the first he's been checked by his new significant other. He's a bit gobsmacked.

Herschel finally centers himself and resuscitates the abandoned conversation.

"Do you think Joseph and the Apostles are finished?"

"Fuck no. They're just withdrawing while they scheme their

next move. I want to strike the Apostles again before they get back on their feet. But where? The only two keeps I know of have been leveled. He's unlikely to be sitting and crying by the remains of either Solid Rock or Fort Caswell. Abraham will have him somewhere secret, even to most of the Apostles."

"When you find him, it's unfortunate you can't just shoot a lamentation blade," Herschel says.

"No, I have to be touching the metal. Unless. Shit. I need to speak with Zeke."

37

Briefly, I duck into Tiff and I's bedroom to slide on a pair of my running shoes. I don't tie them because it hurts to bend down. I strain a bit as I stand and walk over to the coat rack at the door to don my thick, dark-green, down-stuffed coat.

Two French doors give access to the backyard. We have a sizable deck that leads to half an acre out back, which is rare here. Herschel put down an obscene amount of money on this place. And yet, the rise of burgeoning tech and information-based economics continues to make him wealthier by the day. What a clever bastard he is. One might think he learned it in college, but it was really the illicit cannabis industry that carved such a sharp business mind.

Shuffling my way out the back door, I find Zeke sweating from his brow in near-freezing temperatures. He's digging the foundation for a new shop that will mirror the one in Asheville.

Gifted would not be an overstatement when describing Zeke. This is a man with an intricate knowledge of botany and the natural world. Yet, he is also an accomplished master of something wholly unnatural, the sharp angles and straight lines of refined metal. He's down to a pair of blue jeans and a denim shirt.

"Don't you get hypothermic on me, Zeke," I say.

"I'll take this over the heat. I miss Asheville. Here, it's hot and humid as fuck during the summer."

"Eh, it's nothing like Wilmington, especially if you go a bit inland. The place is crawling with alligators and is occupied by mosquitos as though they were an invading air force.

"Yeah, but there's not so much pavement and concrete."

"To get you back there, mountain man, I'm going to have to put Joseph into one of those deep dark holes in the holler. For that, I will require your welding and gunsmithing skills."

"What do you have in mind?"

I put my left hand out, indicating that I want to hold Zeke's shovel. He hands it over. I grip my left hand around the metal neck, below the spade, which allows it to attach to the wooden shaft. I ignite the steel.

Keeping it lit, I say, "I can charge metal into what's called a lamentation blade. It's the only thing I can use against Joseph. Holding the wooden handle with my right hand, I pull away my left, returning the metal to its original state.

"The problem is, once I'm not touching it, the metal returns to normal. A typical gun fires bullets that will bounce off the shielding Joseph's cloak provides. The same goes for his soldiers and their beasts. I need something wholly different."

It takes until mid-April of two-thousand-seven before am I healed enough to begin working out with Herschel and Rebecca. By the second week of May, I'm up and helping Nate, Rebecca, and Zeke finish the interior of the new workshop. Herschel isn't really a hands-on kind of person. He spends most days preoccupied with his laptop. Red and green candles on financial charting software blip slowly across the screen. They remind me of a very boring version of Tetris. But, with a click of his trackpad, Herschel is able to wield large sums of his investment capital all over the world.

Occasionally, I pause, awestruck when I look at a computer screen. Before I was taken away to Solid Rock, in nineteen-ninety-three, my parents still had a rotary phone. For years, I lived in a cabin, away from the world, being taught by Al and Milly with handwritten notes at a kitchen table. A year after Al's death, I was using a modem to access assignments and formulas on my professors' university web pages. Now, Herschel sits on the couch with a portable computer, completely untethered by wires, accessing all the knowledge our world has to offer. I've mostly assimilated. I even have a flip phone now, thanks to Tiffany. I despise it. You're never really alone when anyone in the world can call you at any time of the day, almost anywhere where you are.

On a similar note, I've noticed that since I've returned, someone has always volunteered to go with me anywhere. In fact, I don't think I've been alone out in the community since. Someone is always on the sectional at night. They are determined to prevent me from going after the Apostles alone again. I try to put myself in Tiffany's shoes. How would I feel if she'd done the same? However, I can collapse an entire building by asking the Earth to move and am taller and stronger than most adult men. Tiffany needs help reaching the top cabinet.

The workshop is completed and outfitted by mid-June. That's when Zeke and I get to work on a new weapon. We construct the gun out of a single-shot .410 shotgun with a wooden stock.

To construct it, the barrel is removed from the firing mechanism and stock. Zeke machines a revolver cylinder, four times the diameter of the average .357, and ten inches in length. It's placed between the barrel and stock. Inside there are six specialty loads created from .410 shells. Each is a comically long, slender, shotgun shell, ten inches from brass to crimp. Inside each is a six-inch-long, stainless steel spear, tack-welded to a thin, twenty-foot-long braided wire, attached to the metal base of the shell. This allows the lamentation charge to reach the projectile, even after being fired. When the next shell is advanced forward, a stationary titanium blade severs the former's wire, leaving a clear barrel for a follow-up shot. That's accomplished easily, because of the double-action trigger, which means you don't have to manually cock the hammer. You just keep firing until it's empty. The entire cylinder opens to the left, and has an ejector rod like a revolver, but larger.

What we're doing becomes an open secret. No one talks about it but Zeke and myself in private. My family knows that I must fight the Apostles again, but they don't want to admit it.

It's Friday, July twentieth, two-thousand-seven. It's my twenty-eighth birthday and the one-year anniversary of our ordeal.

I'm almost back to full strength. I've regained a lot of the muscle mass lost while under sedation, which was further compounded during my convalescence. I fed most of that gain with copious amounts of take-out sushi. We have a bench press in the garage, along with a pull-up bar and a set of dumbbells. Otherwise, we rely mostly on body weight resistance and calisthenics.

I go into public less and less. One exception is that I, Rebecca, and Herschel run almost every day. Trips where I'm expected to speak with other people are scarce. That means tonight there will be no festivities out on the town like there were last year, right before Claude was kidnapped by the Apostles. I find it difficult to feel merry with all of this so close in my rearview, on a date that makes me feel as though an unknowable cycle is somehow restarting.

The evening begins with giant sushi trays with plenty of genuine wasabi shredded on real shark skin. I grew up fishing and eating my catch, and thus am conditioned to love the taste. Diane often jokes that I'll turn into one, like Don Knotts in *The Incredible Mr. Limpet*, which is one of her favorite movies from childhood. It's often on cable TV's more obscure channels. I think I've sat through it with her four times in the past year.

We finish with a homemade coconut cake baked by Diane. A horrendous rendition of the Happy Birthday Song is sung by all. At the end of supper, I'm uncomfortably full, but I'm drinking anyhow. I've never been an angry or loud drunk. Mostly I do it to numb my emotions, and to sleep. Some might refer to it as 'passing out'. I almost always execute a well-maneuvered crash, though. Admittedly, I did once fall completely out of the shower at our Wilmington house.

Out on the deck, Beverly, Diane, and Zeke sit at the picnic table that Zeke built out of treated lumber. All of them share a joint. Diane and Beverly have wine. Zeke doesn't drink. Herschel, Rebecca, and Tiffany form their own group by standing in the corner. Tiff smokes her own joint. Rebecca and Herschel each hold fancy bottles of beer. That shit's too bitter for my taste. I usually stick to Pabst Blue Ribbon. Tonight though, I'm having painkillers. Neither Nate nor I use cannabis or like the smell of it, so we form our own non-smoker group in between the other two.

38

Nate looks rather dashing tonight. He's dressed in one of his typical crisp white t-shirts. Over it, he's wearing an open, flowing Versace shirt in a baroque print featuring peach, white, and black coloration. His pants are a pair of white slacks with razor-sharp creases in the front of each leg. I think about how far he's come from the boy who picked me up off the side of the road in Yancey county those many years ago.

"You're not over here thinking of ways or reasons to run off again, are you?" he asks.

I'm shocked at Nate's forwardness, as he's been quiet about my disappearance until now. His demeanor doesn't seem to be one of anger. Nate's one to ruminate until he's finally ready to talk about something.

"What?"

"You just look lost, even though you're in the middle of a crowd of people who love you dearly."

"Today makes me feel guilty about Claude and Ezra. If I had died when I was supposed to, they would still be here."

"'Supposed to.' What the fuck does that even mean?"

"Frieda said that my death was predetermined the night I

escaped from Solid Rock. She said, 'you refused to die, even though you were supposed to'."

"Uh, no. Fuck that stupid hallucinatory witch, Naomi. You did exactly what you should have: refuse to die."

"Frieda's statement wasn't said with malice. She's a bit removed from it all because she experiences reality all at once."

"I don't care. She shouldn't talk to you like that. You're over here hating yourself for living. Every choice we make pushes us into the unknowable. You are not responsible. You did not choose your life over theirs. That is something you could never know."

"For us, time is like reading a book line by line. For the Ceraphirian, it's as though every page is pasted to a wall and can be read in one glance."

"Exactly. There was no choice between yourself and them because you couldn't see it yet."

"No, but I see it now, and I can't forgive myself."

"How many of those have you had?" Nate says, pointing at the glass in my hand."

"I'm not counting. I'll stop when I can't hold a glass to my face any longer."

"I just hope you feel okay in the morning. Camping out by the toilet isn't a good time."

"You're one to talk."

"It is true. I drink to forget my parents, my brother, and my childhood. I was abandoned by them. Now I feel as though Herschel has done the same.

"Bullshit. He loves you."

"Not as much as her. The thing is, I am far from angry. I understand the appeal of having a companion where there is a sexual component. I cannot compete with that. But honestly, I feel terribly lonely."

"You could have come to me."

"I know, but what Herschel and I had was intimate, even before he and I met you. It was a physical relationship, but not a sexual one. We slept in the same bed and held each other for comfort. Now, all I have is an excruciatingly large bedroom populated with emptiness and silence. I don't dare go on dates knowing I cannot be honest about my identity for fear my date could somehow be a honeypot set up by the Apostles."

Holding his hand, I reply, "I understand that. I was without Tiffany for so many years. Your someone is out there. One day, you'll come to that corner in time where you'll meet him. I promise."

Then we embrace. I'm so drunk that I spill some of my drink on his lovely Versace shirt.

"Oh shit. I'm sorry," I say pulling back.

"Do not concern yourself with that. I can take it to the dry cleaners tomorrow. It's just a shirt, a very expensive one, but hardly anything of consequence."

The two of us talk and drink into the night. Everyone else keeps their distance. They know the conversation we're having is important.

By two in the morning, everyone is in a highly altered state. Diane and Beverly are the first to retire for the evening, followed by Zeke. After Herschel, Rebecca, and Tiff disband, it's just me and Nate.

"Back to the Lonely Hearts Club," Nate says.

"Ugh, I hate the Beatles."

"That's because you have no taste, Naomi," Nate says, as he goes back into the house, and to bed."

I realize that due to everyone's penchant for excess, I'm alone for the first time in almost half a year. I look up into the sky. Maybe there'll be a stray meteor. But the city lights are so bright that I can barely see Polaris overhead. I lock the backdoor on my way in. Clumsily, I undress and crawl into bed with Tiffany. I caress her body until she turns around, then begins to kiss me. We make love. Afterward, I curl my right arm around her waist and we drift off to sleep.

I'm conscious, but neither awake nor dreaming. It feels like the space between the Woods of Lamentation and Ceraphiria, but there are no railroad tracks, only darkness.

Something faint appears in the distance. It casts a yellow-tinted illumination from a phantom spotlight, nowhere to be seen overhead. I catch a glimpse of an unhealthily thin blond girl wearing a long dress. I realize the light is the sunrise coming through a window, down onto her forlorn body. As the tableau drifts closer, I recognize the child. It's me. I'm on Maddie Bellew's operating room floor. It's right after she repaired my left hand following the vicious cuts Vernon gave me. At that moment, I was mesmerized by the trauma, contemplating all the unlimited spaces in the universe where I could exist.

In the now, it feels as though a cold steel rod pierces the back of my skull, then continues its path through my forehead. I see a ray of bright white light whose beam behaves as though it's being emitted by a laser. But the tunnel of lumens is large, four inches in diameter. Instantaneously, it makes contact with the back of my younger self's head. I feel all the same emotions again. Even so, I'm still a spectator of my own deja vu. At the time, as a little girl, I was escaping the only way I could, in my mind. After, I would stay trapped, catatonic, within myself for three months.

When I unlock from the time trance, my child self disintegrates into fine gray dust. It swirls into a small cyclone, seven feet tall. White lighting zigzags from the interior of the funnel cloud as a single clap of thunder sounds. As it slows, the gray airborne particles form into Theta.

When she speaks, I hear the faint sound of wind howl in her voice. "Your journey began when you realized that there are infinite places in the Universe to occupy. Your mind's escape attempt led it to pierce the Ceraphirian plane momentarily. Briefly, you saw existence as a whole. That experience altered your thought pattern and is what attracted the light to you."

"What about the ritual Al told me about? Golems are formed from virgin soil, spring water, and long goddamn prayers."

"You forgot the most important part: need. The light saw that. The ritual itself, like so many others, is an attempt to talk with the being who sparked our consciousness. The Ceraphirian believe whatever higher power exists isn't a singular entity. Rather, she is ingrained in every elemental particle and onwards up the chain for all substance and nonsubstance."

"She," I say confused.

"Yes. She gave birth to all. We think of her as a mother without the need for a body. That is simply her identity. Her equation is continually extrapolated as time moves forward on the human plane. Each operation leads to another. New universes and realities form with each choice and spread out like tendrils, continually forking off. With each new tangent, a die is cast because she already knows the decisions and events that will transpire. Your unexpected resilience, which allowed you to continue living, defied her sight. Because of this, it's your decisions that none of the Ceraphirian can see beyond. According to her obtuse logic, you shouldn't be here. The resulting existence has added variables that weigh too heavily on one side of the equation, throwing it off-kilter. My revelation about how I treated Frederick Severe has led me to see that God is completely ambivalent to individual morality.

She treats humans as though they are of no more consequence than pieces on a board game. We Ceraphirian have always been the minders of time and her infinite equation, but I can no longer look away from the suffering such indifference causes."

"Does that mean it's my fault the Apostles have been put in a position where they can take advantage of this shift in reality?"

"Not at all. Survival is an evolutionary train heavily ingrained into your species. Your life has done far more good for other humans than your end could have. You saved many who would have become victims of Odin's Oath and created a family of your own. Without your bravery, Diane would have met the same fate as Milly."

"Yet, the Apostles still thrive."

"For now. They should have faded into obscurity. Joseph was supposed to perish from an overdose last year. Instead, he's become addicted to a new drug, power. But, with your family's help, Joseph can fall."

"He was so strong when we last met. I had to gouge open his left hand and amputate four of the fingers just to slow him."

"His strength isn't his abilities. It's influence. Joseph has perverted the ritual and gained seemingly God-like abilities that have attracted scores of followers. Solid Rock's destiny was to bleed congregants until eventually ceasing operation in two-thousand-fifteen. Each bit of Indigo he creates is a fragment of the Woods of Lamentation seeping into the human realm, further warping our vision. Now the Ceraphirian's ability to view the whole of reality is distorted. It's as though we're looking at a picture through a pane of glass smeared with Vaseline."

"Svangi protects the holy site. I feel his hunger pangs in my hand, even in this world."

"Yes, but they have so much of your blood, pulverized rock, and water already. Their infection is set to spread rapidly if nothing is done."

"I don't know where Joseph is. They won't be at their keeps at Fort Caswell or Solid Rock."

"I know where they are."

"What are you going to do with that information?"

"I'm going to make a choice."

39

"Is your gun ready?" Theta asks.

"Yes. Herschel rented out a gun range on the outskirts of Warrenton for two days to iron out the kinks. Enough money can garner privacy and no questions. Unfortunately, it's only effective up to twenty feet."

"Where you're going, it's close quarters. They've taken over an abandoned light tower, forty miles out to sea. The ocean prevents the escape of Joseph's bastardized creatures. His abilities are weakened and he's nervous about the Apostles' power structure. The substantial loss you dealt them has caused his leadership to come into question."

"Are you supposed to be telling me about this? Aren't you inexorably fucking with the equation?"

"I'm not allowed to tell you any of this," Theta says stoically, but then continues, unphased. "The structure is called Frying Pan Tower. It's a decommissioned lighthouse and Coast Guard station. It's been abandoned for three years. It's a perfect square, rising eighty feet out of the Atlantic, resting on four steel pylons. It measures five thousand square feet and has a single level of living quarters. Above it, a flat roof forms an outdoor platform where a light tower on the southeastern corner can be accessed."

"Joseph squats there, surrounded by a small staff of his loyalist followers. Even though Abraham is providing Joseph with supplies, his faith in Joseph has begun to wither like autumn leaves. But none of the other Apostles know how to create indigo, so they can't just oust him. The thing he fears most is being forced to expose his secret, losing the only thing that has ever made him special."

"Because of the tension, Joseph keeps shooters on every corner of the station in rotating shifts. The best one is always in the tower. Approaching them without drawing their fire is impossible."

"Well, that's inconvenient," I say flippantly.

Without shifting her tone, Theta ignores my comment. "A boat makes deliveries every Monday and Thursday. The Apostles have set up shop in your house, and it's your dive boat they're using for the deliveries."

I'm instantly furious. Besides messing with my friends, nothing raises my hackles quicker than someone fucking with my boat. I'm probably going to have to rebuild both engines by the time they're done abusing it.

"What should I do? Take my boat back and make my own delivery?

"Even at night, it would be impossible. Joseph has them scan with a spotlight from sundown to sunup. Shooting at a target on a moving boat is practically impossible, but they're all quite good; better than you. Even so, Joseph's men have M-16s, so they can spray hundreds of rounds in your direction. If you make it to the ladder, you'll be greeted by guards holding similar weapons, flanked by one or more of Joseph's beasts."

"Would you like to explain what you expect me to do?"

"It's now time for you to make a choice. I can only adjust but so many operations in reality's equation before… well, it would become, let's say, uncomfortable."

"Such as?"

"Time will leak between Ceraphiria and the human plane. Everything would warp. Objects will disappear, only to reappear in other places around the planet. There will be regions where time freezes for those trapped inside but continues normally outside. They'll zap randomly like lightning. The climate will be affected, which will set off catastrophic weather and extreme seismic activity. Most multicellular life will be eradicated. So no, Naomi, I cannot tell you what to do."

Theta then goes quiet but continues staring at me.

After a moment of sustained silence, I scream, "Well, what then? Goddamnit?!"

"Make a choice," Theta says before disintegrating into dust that is blown quickly away as if she controls the wind itself.

It's Saturday, July twenty-first, two-thousand-seven. No one is awake before ten. Of course, the first up is Diane, whose banging around in the kitchen rouses me from my alcohol-induced slumber. I slide out of bed, put on my pajamas, and visit the bathroom before joining her. There is already a pot of coffee on. Diane looks fantastic. Last night has me looking shredded as shit. My eyes are bloodshot, and I appear peaked. This is accompanied by a nasty headache.

I take a seat at one of the barstools.

"Here you go, darling," Diane says, holding out an extra-large bottle of Ibuprofen, TUMS, and a glass of water. After ingesting the entire glass, I lay my face on the cold granite countertop. My headache has dialed back, as I'm less dehydrated. I lift my head, and a cup of coffee, with too much half-and-half, is slid my way.

"You were really mad at yourself last night."

"Why do you say it like that?"

"Because that is what drives you to drink the hardest."

"Yeah," I say, not even arguing.

"Is something bothering you?"

"Yeah," I say again, not even attempting to lie anymore. "One of them came to me last night. Theta told me I have to do something she subsequently informed me is impossible. They've taken over Tiffany and I's house and are using my boat to ship supplies to an offshore platform where Joseph is holed up. There's pressure on him from the Apostles' leadership. Even if I could get to the tower, it's too well-guarded. I'd be mowed down."

"Why not take your boat back, and starve him out, instead?"

"They'll have more boats."

"Not if he's on the outs with enough of them. This may be a convenient set of circumstances for the faction growing against him. Launch a campaign to destabilize the Apostles by making them fight among themselves."

I finish my overly pale coffee in silence, thinking over what Diane said. The allure of the coffee aroma draws in all those still sleeping. With caffeine scaffolding the group, we all sit at the kitchen table and discuss what I was told by Theta and Diane's clever insight.

"We can't exactly drive up to the front door and ask for them to return the house," Herschel says.

"No," Nate replies, "but there's more than one way to travel. They'll never see us if we come by boat. The Intracoastal Waterway goes right by your back door. We can travel through the canals and sounds protected by barrier islands all the way there. Private slips are always up for rent across the bay from your house. This would put you twelve-hundred feet away. That way, we can keep an eye on them and decide how to proceed."

"I vote for we kill them all," Rebecca blurts out.

"It could just as easily be us," I say to her. "I'm not a god. I don't expect you to go, but if you do, know that I cannot guarantee your safety, let alone my own."

"I know," Rebecca replies, sternly. "When I followed you before, I went for myself. This time, I'm going for you."

For the next two weeks, I scour online and print classifieds for a suitable vessel. We take a trip to Baltimore to look at several, but it's Norfolk where we find the tugboat, Camille. She was originally constructed in nineteen-forty. Camille spent the first part of her life in service of the French government. She made it through the Second World War without incident. In the nineteen-sixties, she was decommissioned and has changed hands numerous times since. Most recently, Camille was a research vessel, surveying portions of Greenland's coast.

She has a dark-blue steel body, with a pilot house constructed of darkly stained wood. Below the deck is a galley encased with lighter-colored timber. It has a large kitchenette on the right, a full bathroom on the left, a double bed at the front, two bunks on the right, and a booth across from it. In the back is a door that allows access to a space housing the two diesel engines that propel our elegantly utilitarian vessel forward. It's all a bit shabby and smells of mildew. The rebuild on the engines is recent. There's no GPS or sonar. All are things that can be remedied.

The financials will take a few days. In the interim, we acquire supplies. Those include two sets of binoculars, a night-vision scope, four nine-millimeter pistols, two twelve-gauge pump-action shotguns, body armor, ammunition, burner phones, radios, and food provisions.

By late August, we are ready.

40

We embark on August twenty-sixth, two-thousand-seven. Though the diesel engines were in good shape, the freshwater system and head direly needed repair. New mattresses were required. The old ones were musty and slightly soggy. We had GPS and sonar installed. All in all, it's a fine vessel, but a tight fit for myself, Nate, and Rebecca. Zeke, feeling confident about Rebecca as his replacement, opted to stay back with Beverly, Tiffany, and Diane. That suits me. I'd rather have someone who is fully committed than a reluctant warrior. When the time comes, I'll have the gun Zeke manufactured in my hands, so in a way, he'll be there.

Rebecca and Herschel sleep together in the front double bed. Nate and I crash in the bunks. I occupy the top because my longer limbs make scaling the ladder easier. Nate is afraid he'll fall out of bed, which would keep him from sleeping.

We putter along at three to five miles per hour for ten to twelve hours a day. We rotate shifts piloting the boat, though I'm never far from the helm when it's Herschel's turn.

The Intracoastal Waterway is an assortment of naturally occurring inlets, bays, sounds protected by barrier islands, and canals dug by the Army Corp of Engineers. This section was completed during World

War II to protect commercial vessels from German U-boats, several of which were sunk not far off the coast. I've seen the remnants with my own eyes, as they've become popular dive sites. Today, instead of bringing death, they have become reefs teeming with life.

The weather is hot and humid. Ventilation fans cool our evenings, which consist of mediocre quality food, a call on speakerphone home to Tiffany, Diane, Beverly, and Zeke, and culminating in overly competitive games of UNO. The familiarity of Rebecca's slight snore reminds me of our time in the woods, which leads my mind to Ezra. On those nights, I drink. Typically, this leads me up top and onto the bow. The current cuts across the front of the ship as though we're moving. I watch it ripple by, reflecting a wavey rendition of the Milky Way. Thankfully, some nights in bed, the waves rocking our boat are soothing, much like lulling an infant to sleep. Regardless, I'd rather be home in bed with Tiffany.

At three hundred miles, the entire trip takes just under a week. We arrive on the morning of Sunday, September second, two-thousand-seven. Herschel arranged portage in a deep-water slip, twelve hundred feet across the bay from my house. It's a small marina. There are only eight slots, four on each side. We rented the slot furthest out, on the left. This gives us a clear line of sight between us and my commandeered house. I back the boat in so that we can leave quickly if necessary. Each space is supplied with thirty-amp service and fresh water.

Herschel steps out onto the pier to greet the owner. He's a gentleman in his eighties, with a New York accent, named Howard. He explains the rules. Generally, it boils down to, 'don't be a dick'. According to Howard, he spent most of his working life as a delivery driver, squirreling away money to purchase a marina where he and his wife, Louisa, could retire.

"Now it's just another job," he says indifferently at the end of his spiel.

"Some people are never happy with what is right in front of them," I say covertly to Herschel when Howard walks away.

"I've been guilty of the same," he replies with unexpected honesty.

We have enough food aboard for another week. We'll arrange for delivery once we run low. Doing so exposes us to the fewest people necessary, limiting the likelihood we'll be recognized, either by people we know in passing or the Apostles. I realize it's odd for us to never leave the boat, but at the prices we're paying Howard and Louisa, it's unlikely they'll complain.

After settling in, we train our eyes on the house, taking turns using binoculars from the bridge, which provides some level of cover for our spying. We settled on birdwatching as the official excuse if we're ever asked. We even brought several North American bird identification books.

They've mounted a large antenna on the roof of my house, which is at least six feet in height.

'Great, a hole for water to leak through,' I think to myself.

Other than that, nothing else is different. My boat is on the lift and appears to be better cared for than I expected. Tiffany's gold-colored Camry sits where we left it. There is no movement in or out of the house. The blinds are down, so there's no way to see inside. Nate takes the first shift that night, using a night vision scope with a telescopic lens. It reminds me a bit of a rifle scope whose eyepiece is bent up at a forty-five-degree angle. It was originally intended to be mounted to a tripod. But we hold it in our open palms instead. I take over for Nate around midnight and he heads to bunk.

At six-forty-five the next morning, Monday, September third, I see a plain white box truck back down the driveway beside my house. Two younger white men in shorts and t-shirts step out, one on either side.

No uniforms in the outside world.

They're greeted at the side door by another man. He appears to be around forty, dressed like a yuppie suburban dad who's chartered a boat for a day of fishing. He wears a white, long-sleeved fishing shirt and khaki cargo shorts. Sunglasses hang around his neck since it's not yet bright enough for them.

Another man of similar age steps out onto the second-story deck to speak to the three below. He's dressed in a peach collared shirt and khakis as well. A conversation begins. It continues for several minutes. As it ends, Herschel emerges from below deck, walking up the short staircase into the helm.

I hand him the binoculars as I say, "I think they're making a delivery."

I pick up the second pair of binoculars from the dash and continue looking on with Herschel. The two younger men have begun moving white boxes onto my dive boat's deck. Then I see the man from the balcony exit through my side door. He holds a leash in each hand. At the end of each are dogs. Both are large terrier breeds, likely scooped up off the street. I realize the conversation was about whether there is enough room in the boat to take the dogs to Joseph.

The best place to store cargo would be below deck. There's minimal space unless it's been stripped bare. That can be replaced. What infuriates me is knowing what will become of those dogs. After a very uncomfortable boat ride, they'll be fed indigo and transformed into one of Joseph's eternally hungry beasts. My instinct is to go below deck, install the suppressor on my thirty-aught-six, return and attempt to put a round into the man's chest. They're not wearing protective, indigo-lined uniforms or body armor. If the shot rings true, the man would be dead before he'd have sense enough to ask why. The boat constantly sways in the water, making accuracy unlikely. Even if my shot were true, it would expose our presence.

"Oh, Herschel, I'm going to enjoy watching that motherfucker die," I say with a grumbly voice.

"For people who claim to be so holy, nothing seems sacred," he replies.

After all the white boxes are loaded below deck, the two younger men each take a dog by the leash and lead them down below deck as well. They remain. The guy with the white fishing shirt finishes talking to the peach-shirt-man from upstairs. He then boards my boat and taxies slowly out into the harbor, embarking on his trek to resupply Joseph. I don't expect the boat to return until the afternoon. It's a two-and-a-half to three-hour trip each way, and they have to unload supplies when they arrive.

After the activity stops, I head inside, climb onto the top bunk, and lie down on my stomach. Nate is having a quiet morning cup of coffee. Rebecca is still dozing.

"You just saw them, didn't you," he says.

"Am I that easy to read?"

"It's not your face. It's how you plopped down. Your heart seems heavier, as though there is a new weight inside you."

"You should have majored in psychology, not English."

Nate takes a minute to calmly sip his coffee and says, "Stories tell us more about human nature than any controlled study ever could."

"Too right, sister."

Nate raises his cup in response to me while continuing to examine the worn pages of a paperback copy of *Franny and Zooey* he's had since college.

I place a pillow over my head to block out the light and sound, then doze off to sleep.

41

I expect to be paid a visit in my slumber, but I sleep soundly until noon. I awake in the same position, facedown, with a pillow over my head. Everyone else is topside. After visiting the head, I join them. Rebecca's on watch duty. Every few minutes, she casually picks up a pair of binoculars and has a look.

My house sits on the southern side of Harbor Island. We're docked twelve hundred feet to the east, tucked safely behind the barrier island making up Wrightsville Beach. The Masonboro Inlet is only a mile south, which allows access to the open seas. From my house to the Frying Pan Tower is just under fifty miles.

At one in the afternoon, peach-shirt-man exits the side door and clicks open Tiffany's car, gets in, and drives away. He must have found the spare hiding in my embarrassingly overstuffed junk drawer.

"Well, shit," Herschel says.

"Tell me about it," I reply. "Just make yourselves right at home."

"Using your boat, I understand, but you'd think they'd have their own cars," Rebecca says.

"Who knows? I suppose Abraham won't front the cash unless absolutely necessary after everything that's gone wrong."

Peach-shirt-man pulls back into the driveway around two-thirty.

He hauls groceries in over four trips from the car to the house.

"That's a lot of food," Rebecca says to me.

"It doesn't look like anyone else is there. It's as though he's expecting company. To the outside world, it would appear mundanely benign, like someone preparing for a dinner party."

"A dinner party is only as benign as its guest of honor," she replies.

"My guess would be Abraham Proffit. To stop them completely, we have to eliminate both him and Joseph. They're in a death spiral with one another. Both are equal in standing among the Apostles, and neither can exist without the other. Joseph is the only one who knows how to manufacture indigo, but without Abraham's money, they couldn't afford to keep the lights on in a single-wide trailer."

We watch on as the sun creeps behind the mainland, then darkness. Eventually, it's just Herschel and me. I take over from him at midnight. Instead of heading in for a nap, I've decided to stay up all night. Momentarily, I don't feel like listening to any more Ceraphirian shit in my sleep. Herschel clicks on the night-vision scope when he sees the red and green navigation lights of an incoming boat from the south.

"Yeah, that's your boat," Herschel says, as he hands me the scope.

Looking for myself, I say, "It took them long enough."

In the static green, I see more men than I expected filing out. There are six in total, wearing ACH uniforms. They form two lines, three on each side. Out walks a bald man with a pointy nose, wearing body armor. When I see him in profile, I recognize his facial shape.

"That's Abraham Proffit," I say to Herschel.

"How do you know that?"

"When I was at Solid Rock, we had three deacons, Sheriff Alton Morton, the music director Brent Shoals, and that man. I never knew his name. His presence was an enigma. He wouldn't attend for weeks at a time. Regardless, he was important enough that his chair stayed empty. No one but Vernon spoke to him, and it was always in whispers or behind closed doors. Despite that, who else is important enough to be flanked by so many men wearing indigo-lined uniforms?"

"Can you tell what he's carrying in his hand?" I ask, passing the scope to Herschel.

"It looks like he has an Igloo cooler in his right hand. What's in there, a six-pack of beer," he says jokingly.

"I wish that's all it was. If I had to guess, I'd say it's a pint of my blood, frozen under dry ice.

"Why so specific?"

"Because that's what I'd do. My guess is, Joseph was forced to give Abraham one of the two pints he harvested while I was sedated in the cavern as a condition for continued financial support. That gives Abraham increased leverage."

The six guards and Abraham are followed by the boat's pilot, still in his white fishing shirt, and the two young men who arrived on the delivery truck. Neither of them is wearing any kind of protective uniform.

"It's too many," I say, disappointed.

"Why?"

"Even if I could shoot rounds off without alerting the police, there are seven armed men with indigo armor. Zeke's gun only holds six shells. The other three are likely to have sidearms."

"Zeke made you speed loaders."

Herschel's right. Zeke constructed four round devices that hold to-be-loaded shells in the exact pattern of the shotgun's cylinder. After the previous shells are ejected, they allow the shooter to load six shells at a time. A circular knob on the back is twisted left and they're released in place all at once, greatly reducing reload times.

"Yeah," I say, "but it's not fast enough."

"Not that it would work here, but have you ever considered getting a sword?"

"The perfect way to die is to go into battle with a weapon you have not trained with extensively. Because of my father, I've had a gun in my hands since I was four. He taught me basic hand-to-hand combat and knife fighting. I don't know jack-shit about swords. It takes years to become remotely competent with one."

"That's fair," Herschel concedes.

"We have to let him go. It's more important that we stop Joseph's production of indigo than cut off his money. Abraham knows the ritual's vital ingredients are—rock and water from the cavern, as well as my blood.

"Didn't they use Claude's blood?"

"Blood from people exposed to the use of my abilities, like Claude, can be used, but now that the Apostles have the genuine article, all they have to do is preserve it. Theta told me that one drop of my blood could make as much indigo as the entire volume of Claude's body."

"That's even more reason to get him now, Naomi."

"He doesn't know how to put it all together. Abraham is an unassembled bomb, while Joseph is a live one. Could the parts eventually be assembled? Yes. But will it happen anytime soon? It's unlikely. The risk level isn't worth betting on our exposure. After Abraham leaves, we take back the house while it's guarded by men not wearing indigo armor."

This doesn't sit well with Herschel emotionally, but I see logic gloomily drift across his face upon the realization that I'm right.

"It burns to see him walk right past us," he laments.

Around midnight, Herschel retires to bed.

For the rest of the evening, I watch through the night-vision scope. A few men enter and exit the house, but Abraham stays out of sight.

At seven the next morning, Tuesday, September fourth, two-thousand-seven, a large black limousine pulls up to my occupied house. It appears to be abnormally robust, as though it's armored. Abraham and four of his guards get in. The other two get into the back of a black Mercedes that follows behind them. They drive away just as the sun crests above the open ocean to our east. Not long after, the two young men from yesterday drive off in the white delivery truck. That only leaves peach-shirt-man and fisherman-dad behind. My guess is, one will be occupying the guest room upstairs, and the other will be in Tiff and I's a larger bedroom on the ground floor.

I need to see what that antenna is connected to.

About this time, Nate walks up the steps into the galley. Knowing that Nate has arrived to take over allows me to feel the weight of the previous night. For the first time in a few days, I brave the cruelly tiny shower where I have to squat down just to get under the nozzle.

Finished, I crawl onto the top bunk and return to a restful, rocking slumber.

42

I awake later today than yesterday, around two in the afternoon. Either way, Nate is exactly where he was when I woke up yesterday, sitting in the booth and drinking a cup of coffee.

Upon seeing my eyes open, he says, "Watching you sleep reminds me of when we first met. We slept in that hospital chair together after Herschel lost his pinky to the Mace brothers."

"The day Herschel's non-existent dream to play guitar died," I say jokingly.

"The Mace brothers spared all of us from a sonic atrocity," Nate quips.

My laughter fades into the gravity of our situation.

"Tonight, I'm swimming across the bay to my house and taking it back. I want to be there on Thursday when their next shipment arrives. I need you to accompany me. You're our best swimmer and the lightest. We're going in through the second story. You're better suited to climbing the post up to the elevated balcony outside of our living room."

"You can't carry your gun through the salt water."

"I don't think I'll need it. Neither of them appears to be wearing indigo-laced ACH uniforms or body armor. Even so, I can use my dive knife to cut through the protection indigo gives them. The point is, we do it quietly."

The remainder of the day sees no one enter or exit the house. It's as though they're cautious about being in public view any more than necessary. I think they're afraid of me.

———

Around two in the morning the next day, Wednesday, September fifth, we gear up. Despite the warm temperatures, we both wear full-length black wetsuits, not for thermal reasons but to make us harder to see. They're not too thick, so we should be comfortable, plus they add buoyancy.

On the deck, before we leave, Herschel embraces Nate tightly and cries softly.

"I'll be okay," Nate says.

They stay bound together for a little while longer. As Herschel releases his powerful grip on Nate, he says, "Come back to me."

We sit side by side on the starboard gunwale with our backs to the bay. Both of us slip on fins, pull down our masks, hold them tight, and tumble back into the water. The only things we carry are dive lights and knives.

It's eerie. We have to snorkel with our face masks half out of the water. Otherwise, the only thing we'd see is the black void below us. My biggest concern is boat traffic. At night there are fewer vessels, but it's not absolutely absent. We keep our long fins submerged, to minimize splash that could draw attention. Nate stays on my left and we keep a slow, even pace. It's best not to be completely out of breath when we get there.

It takes eighteen minutes to arrive at my dock. The structure begins as a wooden pier, twenty feet behind my house, then splits in two, providing a walkway on either side of the boat lift. This allows the pier to cradle it like a U. My dive boat is suspended four feet out of the water on carpeted, wooden bunks. This keeps the barnacles and other crawly things from taking up residence on its hull. On the other side are identical aluminum ladders attached to the end of each wooden walkway.

We're still in the water, directly under the boat now, for cover. The spotlight from above the house's raised balcony ripples across us and the underside of the white hull. With our masks up on our foreheads, we're able to speak to one another.

"The light needs to go," Nate says.

"I can handle it, and half the lights on our street."

"Perhaps don't make it so the power company shows up?"

"Of course. I believe we long ago established my zeal for overkill."

Nate doesn't respond verbally, rather, he cocks his head, raises his eyebrows, and gives me a half-smile.

We swim under the right side of the dock, coming up just off the beach where my property begins. Both of us crawl onto shore while removing our masks and fins. We each wear thick-soled booties, typically used for surfing. This gives us the advantage of better traction and protection. We stow our gear on the sand under the beginning of the pier.

Staying low and still, we assess the situation. Even though the spotlight is on, all the lights are off in the house, and the blinds are down.

Placing my left hand on the ground, I begin to build up a static charge. It's similar to the one I used against my father through the metal rod, except at a much lower voltage. I send it creeping along in an expanding latticework of blue that ever so slightly illuminates the grass from underneath as it spreads out from my hand. With low crackles, it courses under the house, coming to rest beneath it like a fishing net made of electricity. I concentrate my effort, envisioning the outcome, then force a surge of pulses through it. The spotlight flickers and then is extinguished.

"What was that?" Nate asks.

"An electromagnetic pulse caused by static electricity. It's like thousands of tiny lightning strikes happening under the house at once. The bursts cause an electrical outage and can damage semiconductors. If we're lucky, they won't be able to contact the power company because their landline is down and their cellphones are trashed. That means no one will be coming to help them if we do this stealthily. Hopefully, they're still asleep."

We wait to see if there's movement in the house related to the power outage. Time is against us now. In an hour, the house will be stuffy from the late summer's heat, which could wake them up. I keep time on my dive watch. For ten minutes, there's been nothing to see but darkness, occasionally pierced by a flickering lighting bug. Everything, except for a chorus of chirping frogs, remains quiet. Still encased in black wetsuits, both of us crouch low as we dash across the yard and underneath the balcony. It's built of an array of treated four-by-four lumber. We focus on the ones holding up each outside corner. I take the one on the left side of the house, Nate on the right. We each use our sinewy, lanky builds to our advantage, climbing them like lumberjacks. The most difficult part is making the transition from the pole up onto the balcony, fifteen feet in the air.

Swift Nate is already waiting at the top to help pull me over the rail.

After getting my bearings, Nate asks, "Are you going to melt through the lock?"

"No. I've never been able to get it to close well. I probably could have tried harder. Besides, who's crazy enough to climb a possible bone-breaking height to steal my flatscreen?"

"Us, it seems."

We shed our wet boots on the porch, so as not to make squishing sounds when we walk across the wooden floor. I wiggle the door while holding the lock-releasing mechanism. I feel the loose hook securing the door begin to slip over the holding pin. Then comes the soft sound of rough metal pieces sliding over one another as the door pops loose.

I slide the glass door open just wide enough to get my left hand through. Placing it on the wooden floor, I feel for movement throughout the house.

"Whispering to Nate, I say, "They're both snoring, which vibrates through the structure just slightly. There's one in the upstairs guest room and another in the downstairs bedroom."

As I slide the door open, I pull my dive flashlight from its belt holster and ignite it on the lowest setting. The glow faintly illuminates the space. Everything is the same as we left it, only now there's a dank cigarette smell clinging to the walls. We take a right in front of the sectional, toward the guest room. The door is cracked ever so slightly. After opening it, our feet hit the bedroom's comfortable, seafoam-colored carpet, further dampening our footsteps.

A man lies face down under disheveled sheets. Without hesitation, I leap on him, straddling his body with my knees. Before he wakes, I already have the knife to his throat.

43

I place my right hand over the man's mouth and use my left to hold the knife.

I whisper in his ear, "I'm sure you've heard the fairytale of the Three Bears. In the original story, the bears lit Goldilocks on fire, drowned, and impaled her when she was found sleeping in Baby Bear's bed. One of you is going to burn tonight. It can be you, or it can be your friend downstairs. I'm going to uncover your mouth and I want to hear you say, 'I understand.'"

Releasing his mouth leads to a slight sputter as the man tries to get words past his terrified, quivering lips.

"I-I wu-wu-will do what you say."

Keeping the blade to the man's throat, I run the fingers of my right hand through his medium-length, dark hair and grasp it as hard as I can. He winces.

"Get up," I say, snatching him off the right side of the bed.

The sound of him hitting the floor causes movement to begin downstairs.

Standing now, I have him in front of me, knife still at his throat.

"Nate, hurry, switch places with me."

He walks around behind me and the man, then uses his right

hand to hold his own dive knife against the man's throat. I step to my left, exiting the entanglement of our three bodies.

Continuing to whisper, I say, "You're going to scream for help when I tell you. If you say anything else, you'll bleed to death on my nice carpet. Are you ready?"

The man nods his head, then shouts, "Help Jeremy, help!"

I hear clanging like the man downstairs is looking for something, perhaps a flashlight. Maybe a gun? I walk light-of-foot through our dark living room by memory. I pass the sectional couch on my left. A few feet later, I place my hand on the pool table. I crouch and lie face down underneath.

When the man from downstairs reaches the top of our spiral staircase, he shines his light in my direction. The couch impedes his view. As he pauses to look at the opened sliding glass door, I get to my feet. After moving past the right side of the couch, I turn and place myself behind him, just before he steps foot inside the guest room. With my left hand white hot, I reach around and grab a fistful of his throat and rip it out, Adam's apple and all. The wound cauterizes because of the extreme heat. His body falls forward into the bedroom, where he writhes on the floor in front of the man Nate's holding captive. I make sure to shine my flashlight down on the dying man as he holds his throat and suffocates to death. I want his surviving friend to see what can happen. Then I raise my left hand, still white hot, and show it to him.

"Do you know what this means," I ask?

"That you're Naomi."

"What do they say about me? Be honest."

"That you have the stolen light of Abraham's prophecy and believe you're God."

"The only thing I believe is that I'm annoyed with y'all."

After thinking for a second, I say, "Nate, go downstairs and search through my junk drawer. There should be duct tape, needle nose pliers, and a roll of baling wire buried somewhere. I don't think the intruder is going anywhere unless he'd like to see what other talents I have."

Bereft of spirit, the man sighs and looks down. Nate makes sure not to put his knife away until he's safely past me and out the door.

"What's your name?" I ask the man.

"Levi."

In a demanding voice, I say, "Why are you in my guest room?"

Trembling, Levi says, "I'm staying here while the Prophet Joseph is on his oceanic pilgrimage. Fewer distractions make God's messages clearer."

"And you do what for him?"

"I help Jeremy arrange acquisitions," Levi says, looking down at the corpse on the guest room floor. "And I operate our HAM radio."

"That explains the antenna. But I reckon it's busted now."

"Why?"

"Because of the electromagnetic pulse I sent under the house."

"It was off."

"But what about the semiconductors?"

"It's tube operated, just in case. Even so, if you created the pulse underground it may not have reached it. We're on the second story of a rather tall house."

"Why a radio?"

"There's no cell service that far out to sea. Prophet Abraham wants a single point of contact. He writes letters that are sent by a personal courier. We read them to Prophet Joseph."

"On the open airwaves," I question.

"Yes. It's mostly scriptures he wants Joseph to focus on when he talks to God. Joseph's replies are mostly grocery and supply lists. It's not exactly scandalous."

"It looked to me like Abraham was just here. He's a rich guy, why did he take the rough trip in my small boat when he could have chartered something larger?"

"Abraham arrived at Frying Pan Tower by personal helicopter. Before it returned to pick him up, the engine developed a mechanical problem. He had no choice."

While not clever, I can't help but notice that Levi is not as dim as many of the others. I find that puzzling and disconcerting. How can someone with a reasonable level of intellect fall for the sham Joseph and Abraham are putting on?

"Why did you join the Apostles?"

"When I witnessed Joseph's miracles, it changed me. I knew that I had found the one true Christianity. Others think of Christ's miracles as something that doesn't happen anymore. But I've seen Joseph perform them."

"You've seen me do the same."

"Joseph says your miracles are blasphemy against God."

"Joseph says, does he? What about you? Why are you trying to redirect?"

"Are you going to kill me?"

"Perhaps. But you've been cooperative thus far."

I peek over my left shoulder to see Nate standing in the doorway.

Shaking his head, Nate says, "You need to do something about that drawer, it's awful. On a positive note, I found Tiffany's car keys hanging up at the door."

"Levi, turn around and put your hands behind your back."

He does so with no delays. Levi is likely experiencing true existential terror for the first time. He's out of options. The only thing Levi can do is ingratiate himself with his captors.

Behind Levi's back, Nate wraps his wrists together with five loops of duct tape.

"What's with the baling wire and pliers," Nate asks.

He hands me both. I pull three feet of the wire into a loop, then bend the end of it around the wire, creating a metal slip noose.

Holding the loop of wire up to the man's face, I ignite it as a lamentation blade. It glows indigo and crackles.

"Your neck will put up no more resistance than brie does to cheese wire. When it happens, you'll feel as though you're falling. Your instinct will be to throw out your hands. But they won't move because all that's left of you will be a head plummeting toward the floor."

I slip the loop over Levi's head. After, I unfurl about eighteen feet of wire. I make a loop on my end for my left wrist and show it to him.

"Are you expecting anyone else," I ask.

"Not until tomorrow morning. It'll be the same two delivery drivers."

"Are they armed?"

Each carries a concealed, five-shot, thirty-eight revolver in their waistband.

"Why Monday and Thursday?"

"So we can avoid weekend boat traffic."

"What are you delivering?"

"Food for Prophet Joseph's men and meat for the holy beasts he creates."

"Why does he use dogs to make them?"

"They're hearty and can survive the transition. Dogs are easy to obtain, smart, and a reasonable size. They instinctively want to please humans. That means we don't have to wrangle them like wild animals or house cats. Felines don't grow much larger. Chickens and other birds die during the transition. Most livestock animals are too large."

"I've heard enough of this shit. Take a seat on the floor, in the corner behind you."

Levi puts his back into the corner of the bedroom furthest from the door.

"The three of us are going to wait in this room until morning. Okay?" I say, patronizingly, as though there's an illusion of choice.

Standing over him, I begin wrapping duct tape around Levi's head and across his mouth.

44

The sun breaks over the horizon. Light from the western upstairs window seeps into the living room, illuminating its now tar-colored stained walls. Even when I smoked, I had the courtesy to do so outside.

I left Jeremy's corpse where it fell all night, so when Levi looks down, he sees the dead man's stare. The body is on its stomach, with his right hand clutching at the void where his throat used to be. The expression on Jeremy's face shows that his final emotions were surprise and disbelief. It says to me that Jeremy was so confident in Joseph's word, it never occurred to him that there could be consequences.

Levi speaks in mumbles from behind the duct tape.

"He probably has to take a piss," I say, looking at Nate.

At that moment, Levi nods his head frantically. With the baling wire still in place, we escort him to the upstairs bathroom, between the guest bedroom and Tiffany's office. Nate pulls our captive's pants down and Levi sits facing forward on the toilet. Levi's hands are still bound behind his back. He lets out a stream that lasts for more than a minute.

At that moment, the electricity blinks back on. I hear the stove downstairs beep and a rush of cold air from the bathroom vent.

"You must not have done as much damage as you thought," Nate says, as he turns in my direction from inside the bathroom.

He has the unceremonious duty of pulling Levi's pants back up. I lead Levi by the wire, to just outside of the guest room door, where I can see in.

Kneeling on the opposite side of Jeremy's body, so I can keep eye contact with Levi. I place my right hand on him and begin to draw water from the stiffening corpse, just as I did sweet Ezra. Soon, all that remains is a fluffy, gray casing resembling an ashy statue. I stand and tap it with my bare toe. This causes the familiar shape to collapse into nothing but a pile of dust.

I walk to the sliding glass door, open it slightly, place my left hand through, and release a plume of water droplets that mix with the morning fog.

Looking at Levi, I say, "All I have to do now is vacuum up and it's like Jeremy never existed. Lie to us, or worse, and instead of the mercy I showed your friend, I'll remove your appendages bit, by bit, the way I did Jeremy's throat. The wounds will cauterize, allowing you to live far longer than you'll want to."

All Levi does is look down.

"Now, get back in that corner," I say pointing.

I stand at the guestroom door, still holding onto the wire around Levi's neck, and speak with Nate. "Go see if the car starts. If it does, get Herschel and Rebecca. They're likely petrified with dread by now."

A few moments after Nate leaves, I say to Levi, "Let's go look at this radio of yours."

I walk Levi toward Tiffany's office on a leash, the way he did the two dogs he sent off to Joseph. We find the door closed.

"Open it," I say flatly, preparing to be angry at what I'm about to see.

It smells worse in there than the rest of the house. It's as though old smoke clings stubbornly in midair, mixed with sweat, and stale fast food. There are coffee stains all over the floor. Both of Tiffany's drawing tables are gone and so is all her art and painstakingly handcrafted calligraphy from the past two years. You can still see the scratches in the wall paint where the men who took over our house tore them down as though they were angry such a thing was allowed to exist at all.

The only thing belonging to Tiffany that remains is her writing desk, upon which, a battleship-gray metal cube rests. It's two feet wide, one tall, and one-and-a-half feet deep. The front has several knobs, and two displays with frequencies embossed on them in black decades ago. In the top left corner is nestled a square analog clock. Next to the HAM radio sit at least a dozen notebooks full of handwritten notes. They're incoherent facsimiles of religious texts.

The first verse I read states, "Let him be as a bird in heaven as a worm in the soil."

Whoever wrote it deluded themselves into believing their words to be profound. But it's just piles of congealed grammar salad with ambiguous meanings that could be interpreted in countless ways.

I begin unwrapping the duct tape from around Levi's mouth. He winces in pain as I pull clumps of hair off of his head.

"Who wrote these?" I ask Levi, throwing down the first notebook.

"Joseph dictates to us, beginning at noon on days we don't send supply boats. It can go on for an hour, or until early in the morning. It just depends on what God has in store for his revelation that day."

"Why over the radio?"

"Prophet Abraham thinks that all scripture should be broadcast over public airwaves for all who follow the Apostles of the Cloven Hand to listen. He forbids private communication from Frying Pan Tower."

For some reason, it isn't obvious to Levi that Abraham does not fully trust Joseph. It's as though a self-regulating delusion has been uploaded into his mind. He's by no means a stupid man, but slow drips of ignorance can fill pools where reason can be drowned.

"I'm going to make sure you make your lunch date with Joseph. Convince him everything is normal, and you might get out of this with your life."

"I'm really thirsty."

"When they return, I'll get you some water."

———

Nate calls my name from the front door. Next, I hear the familiar sound of car keys hitting our kitchen island.

"I'm fine," I shout.

I hear rummaging around downstairs. They're looking for anything out of the ordinary, such as hidden surveillance, weapons, or sabotage. After a few minutes, I hear Herschel's heavy feet bound up the metal, spiral staircase. He walks across the upstairs living room, stopping at the entrance to Tiffany's office, where Levi and I are. Except now, it's a communication headquarters for the Apostles. I meet him just outside of the room.

"What the hell happened to Tiff's office," Herschel blurts out.

I shrug, saying, "I guess, they needed a room for their HAM radio."

"Besides being filthy, downstairs appears unchanged. There was a Glock nineteen pistol in his, rather your, dresser drawer."

"That's their preferred model. There's likely another in the guest room."

"I'll look for it on my way back down. After Nate changed, he and Rebecca began to tidy up. I'm heading back to help them in a few minutes."

"Y'all don't…"

"Just hush, Naomi," Herschel says, putting his right hand up, then walking away.

I watch as he ducks into the guest room and walks out with an identical handgun in less than thirty seconds. Herschel cocks the slide halfway open and drops the magazine from the polymer handle into his left hand.

"One in the chamber, and fifteen in the mag," Herschel says, as he slaps it back into the pistol so he can fire it if necessary.

After he walks back downstairs, Levi asks, "Water, please?"

"You can drink out of the sink. Come on," I say, leading him with the wire slip-knot to the bathroom. I turn on the water and allow Levi to drink until he's sated.

When we return to the office, I lay out simple ground rules.

"When Joseph calls, you are to act like everything is normal, including writing down all he says. Otherwise, you may not sound genuine. After, you'll tell us everything we need to know about Frying Pan Tower. If you behave well enough, I'll even feed you dinner."

In a seemingly compliant statement, Levi says, "How do I explain that Jeremy won't be taking over for me at some point?"

"The flu."

"Joseph is terrified of germs. If I say that, he'll cancel the next shipment."

"Fine. That gives me more time to plan."

45

"Who got you involved with the Apostles?" I ask Levi.

"My father, I reckon. He's always been big on church. My mom, not so much. Their disagreements about religion led to fights about bringing me up in his church. Mom left dad when I was seven, retaining full custody. But it was my father I always wanted to be with. When I turned fourteen, I was old enough to choose, so I went to live with my old man."

"And where was that?"

"Nearby, in Wilmington."

"What church?"

"For most of my life, we went to a church called Avent's Chapel, right outside of Burgaw. It's where my dad went to church from the time he was a boy. All my relatives go there. So I was surprised when, after going on a men's group retreat up in the mountains for a week, he came back insisting we had to begin attending First Baptist in downtown Wilmington."

"The one across from Spectrum?" I ask with my ire up.

"Yes," Levi says, attempting to fake remorse.

"You were the sentry who saw us in the alleyway, then followed Claude home, aren't you?"

Looking down, he mumbles, "Yes," again.

———————

Around ten in the morning, Nate takes a break and pays me a visit. I'm glad it's him. He should hear first.

When he approaches the door to Tiffany's office, I stand up and greet him before he can enter. I run the baling wire under the door and shut it behind me.

"It's him," I say to Nate.

"Whom, exactly," Nate says confused.

"Levi was the sentry who spotted the attack in the alleyway last year. He's the one who followed Claude home."

Nate's pale face turns bright red. Tears stream out of his eyes. His raw feelings from the aftermath of Claude's death are reanimated. Nate calmly walks around me and opens the door. He approaches Levi sitting in front of the radio in a metal folding chair, hands duct-taped behind his back, baling wire noose still in place. I hear an energetic slap followed by another, and then several more. At this point, Levi is crying. Then come deep, wet thunks. Nate has moved on to fists. It's not until hear the chair fall over, that I enter the room. Nate has the heavy radio microphone held above his head, preparing to bash Levi across the brow with it for a second time.

"Nate, stop! We need him alive."

Nate gently places the mic on the desk, standing it up on its base, just as it had been before. He looks at me and walks out calmly, leaving Levi laying facedown under the desk. He's bawling into the dirty carpet, leaving tears, slobber, and snot mixed with blood smeared across it.

"If you plan on getting out of this alive, Levi, you're going to have to pull yourself together."

Not long after Nate disappeared downstairs, I hear heavier feet on the spiral staircase. It's Herschel. The slighter footsteps right after belong to Rebecca.

They look in to find Levi where Nate left him, under the table, snotty and bleeding.

"He doesn't look like much," Rebecca says.

"That's because he's not," Herschel responds.

"I was concerned momentarily that you were going to hit him too," I say.

"From the looks of things, Nate did enough beating for two people," Herschel jokes.

After they leave, I say to Levi, "Come on, let's get you cleaned up."

I pull my knife out of its sheath, which makes Levi squirm.

"I'm not going to kill you," I say, as I cut his bindings.

I take Levi to the bathroom and let him wash and bandage his face. After he's done, we return to Tiffany's office. I call down to Herschel and Nate, telling both of them to bring their pistols.

"What's wrong?" Herschel says from the top of the stairs.

"I need to shower and change. But I can't exactly leave Levi without babysitters. And both of them need to be armed."

Reluctantly, I pull the baling wire noose from around my wrist, leaving Levi in the boys' hands. I don't want to, but I really need to get out of this wetsuit. After showering, I dress in a pair of green pants, boots, and a black t-shirt. My short hair is still wet when I venture downstairs. It looks better down here than on the top floor since it's been preened over by Nate, Rebecca, and Herschel. I find myself feeling guilty that they spent all this time tidying up. It could have waited.

I find Rebecca sitting on a barstool at the kitchen island. In her hand, she's holding a copy of today's paper. The name on the delivery address still says Hannah Sillman.

"It must still be on auto-draft," I say.

"They really did help themselves to everything, didn't they?"

"The Apostles tend to do that, just like Solid Rock before them. The world belongs to them because God said so. They still hold onto control of the land where Milly and Al's house once stood, even though it legally belongs to me."

"It's past due that someone starts taking from them. Maybe you should keep Frying Pan Tower after?"

"It's not theirs. Frying Pan Tower belongs to the United States government. Despite being a worthless rust bin teetering above the open sea, Uncle Sam always keeps up with what he owns. I don't want to be there when he comes around. Nor, do I want anything more than I already had."

"Unfortunately, there's nothing in this kitchen I would recommend you eat. By the looks of the trash and paper cups they left around, they've mostly survived on fast food and cigarettes. There was moldy bread and chunky milk in the refrigerator. That's about it. We're going to have to do the same, maybe we order pizza after we're done on the radio."

"And Levi, I'll have to feed him so he'll keep working for us."

"I'd rather watch him get run over by a bulldozer, feet first," she says chuckling.

"Zeke could probably arrange that," I respond, tilting my head while raising my eyebrows.

Rebecca smiles at me. I can tell she's spinning tires in mud, waiting for something to act on.

When I return upstairs, neither Herschel nor Nate haven't budged. I'm re-tethered to Levi, and we sit and wait for Joseph to reach out on our frequency.

At ten minutes to noon, everyone gathers outside the door. They don't come inside the room to minimize background noise. At precisely twelve in the afternoon, Joseph's static-riddled voice comes through, lighting up both displays of the radio with an orange glow.

"Levi. Are you there, my brother?"

"Yes," Levi answers.

"Brother, I just don't feel the spirit moving within me today. There are no verses forthcoming, so I'll get straight to business. Are you aware there's a tropical storm coming? You'll have to cancel tomorrow's shipment. We should be fine. The tower has been through many storms, and there's a surplus of food. Today, I want to talk about getting new tributes. I've grown tired of these two."

"It will take a while, so don't do anything rash, or you'll be without until it can be arranged."

"Yes, you are wise brother Levi. Perhaps you both can start tribute shopping Friday and Saturday nights?"

"Yes, Prophet, we certainly can."

"Good, my brother," Joseph says.

Then the radio goes silent.

"What the hell are tributes?" I ask.

Levi looks at his shoes, then says, "Young men we take to Joseph on Frying Pan Tower."

"Why?"

"For fleshly pleasures. He has to get the sin out so that God will speak to him."

"Joseph is gay?"

"No. The devil tempts him. That's all. Without yielding to it, Joseph cannot be open to the divine words God sends him. They're just a means to an end. Much like how the Israelites sacrificed lambs and goats to Yahweh, Joseph sacrifices his body's purity."

Seething, I ask, "How do you transport them?"

"Usually locked in a wooden box. They are men Jeremy and I meet at clubs like Spectrum. Sometimes we drive up to Raleigh. They have more gay bars. After luring them to our car, we dose our unsuspecting guests with a syringe filled with ketamine."

"And now that he's bored, Joseph needs you to kidnap two more men to be trapped as sex slaves, fifty miles out to sea," I say with an indignant, raised voice.

"When you say it like that…," Levi says before my open left hand slaps the remainder of the sentence from his mouth.

"There's no other way to say it," I respond.

46

After radio silence, I turn to the door and say, "Herschel, go turn on the Weather Channel.

Thankfully, Nate was right. I'd done less damage than I originally thought, and it powers on.

I don't move much past the doorway because I'm still tethered to Levi and prefer the added security a room with one door provides. The segment that comes on is about NOAA's Hurricane Hunters. In it, scientists fly high above a hurricane's eye and drop a probe down into it. After a few advertisements, the storm of interest is named. It's Gabrielle. The cyclone is a few hundred miles southeast of us.

"Surf should be kicking up soon," Herschel comments.

"Wouldn't the rain kill his creatures, since they can't be exposed to water," Rebecca asks?

"They can get wet because they're created from an animal that's been transformed by ingesting indigo. But they can't be fully submerged. When that happens, it's instant death. The universe can't reconcile them being totally immersed in an environment where they couldn't feasibly exist. It's much like a robot getting its power switched off. They instantly freeze like a statue and sink."

"This could be the opportunity we need," Nate says in a huff.

I can tell he's ready to be rid of Levi, and I agree. But mostly, he wants vengeance. And Nate deserves it.

"It's too dangerous," I say. "Sure, their snipers will have retreated inside, but the waves coming in ahead of the storm are going to be rough. What if it takes longer than we expect and we get trapped out there? The ocean's erratic movements will be far worse once the storm moves directly overhead. What good would it do if we capsize and are lost to the sea? There'll be no one left to stop Joseph."

I turn back toward the room and shout to Levi, "What are the names of the two men Joseph has trapped in Frying Pan Tower?"

"I don't remember. One is white, the other black. Both are in their twenties."

"They mean so little to you, that you can't even remember their names?"

"I'm sorry," Levi says with reluctance.

I can't tell if he's saying that because he feels remorseful, or just doesn't want to get hit again.

It's four in the afternoon. Since we aren't expecting any more radio correspondence, I suggest calling in the pizzas.

I allow Levi two slices and water. He chooses pepperoni, eating it at Tiff's commandeered writing desk. Levi doesn't leave the room unless it's to visit the toilet. At seven in the evening, my crew assembles in front of the upstairs TV to watch Wheel of Fortune. Nate, Herschel, and Rebecca have a love for board games and trivia shows. Tiffany is the same way. I just kind of go along with it since it's a lot of fun for them. Still guarding Levi, I watch from the door.

Right as the wheel spins for the first time, Joseph's voice rings out of the radio.

"Brother Levi, there's something wrong with the metal."

"What is it, sir?" Levi responds.

"Every surface that we painted is beginning to thin. It must have been doing it all along, but the amount of rain coming down is causing it to accelerate."

Joseph stops, as a creaking sound can distinctly be heard in the background.

"You and Jeremy come get me right now!" Joseph screams over the radio.

I write on a piece of notebook paper, and slide it over to Levi. Levi reads what it says, "We're on our way," then signs off.

"We're not seriously going out there," Herschel says, pointing to the eastern window.

The gray sky is on the crest of darkening. The southwestern wind is ten to fifteen miles per hour, and it's only going to increase.

The three of them train their eyes on me.

Looking back at them, I say, "He's holding two innocent people captive. We can't let them go down with the tower."

I lead Levi to the staircase, sending Herschel down in front of him as a stopgap in case our prisoner tries to run. Sure, I could kill Levi with one lamentation charge through the wire, lopping his head right off. But, for now, I need him alive. Downstairs, I dig through Jeremy's closet until I find his rain jacket. It's dark blue, with a hood on it. In the living room, Rebecca, myself, Herschel, and Nate don our body armor followed by rain gear. I cover myself in Jeremy's rain jacket.

"Can I at least wear my own?" Levi asks about the jacket.

"It would look strange, otherwise," I say.

Nate goes upstairs and retrieves Levi's. It's the same brand and make, except that it's bright yellow. I run the wire underneath and out behind it. We each carry a radio and a sidearm. Also along are two shotguns and my rifle. Most importantly, I have Zeke's gun and the four speed loaders he made for it, each with six cartridges. Lightweight zip ties affix them to my belt. They are easy to break away when needed using a sharp tug.

Nate goes ahead of us. He uses the lift to lower my dive boat into the water and starts up the outboard engines. Despite being smaller than the Camille, we have to take it because the tugboat would be too slow. When I exit the side door of the house, I don't even bother locking up. The rain isn't terrible. At the moment, it's a fine mist flying on a cool breeze.

I push Levi firmly forward onto the boat before following. His hands are still untied. He may need them to brace himself against something as we navigate what could become a roiling hell ahead.

Looking at Nate, I say, "I'm counting on you to navigate."

I nudge Levi below deck then follow. It's been stripped clean except for the exposed head. Rachel and Herschel follow behind me.

"Can you two make sure Levi behaves?" I ask them both.

"You're kidding, right?" Rebecca says.

"Sounds like a yes to me, Levi. If I were you, I'd do exactly as I was told. All it will take is for one of them to say the word, and I'll yank on the wire from the helm. We'll dump your separated head and body overboard for the tiger sharks to eat."

I return to the deck and slide into the pilot's seat on the starboard side. Nate, in turn, sits port, which is to my left. All that blocks out the drizzle is a green T-top canvas overhead. It's supported by a sturdy aluminum frame bolted to the deck. Affixed to the front of it is a sheet of polycarbonate blocking the wind and rain from hitting us in the face. An overhead compartment holds a GPS and a marine radio. I typically keep it tuned to sixteen. It's the international distress channel. Anything that goes out over that frequency will be heard by the Coast Guard.

Nate inputs the coordinates into the GPS, and I look down at my gas gauge. It's nearly full. They must have fueled up on their way back in to prepare for their next trip. The sky isn't completely dark yet. Regardless, I turn on the two large spotlights attached to the aluminum frame, directly overhead. I'll need them soon enough. I back the boat out of its dock, then head south toward the Masonboro Inlet. I keep a moderate pace, probably a bit too quick for the circumstances. The sound is higher than usual because of the impending storm. Miniature waves roll across its trapped water, creating an unpredictable and uneven surface profile to navigate.

At the Masonboro Inlet, I have to apply a lot more throttle than I typically would against an incoming high tide. This is different. There's literally more water in this part of the ocean than usual because the storm is pushing it toward us. It's a small inlet. Even on good days, navigating its shallow waters can get one run aground. Once I pass the breakers, the waves become smaller, and the ocean is more chop than rollers. Because of the deep hull on our vessel, I'm able to get on a plane and cut through. After the last channel marker, all Nate and I can see is the great darkness ahead of us.

47

We cut a path southwest. Our lights illuminate an endless tableau of shallow, brown coastal water in front of us. Its chop skitters underneath us with an endless pop-pop-pop rhythm. Both outboards hum a familiar, droning tune. After killing Vernon, it's always been a sound reserved for nice, sunny days diving on wrecks or fishing.

Here I go again, slipping into bad memories. I feel as though I'm back at the same point I was two years ago when I threw Vernon onto the carcass of a dead humpback and left him to be devoured by whatever put their teeth into him first. I often feel as though I'm living in a loop whose consequences escalate with each cycle. Will I have peace again once this is over? If so, how long will it last? I only got two years before. Then my life unspooled and tangled like a bird's nest of fishing line on a baitcasting reel.

After an hour, the waves increase in size, getting as tall as two to three feet. The wind is between fifteen to twenty miles per hour. Then, we spot a glimmer of light ahead. It's not the illumination from the lighthouse tower. The Coast Guard deactivated that years ago. It's the lights illuminating the exterior of the structure.

I slow down a bit and have Nate peer through the night vision scope the best he can. Nate analyzes the bouncing image for two minutes before speaking.

"There's no shooter on the tower or anywhere else, for that matter. There's no one outside. Something is very wrong."

The closer we get, the more the metal of the tower appears to be illuminated with a flickering indigo glow. Joseph said the indigo in the paint is deteriorating the structure. I think back to Theta's remarks about how indigo is tiny particles from the Woods of Lamentation. Because indigo shouldn't occur on a plane with water, each particle will fall out of existence, and back into the Woods of Lamentation when it's exposed to moisture. However, it will take whatever dry matter it's touching along with it. In this case, it's the metal of Frying Pan Tower structure.

I direct the boat to the northwestern corner. It's the only section of the tower's lowest level to have a walkway. That walkway leads to a set of stairs ascending twenty feet up before turning into a spiral, spinning right up the northwest pilon. Nate and I tie off on the side of that walkway, against large boat fenders. The boat is taking a beating. Hopefully, it will be here when we return.

We see figures beginning to descend the spiral stairs in the distance.

Sliding on Vincent's brass knuckles, I say, "Nate, go below, get the gun Zeke made and send Levi up. After, stay out of sight. If I'm lucky, I can get a shot off at Joseph before he realizes it's me instead of Jeremy standing behind Levi."

Nate aggressively pushes Levi up the stairs to the boat's deck. All the while, Levi is bawling. Nate hands me the gun Zeke built for me out of a .410 shotgun. It's a six-shooter long gun that catapults six-inch metal spears while still tethered to the gun via thin braided wire. Theoretically, if the spear point is charged as a lamentation blade through the wire, it should pierce the field protecting Joseph or his men.

Considering the sheer amount of indigo he has in his cloak, you'd think it would be heavy, but it seems to add almost no mass as his shimmering cloak flows as Joseph's outline descends the stairwell.

"If you want to live through this, shut the fuck up, and act like everything is okay," I say to Levi as I push him onto the metal grate walkway.

"The blond man said he was going to kill me by stabbing my face repeatedly. He even showed me the knife."

"Don't worry about him," I feign, "he's justifiably emotional about what you did. But I promise to keep you alive if you help us save the two men being held captive up there in the tower. I'll take you back with us, and you can make a run for it. I advise you to get as far away from this cult as you can."

"Okay," Levi says, snorting and sniffling from where he's been crying.

The party stops thirty feet from us. I feel deep down for the ocean floor. But I can barely sense it, like something just out of reach that the tips of your fingers graze against. The entire structure above the waterline has been coated with clay-colored paint laced with indigo. The effect is much like the shackles the Apostles used to cuff me to my hospital bed back in the cavern. I can't affect it directly with my abilities. Despite being too far from the Earth's surface, I'm still able to ignite lamentation blades because they're forged by the light inside me. What good would manipulating the metal do anyway? I don't want to damage its structural integrity. A gun, knife, and Vincent's brass knuckles are all I have.

There appear to be four human figures and one beast. Two of the men continue forward. Their beast follows directly behind them. As they get closer, I see they're wearing "ACH" uniforms, like the men at Fort Caswell and the entrance of Severe Mine.

When they reach us, the one on our right says, "Hello brother Levi."

"Why is Prophet Joseph waiting all the way back there," Levi responds pointing over their shoulders.

"Joseph wants us to check the cabin of the boat. After Abraham's visit, he's being cautious."

I begin to draw the gun up when the beast firmly latches its teeth into the right thigh of the man Levi was just speaking to. He screams out in pain and terror, as his leg is pierced through and through by the creature's elongated teeth. The guard is shaken like a dog's toy. The sounds of his femur shattering and hip popping out of the socket accompany his dying screams. The beast then begins to feed.

"It's happening again," the uninjured uniformed man on the left yells back at the other two figures.

The third guard runs toward us as the beast finishes consuming the first man's body. Once done, he'll kill whoever is closest next. Knowing that's us, I raise my gun over Levi's right shoulder, charge it, and pull the double-action trigger. The barrel, cylinder, guard, trigger, and frame glow with crackling, electric indigo in my hands. The glowing mechanisms automatically cocks, fires, and advances the next round in the six-shot cylinder. The spear cracks the air, buzzing, with the charged braided wire trailing behind it like a diminutive lighting bold. The shot rings true and the monster turns to dust. The plume disperses down through the metal grate walkway and into the water below. I pull the trigger again after leveling the gun on the uninjured Apostle. The metal spear enters his forehead and exits out the back with no discernible resistance.

I train my sights on the third Apostle, but he already has the drop on me. I hear a gunshot. I expect the searing pain I felt before when I was shot through my body armor, or worse. But there's nothing. Rather, I hear the round whizz past my left ear. Directly after, I see the man fall. I turn to glimpse Nate standing on my right with his recently fired Glock in his hand. He hit the man directly before he fired his gun, causing him to miss my skull by inches. Realizing the three are dead, Joseph turns and begins running back toward the spiral staircase. In vain, I charge the gun and let off the remaining four rounds. Disappointed, I join everyone on deck, leaving Levi standing on the walkway. He's still tethered to me by baling wire. There, I eject the spent shells. I snatch my first quick-loader free from the right side of my belt and insert the six ready cartridges into the cylinder.

"The one guard screamed, 'It's happening again,' after the beast attacked his comrade," Nate says.

"The water is breaking down the indigo in their suits. With it gone, the beast was free to attack him," Levi says.

"That's why the guard was susceptible to conventional bullets, meaning Joseph is weaker than we initially thought," I say.

"No," Levi replies, "Joseph waterproofed his. Exposure to light amounts of moisture doesn't matter much, but the guards have been standing out in the rain for hours, which would slowly leach the indigo out of their uniforms. The small amount in their clothing slowly breaks down the fabric, but larger quantities would severely burn someone when exposed to water. If the beasts got out of control, the men Joseph was holding captive are likely already dead. We can leave and let the tower fall with him in it."

"No, you fucking coward. You're going to lead us to them."

48

As I follow behind Levi, it dawns on me that's the first time Nate has killed anyone.

Two years ago, when he kicked the shit out of Odin's Oath leader Marx Klein's head, I pulled Nate away while telling him, "That's not for you."

It turns out I was wrong. Nate pulled the trigger without reservations. Now, he follows directly behind me. Next in our precession is Herschel. Rebecca is at the end of our single file line.

When we're twenty feet from the eighty-foot tall spiral staircase, three more creatures begin hurdling down. I raise Zeke's gun over Levi's shoulder and unleash a round into the first, killing it. I line up the next shot, only to have it misfire. Panicked, I pull the trigger again, which elicits a blast, turning the monster into dust. My next shot misses the final beast, but the fifth round causes it to evaporate.

We stand stationary, anticipating more. None come.

"How many does he have, Levi?"

"He had five before I sent the two dogs on Tuesday. You've killed four. That means there's at least one more, but likely three."

The wind and rain begin to noticeably increase. The precipitation hitting us comes down with force. Though it is not yet unbearable, it certainly is uncomfortable. The jackets do make a difference.

Upon reaching the base of the staircase, I take a long glance up. The number of close-together, winding stairs is an almost inconceivable sight as the circular column is juxtaposed with the storm brewing above. I keep my gun over Levi's shoulder because I won't have the room to draw it once we start ascending.

With reservations about having one more round in the chamber, I eject the shells. Catching the unspent one, I slide it into my left pocket. I can tell which one because it's the only shell that doesn't have a dent in the primer. Plastic snaps as I pull my second speed loader from the right side of my back. There are two remaining, one on my left hip, and the other on the left side of my back. I load up and throw the now empty speed loader onto the grate with a heavy clunk.

As we climb, it doesn't take long to become overwhelmed by a feeling of being perilously exposed. If it weren't for seeing those three creatures bound down them, I'd worry that the staircase wouldn't hold our weight. Halfway up, we hear a loud creek followed by a deep groaning sound. We brace for the inevitable, but it stops. After, there's nothing to fill our ears but the rushing wind. The tower's structural integrity diminishes by the moment, as the indigo in the paint pulls metal flake by flake into the Woods of Lamentation.

At the top of the northwest tower, the walkway around the square structure forks off at the corner, going both east and south. Levi begins to take us east, but I know that as soon as we turn right around the next corner, and head south down the western side, we'll be in the direct line of sight for a sniper in the southwestern tower. We didn't see one earlier, but that doesn't mean there isn't a sniper now. Going south from our position keeps the flat roof of the structure in between us and the tower. The walkway is wider up top, so we no longer have to stay in a single file. However, everyone remains behind me and Levi since their guns are ineffective against the Apostle's beasts. Despite this, both Rebecca and Herschel are armed with twelve-gauge shotguns and side arms. Nate only carries a pistol. Being so light, he lacks the body mass to effectively brace against the kickback of a twelve-gauge.

At the mid-point between the corners, there's a metal door on our left. It's locked. I place my hand on the wall, but the indigo and my physical distance above the Earth's surface, make it impossible for me to sense anything. I don't want to risk injury kicking the door in, even though there's only a keyed metal doorknob.

I look at it and say, "Herschel, would you do the honors?"

We all step back as he places the muzzle of his shotgun in the crease of the door and frame, right where the latch is located. He pulls the trigger. It's loosened. Herschel rears back and gives the door a resounding kick. It flings open, revealing a dimly lit hallway with the red light of an emergency sign flickering overhead.

Thinking about the lighting up top and the red sign, I ask Levi, "How do they power this place?"

Still sniffling from crying, he responds, "Solar during the day, and a diesel generator at night. It's located in the southwest corner, inside a workshop. The exhaust is piped up through the roof. It's just enough power to keep a few lights on, a fridge, and a HAM radio. More than that puts too much strain on the system.

Nate, Herschel, and Rebecca ignite the flashlights on the rails of their firearms. Mine is custom installed on the wooden stock so that it's insulated from the effects of a lamentation blade.

Herschel ejects his spent shell from blasting the door open and steps back to give Levi and me the lead.

Our lights expose arterial blood sprays crisscrossing the light tan walls. Seeing this, Levi begins to shake uncontrollably. The hallway is twelve feet wide and nine high, likely because the Coast Guard designed it to be staffed with a sizable crew who would need to move around each other without obstruction. The only way we can go is forward. There are doors to small rooms lining the hallway.

As I try to open the first on my left, Levi says, "They're not in that room."

Upon reaching the center, we come to a large open-air space in the shape of a square. It's split in two by the hallway. On the right are the remains of the recreation area. There's a run-down pool table, a small television, and tables for playing board games. On the left is a kitchen area. The only thing that seems to function is an all-too-new refrigerator. Its bright white color stands out inside the dingy space. I move forward, cautiously opening the door, and peek inside. It's filled mostly with junk food and soda. I notice a tiny airtight bag in the back. I pick it up to find a red substance swirling around inside. It's my blood. Opening the freezer exposes dozens more pouches, all rock hard. I don't have a way to carry them. I close the doors. It doesn't matter, everything will go down with the tower, as its collapse creates a miniature environmental disaster.

I hear the door we entered from the outside bump against the wall. We see a pair of indigo eyes staring through the dark, cast in the red flickering light of a malfunctioning exit sign. It's one of Joseph's beasts who eyeballs us as it snarls.

"He must have come down from up top," Rebecca says.

I rush into the hall to get a clear shot. The round wizzes over the thing's head. It's in a full sprint now, crackling indigo eyes focusing on me. The next blast severs the beast's front right leg. The creature continues pushing itself forward, scooching on its chest across the floor, oblivious to pain. I fire again, piercing its head.

Grabbing a shaking Levi by the throat, I scream, "Where are they!"

"The northeast corner."

We continue down the hall, past closed door after closed door. Three-quarters of the way, Levi comes to a stop. He reaches down and turns the knob of the door to our left. It opens to rundown living quarters with a small bed and desk.

"There's no one here," I say angrily.

"They're here."

Levi walks over to the tiny closet in the far-right corner of the room. He opens the door, reaches up, and pulls down a telescoping ladder. Without asking, he begins climbing. I pull the baling wire leash around his neck, reminding him that I can end his life at any moment.

"I'm not sure what's up there, but I'm not risking it being a gun," I say.

He comes back down, and I climb up alone. It's a secret room with a four-foot-high ceiling, which means most people have to crawl or hunch over. There are several mats strewn about and five dingy white buckets. There's no doubt these men have been relieving themselves in them. The entire place is spackled with the odor of putrefying feces comingled with ocean salt floating in the moist air around us.

Crouched, I move toward them. I feel the wire around my wrist become taut, pulling against Levi's neck. Desperate, I remove it.

The man with a light complexion had obviously been dead for a few days. He's bloated with gas from the bacteria devouring his carcass from the inside out. A man with a dark complexion lies to the left of him.

He jumps from the shock of seeing me.

"Come on," I say, "I've come to get you out of here."

The man lifts his right arm up and I guide him toward the stairs.

"What's your name?" he asks straining and out of breath.

"Naomi."

"Thank you, Naomi, I'm Malcolm," he says, his voice becoming raspy.

When we reach the ladder, I call down to Herschel. He helps guide Malcolm to the floor. Once there, he and Rebecca hold him up.

In the commotion to help Malcolm, I forget to put the wire back around my wrist. When I reach the bottom of the ladder, Levi sees my end of the loose wire fall down from the ceiling entrance. He takes his chance, grabbing Nate's pistol off his side. Instead of fighting Levi for it, Nate unsheathes his knife and begins stabbing him in the face repeatedly. At first, Levi emits high-pitched screams. That soon gives way to muted gurgles. Nate continues as Levi lays supine on the floor, unrecognizable, and obviously mortally wounded. None of us say anything. We stand in silent vigil and let Nate savor his vengeance.

49

When Nate ceases plunging his dive knife through every orifice of Levi's face, he looks up to see the three of us stunned. Malcolm's consciousness is nebulous, so he doesn't react.

"That was for Claude," Nate says, breathing heavily from the exertion.

His face and chest are splattered with blood. When Nate stands, he places his knife back into its sheath, then wipes his blood-slathered hand on his right pant leg. He slaps it back and forth for good measure.

"We have to get Malcolm out of here," I say. "It's going to take a long time to guide him down the staircase and back to the boat. Nate and Herschel, that's going to be up to you. Rebecca and I are going after Joseph."

Rebecca turns and looks at me surprised.

"There are two beasts unaccounted for. They could be anywhere," Herschel replies.

"No. Both are going to be with Joseph. They're the last line of defense before using his abilities. Joseph's are much different than my own. They seem to be derived from the atmosphere, not the Earth. He can likely still use them up here. But I speculate Joseph is much weaker because of the severe injuries I dealt him last time we met. Why else would he be hiding out at sea? If he were at full strength, Joseph would have already confronted us. He's going to be in the one place that's advantageous, the light tower. There, he can see anyone coming, and shoot from a distance."

"How are you planning on countering that?" Nate quips.

"We'll turn off the power so he can't see jack shit."

"The generator," Rebecca says. "All we have to do is flip the switch, and we plunge the entire structure into darkness."

"Just let him go down with the tower," Herschel argues.

"I want to be sure. I have to see him die with my own eyes or else I'll never rest. We're not the only ones with a boat. And if he gets away this time, I likely will never get another chance."

Herschel shakes his head in disagreement.

I continue, "Once you're in the boat, if a creature comes, you can escape by unmooring yourselves and riding out into the chop."

Nate takes over holding up Malcolm's right arm from Rebecca. She walks over to Herschel and kisses him on the lips before whispering, 'I love you', in his ear.

We walk with them back to the top of the staircase.

Right before they descend, I say, "Radio me when you're in the boat. I'll cut the power then."

Rebecca and I head back to the western entrance. It's the one Herschel opened with his shotgun. The only exit is all the way through the hallway to the western side of the building. An identical metal door is there. Making a right on the other side will put me one hundred feet from the base of the tower. It starts on the corner of the southeast metal walkway and extends up eighty feet, overlooking the square, flat top of the structure.

Rebecca and I rummage through most of the rooms together. Many of the lodgings are just as they were left by the government: empty bedframes and institutional furniture. However, there are rooms with new mattresses and furniture pushed against the wall. At least two guards were eaten while sleeping, evidenced by huge blood stains on their beds. Interestingly, there are only a few bullet holes in the walls. The men barely had time to fight back. Most of their bedside tables have framed pictures of family on them. What kind of fanaticism could cause men to risk it all and abandon their families for a charlatan? Are their families proud of them? Will they be considered martyrs?

Forty minutes later, we hear Herschel's voice over the radio.

"We made it. Malcolm's still alive. Nate's getting him hydrated."

"That's wonderful news," Rebecca responds back to him, through her radio.

I click the talk button on my walkie, saying, "Keep him and yourselves safe. After this do not radio unless it's an emergency."

The generator room is the last on the right before exiting the western door. Inside, there's a circuit breaker.

"I want you to stay here, Rebecca. This way, we control who sees what and when."

After opening the western door, I give Rebecca the go-ahead to flip off the main breaker.

She enters the deafening room, and a few seconds later, darkness. We don't turn off the generator. It's easier to flip a switch than start a dodgy old engine. Rebecca comes back into the hallway with her headlamp illuminated with a red-light-spectrum bulb. This allows human vision to transition quickly between bright and dark. It's the only point of light besides what the moon reflects, vaguely piercing the soupy peripheries of the oncoming tropical storm.

"Kill him, Naomi," Rebecca says calmly, patting my shoulder and looking me in the eyes.

Once outside, I walk slowly south, toward the tower, with my back to the wall. There's a slight overhang, giving me just a bit more camouflage from above. I use the wall as a guide in the visual conditions. I can see things in front of my face, but nothing more. Joseph definitely can't see me from eighty feet above the walkway.

The door to the tower is locked. I contemplate opening it with my pistol. Then I hear something tumbling down the metal stairs inside. I back up and raise my gun. The metal door smacks the wall when it's smashed open by the beast. Out of the dark appear two sparking, indigo eyes. I charge the gun, aim in their direction, and pull the trigger. They vanish in an instant. As I approach the door again, another set of footsteps begins to bound down. I shoulder the gun, but the creature is too fast. It breaks down the other door inside the square tower, opening to the southern walkway. That could let him circle back to Rebecca, or continue down to the boat where Herschel, Nate, and Malcolm wait.

I get on the radio. "The last beast is loose. It could be heading for either of you. Rebecca, get to me now, Nate, unmoor yourselves and throttle away from the structure.

Fully knowing it will expose her while running in my direction, Rebecca turns on the lights again. Without them, we'd be fighting in the dark. I watch her sprint toward me. From above comes a muzzle flash, then sparks where the rounds hit the metal walkway. I run up the first full spiral of stairs, charge the gun, and fire upward. Joseph is startled, causing his next shot to land fifteen feet behind her.

Rebecca rounds the first flight of stairs, meeting me just inside the tower door to the five-thousand square foot platform's flat roof. On the north side, there's even a helipad. We're trapped.

The metal staircase blocks our line of sight to Joseph, and his to ours. If we walk out onto the platform or back down the lower walkways, we'll be shot.

Herschel comes over the radio, "The beast is heading in our direction. We're starting the engines now."

Furious, Rebecca fires all sixteen of the rounds in her pistol up in Joseph's direction. He fires a round in retaliation. The bullets clink and ping around inside the tower. As she drops the magazine to reload, we hear a groan similar to the one earlier as we ascended.

"It's coming down," I shout.

I grab her hand and scream, "Let's go!"

We run toward the northern end of the open platform, in the direction of the empty helipad. At a safe distance, we watch as the tower crumbles slowly in our direction. The sound of metal on metal plays an unwelcome symphony as it splinters to bits.

"He won't be dead, I say to Rebecca. The indigo protects him. But he can be trapped."

We sprint toward where the peak of the tower has fallen. Thirty feet away, we see him break out a window and clumsily fall three feet onto the platform's roof, rifle still in hand. Joseph is too weak to walk through walls. He looks tired and sickly. Slicing open his left hand and cutting off four of its fingers has caused his abilities to recede somehow.

"I have to get closer," I say to Rebecca before I begin to run at him.

If I can get in range before Joseph rises to his feet, I might be able to fire first.

I shoot. The spear tip's wire breaks loose and becomes an uncharged projectile that bounces off Joseph's indigo layer of protection. I'm too far away.

As I sprint to close the gap, Joseph ejects his last round and closes the bolt. Before he can point his muzzle in my direction, I fire again only to hear a click.

'I'm out,' I scream in my own head, furious at myself.

Then I hear another click. It's Joseph's rifle dry firing, just like my own. He casts it aside and begins walking hurriedly in my direction. Before I can snap a quick loader off my belt, he pulls a large plastic storage bag from his cloak. It's filled to the top with indigo. He opens it and swiftly flings the contents in my direction. I experience horrendous, scorching pain as it showers down on me. It's as though my skin is sloughing off. I'm caked in the stuff and am simultaneously drenched with rain. Every bit of me it touches is disintegrating and being transported into the Woods of Lamentation.

As I fall to my knees, Joseph pulls out a knife. Rebecca comes to my aid, firing round after futile round into Joseph's chest. While she does this, I eject the empty shells and load the one I have in my left pocket, lining it up one position to the right of the breech.

No longer able to stand, I hold the gun up to Rebecca, saying, "Only touch the wood and aim for his heart."

When Rebecca has the gun lined up, I reach up to the metal trigger with my left index finger, charge it and pull it back until the gun fires.

The projectile goes through Joseph's chest. The force of the ejection out of his back pushes him forward. His body crumples face down. He is dead.

"The beast," I raspily say to Rebecca. "It will come back. Reload the gun."

––––––––

That is Naomi's last conscious thought. Rebecca watches in horror as her friend disintegrates into flakes that fall onto the metal platform, melting a hole three feet wide into it. The destruction doesn't end there. It continues through the floor and supports below.

Rebecca hears the beast's shriek as it pounds up the tower's tall, spiral staircase on the northwest side. The structure groans, further destabilized by Naomi's fragmented body, sheering off important pieces of metal.

Rebecca picks up her walkie and hits the talk button, saying to Herschel and Nate, "I'm jumping off the western side."

"What?" Herschel screams back at her, barely processing the reality of what she said.

It's too late to reply. Rebecca throws down Naomi's gun, tears off her body armor, and runs toward the western edge. She jumps into empty space. Straightening her body, Rebecca dives like a spear, feet first, hands flat against her side. A fall from one hundred feet seems like an eternity. At impact, water rushes up Rebecca's nose. She instinctively swims toward the surface, uninjured, but far deeper than she'd like to be. Taking a deep breath, Rebecca sees the red and green navigation lights of the dive boat. Nate navigates it to her position, and Herschel pulls Rebecca over the transom swim platform.

"Where's Naomi?" he says.

"Gone," Rebecca sobs.

Upon hearing this, Nate begins to break down. But he has to steel himself against the horror so he can get them home safely.

Herschel and Rebecca tend to Malcolm below deck, occupying themselves before they have to be alone with the truth, Naomi Pace is dead.

Epilogue

I awake, not on train tracks, but in a forest. Around me, there is lush growth, healthy trees, and a bright, clear sky. A circular periphery encompasses me, much like a wall. It's five hundred feet in all directions. Beyond it, everything appears fuzzy and gray.

There are screams coming through the barrier. Then I realize. I'm in the Woods of Lamentation. My light must have caused the change in this part of its environment. I walk toward the commotion. Beyond the veil are innumerable types of beasts stalking and eating the live prey of depraved men's souls.

Without fear, I step through.